ANALOG HEART

ANALOG HEART

SAWYER BLACK

AVERY BLAKE

STERLING & STONE

Chapter One

Of all the slums in the Rundowns, the fourteen-story tenement before him was the slummiest. Royal Heights was a lie of a name, a stain upon a festering patchwork city of grease, trash, debris, smog, and crime. The building served as a squatter's paradise to some of the most notorious thieves and murderers in the Rundowns, making it a place that any sensible law enforcement agency avoided.

And of course this hellish fortress would be where the kid was being held.

Bronson Dodge wondered why he couldn't ever get an easy job.

As he readied himself for combat, he could barely get his heart rate or breathing under control. He approached the wall around the tenement and pretended to use the barrier wall as shelter from the cold, dirty rain to light a cigarette.

Nothing to see here, folks, just another degenerate wandering the streets.

He tried to steel himself for the mission ahead. It was one thing to be getting older, but a completely different thing to be getting older too goddamned fast. Seemingly overnight his body felt like it was squeezing six seasons into two. He had known it was going to happen, and that it would be sudden, but still it was unexpectedly like crashing into a wall. Almost everything that Bronson had learned to rely on in the last five years was suddenly broken. The tricks up his sleeve all tainted and faulty.

He planted his back against the rampart, sank to the ground, and collected his breath, letting the rain extinguish his prop. All around him was a cacophony of auditory misery from the nearby apartment buildings — dogs barking, music thumping, babies crying, drunks and addicts fighting. Just another night in the Rundowns.

A few people were cruising the streets looking for drugs, sex, or someone to steal, but they ignored Bronson, who looked like a harmless, if not a bit crazy, vagrant in his old black trench coat over too many layers of clothing hiding his bulletproof armor. His old shock-resistant armor had worn out and it was impossible to get a hold of it since it became illegal.

Two men turned out of the apartment building across the way, twitching and jerking as they noticed him and started their approach. He didn't think they were part of the crew that kidnapped the kid. Probably V-heads looking for someone to rob to fund their addictions.

The closer they drew, he noted their stench, their

dirty clothes, and that familiar tweaky look in their eyes. And the telltale implant scar from temple to temple. Definitely V-heads. They'd usually try a hustle with their attempts at charm before committing an outright robbery. But he didn't need any attention on him.

As they closed in, he lifted his jacket, revealing his weapon.

He needn't say another word.

They both turned almost in wordless unison, and continued down the street in the other direction.

He continued searching inward for the focus he would need.

Cracking skulls had never been easy, but these days Bronson was feeling like he'd taken a beating before the first punch. His body was more brittle than it used to be, but that's what happened when the critters inside you were starving, and you couldn't do shit to feed them.

Bronson was like everything else in this part of the Rundowns, well past his prime and broken beyond repair.

His target was somewhere in one of the rooms, on one of the floors of the fourteen-story tenement behind him. But with his back to the wall, he could stare out at the lounging landscape of structural decay, technological purgatory, social disease, and general apathy that colored the Rundowns in darker shades of rust and black.

Concrete had been cracked for more than a century, and the majority of the enclave's glass shattered for half as long. Migration from the hellhole was mostly for the grapevine, gossip passed among the transients trapped in their twilight of misery, hovering at the edge of a permanent midnight where despair sat fat and glowing like the moon in a starless sky. Hope that Empyrean Flats wasn't the figment of a collective yet quickly dying imagination, supposedly just one city over and a whole world away.

It was either imagination or memory, but something was fading.

Something was wrong, and Bronson had been feeling it for a while.

It wasn't just him. The way conversations swam in and out of logic, no matter who was on the other side. He wasn't even sure how long it had been going on, maybe a year or so, though he couldn't ever fix on the question in his head without everything going all fuzzy.

Maybe it was this part of the Rundowns. It was a long fifty kilometers from Lab #224, in the Boundary, sandwiched between High Town and the Rundowns.

Things had always been different there, this place where people gave up in utero. A hotbed for black market activities, smuggling — girls, drugs, and all the expired bots and bleeding-edge tech that Cascade Labs didn't know how to track, but only because they were a blink behind.

Bronson had done everything he could to keep the streets safe while working for Cascade, but those days were behind him. Without the company to constantly credit his account, he had to take whatever odd jobs and unsavory assignments came his way, fully reliant on illegal tech and underground friends to keep him alive. Fortunately, Bronson had plenty of both. He did whatever he had to. Within reason, of course. But the list was long. The era of him having to discuss his days around the dinner table were dead.

That had been a great job with even better benefits. He enjoyed the work, demanding as it had been, and the world's best upgrades. After a big promotion around a decade ago, Cascade juiced him with an army of nanos. Critters, they called them. Turned him into a super soldier, perfect for maintaining law on disorderly streets.

Except it wasn't a promotion.

Bronson left the gig five years ago. Had a hard time remembering why, exactly, other than he *didn't want to do it anymore.* He had to get out of there. But without a contract, there was no way Cascade could help him with the critters inside him. Because officially, they didn't exist. And now that Bronson no longer worked there, he couldn't get anyone to admit otherwise.

He eased himself up onto the balls of his feet and stole a glance over his shoulder, eyeing the building from the floor of its blown-out lobby to the plummeting slant of its dangerously caving roof. A big place to get lost in, acres of stacked concrete, waiting for Bronson to explore, and die in if he wasn't careful. But the kid was in the building somewhere, and Bronson would be bringing him out.

He remembered the promise, someone from the

Cascade board saying that he would live like a super-man. But he didn't remember who, or them saying shit about him being their slave to keep it that way.

But, in truth, he'd die without them. So Bronson and the law were taking some much-needed time apart.

He took his Tonic, fast and without a second thought since the drug hit his ailing body like a bolt of lightning. It wasn't *supposed* to fry the brain, but it sure as hell felt like it every time. Still, it was worth it in the end, seeing as how it gave him everything he needed to still feel like a superman for a few more minutes.

The Tonic worked fast, like always. He winced through the worst of it, the pain lancing through him like a flaming arrow. Then it was over and he felt the strength of a quarter god filling his body again, critters inside him turning the crank, rolling his inner engine over from *dying old man* into the aging machine fighting for life that it was.

Most of Bronson's enhancements were either dead or defective, but he had what he needed to make it through this next part alive, if he was careful. A relative term for sure.

His body was buzzing, hungry for Bronson to feed it with action and information.

He activated his Aversion chip. One of his oldest add-ons, and one of the few that had yet to fail him. It was a misnomer, since the chip was designed to keep him going forward in the face of fear, no matter what. However, it did nothing to help him deal with the PTSD that sometimes followed.

Then he activated a second enhancement, Locus4. The add-on was supposed to offer him a visual overlay displaying data such as the details of his environment, heat maps to alert Bronson of potential danger, and relevant environmental factors like menacing weather or physical threats. But the chip barely worked, blitzing out well over half the time, and right now it was showing Bronson only what he could see with his own eyes.

He lowered the black mask over his face, stood, and circled the broken wall, his body now warmed with its latent potential.

Bronson approached the tenement, wondering if today was the day it might finally fall over, surveying the situation as he crossed the parking lot, heading directly for the only threats standing between him and the entrance.

There were five of them, including two older-model bots. The older they got, the worse they listened. The more mistakes they tended to make. The more dangerous they tended to be. That's why recycling laws were so strict. But around here Bronson had seen plenty of bots living in the fringes, off the grid and well past their dates.

He would have thought some of them were more than fifty years old, if that were possible. But the technology wasn't that old. Except that it was. *And* it wasn't. Then it was all over again and that didn't make any goddamned sense.

There was a schism of truth that felt like jagged glass dragging its edge deep into his brain.

It left a deep ravine in his mind. These days, half of Bronson's thoughts felt more like contradictions.

From behind the rampart, Bronson thought the men warming themselves at a burning trash can in front of the tenement might have been a few unfortunate homeless and a couple of scrapheaps, living on borrowed parts and barely hanging on. But up close he saw the danger. Thugs, two of them armed, with the bots positioned around the perimeter to keep the three humans safe.

Few people owned anything around here, so it was easy to kill for the nothing you had. This building belonged to them, and nobody was getting in without paying their entrance fee.

But Bronson didn't have what they were going to want.

He would probably have to kill all three of them. But that was fine, because killing fed the critters.

Bronson stood in the open, forcing one of the men to make the first move. Reveal their party's weakness.

The largest among them approached. An absolute bear at six-feet-six — according to the Locus4, before the overlay display started glitching and he had to shut it down — he had a half-foot on Bronson. His shoulders looked like they weighed twenty-five pounds each, and his few teeth looked a lot like fangs.

"The fuck you doing here?" he growled with a smile, eyeing Bronson like the entertainment he wanted him to be, letting his jacket open so Bronson could see the butt of his illegal Stomper. That thing could send an energy blast big enough to level any one of the empty husks nearby that used to be single-story buildings, and take a wallop out of the ancient apartments behind him. He could pull the trigger and send a tornado of plexiglass and broken metal tearing through the street.

But only if it was charged, and Bronson would bet his life that it wasn't.

That's why he was packing a second weapon, the one he probably thought Bronson couldn't see. It was illegal, too. But he wanted to make Bronson afraid of his impotent handbomb, while certain death waited on the other side.

They get you to cower from one blast so you can't mount an attack, only to rip you apart with a quicker strike.

In the old days, the dude would already be dead. Bronson would've hit him with speed and precision that married both his human talents and his robotic and nano enhancements to their fullest potential.

They stood like gunslingers, in stance and distance.

Bronson spoke, the voice modulator dropping his words by a handful of octaves, making them rumble like an air conditioner coming to life. "The boy. Where is he?"

The bear insulted him with a shrug, followed by a shake of his head. "I got no idea what you're talking about."

He sneered, then his buddies hunched forward, thinking they were getting ready for what was coming.

The bots behind them whirred and buzzed.

"You're making a mistake," Bronson warned them. There was no joy in killing.

But as expected, the bear laughed, enjoying the show that he thought he was writing, no clue that the curtain would fall on his life in just seconds.

"Or what, grandpa?"

"Tell me where the boy is, and I'll let all of you live. Don't, and I'll start with you. I'm not worried about the Stomper, because you don't have the energy to charge it, and you wouldn't waste it on me if you did. I'd be worried about your sidearm if I wasn't a faster draw. The two bots behind you can protect your friends, but you're dead no matter what. It's hairy for me after that, because that'll make it four of them and one of me. The two humans have big metal shields, but that's all the robots really are. I don't care what kind of mods they might have, you're not bypassing the Asimov Laws, so they're never gonna be swords. Fortunately, only one of your two goons is armed. So I figure that makes us even."

The bear's hand made it halfway to the butt before Bronson pulled the trigger on his Solacer — the same piece he'd used to drop bodies for his entire career.

The bear's face blew out the side of his head, the jagged edges flapping like the skin of a shredded balloon.

Bronson charged, quickly closing the short distance between them.

The robots protected their masters, or at least they tried to. Maybe could have, if one of their masters wasn't an idiot.

He should have been smart like the second goon, who was trying to go fetal.

Instead he went for his weapon. He was fast enough to draw, but not nearly enough to use it.

Bronson was already there, snapping all four of his fingers like pencils, the first two in retrieval of his gun, and the second two for pissing him off.

Looking closer, the situation was laughable. His robot protector was strange, and the kind of bot that Bronson saw a lot around this crumbled part of town. The design looked brand new, but beat to shit. Like someone brought a brand new car back from a demolition derby.

A single squeeze of his Solacer and Bronson put the man down.

To the bot protecting the coward he said, "Stand back and I won't shoot him."

"Better do it, Merit," said the second robot, a large disposal unit.

"You too," Bronson ordered the second bot.

They both stepped back.

"The kid. Where is he?"

And the coward said, "Ninth floor … 9L."

"Thanks." Bronson nodded. "Hey, you ever steal from a family, fuck a girl even after she said no, or creep on any children?"

The man stuttered, but that was fine. The heat map gave Bronson all that he needed.

"That's what I thought," he said, then sent a slug into the thief, rapist, or pedophile's forehead, nodding to the bots as he passed them. He'd have ended them too if he'd had the firepower.

Bronson entered the keeling tenement, gun tight in his fist, grateful for the Aversion chip.

The shadows were dark. Tangles everywhere. Too many of them the size and shape of a human. But he kept taking one step after another, refusing to stop, first to the stairwell, and then up the stairs.

Bronson had to kill another three men before making it to the stairwell door. Fortunately, he saw the first one just as he was rounding a corner. The guy barely flinched before his body smacked the ground. He never came close to getting his gun.

That shot brought another two running, one from each direction. He aimed for the forehead on both, one bullet each because waste not want not and shit, but the second guy tried to juke and Bronson had to correct, so the shot went right through his throat and, thanks to the angle, cleaved the man's head from his shoulders. The second bullet did its work proper, landing right between his attacker's eyes.

The world went temporarily still after that.

Nine floors were a horror show of patience and waiting as Bronson slowly climbed, needing another hit of Tonic halfway up but refusing to take it, and still doing so even though he was practically dying for the sweet relief and surge of strength that would follow the inhalant into his lungs as he stepped into the ninth-floor hallway.

The world was still silent, but that quiet meant

nothing. A lot of killers lived in a hush. Especially here.

9L was 150 feet at that, but it took Bronson five full minutes to get there.

He didn't make a sound on the way, and with the Aversion chip stripping fear from the encounter, he had all the patience in the world.

Bronson pressed his ear to the door and, thanks to the critters, knew there were just two hearts beating behind the door.

So the next part was easy.

He kicked open the door and caught the lone guard unsurprised. He shot up from his chair where he was reading from an old tablet, but a pair of bullets sent him crashing to the floor.

And that left the target. A little boy, eight years old. Tied to a chair.

"Come on," Bronson said. "We're getting out of here."

But the kid didn't want to move.

He sat frozen — not like Bronson was his savior, but like he was just another of Hell's demons sent to torment him.

"I said let's go. We need to get out of here." His voice modulator was still on, and that gave the kid every reason to see him as monstrous. Same for the black mask. He took it off and approached the kid, but Bronson wasn't sure how much better that could have made it. Maybe he looked more like a demon without it.

"Sorry, son," he said, kneeling down to look the

kid in the eye. Hopefully he'd stop shaking by the time Bronson untied him. But probably not.

"Are you … going to hurt me?" The kid choked as he said it, but still managed to sound brave.

"No. Of course not. I'm here to take you home. Your parents hired me."

At that, the kid smiled. "What's your name?"

"Bronson Dodge."

The kid used his freshly freed hands to give Bronson's a hearty shake. "I'm Peter."

"I know. Now let's get out of here. You need to stay behind me and listen to every word that I say. The only thing more important than keeping you alive right now is keeping myself alive, so follow close. It was a little too easy getting in here, and that's probably bad news for the way back down."

Peter nodded.

Bronson turned around and the kid followed, both of them pausing at the door.

He looked back over his shoulder, shaking his head and putting a finger to his lips.

The hallway was quiet on purpose. There were at least two bodies on the other side of the door, and for now both were still breathing. Bronson pulled the hood back down over his head and whispered for Peter to wait.

He counted to three, kicked the door off of its hinges and into the hallway, waited for the bullets to blaze on both sides, then rolled into the hallway, eliminating the left attacker with instinct and aim before letting the AI inside him take care of the one coming in on his right.

Bronson sprung back to his feet. Felt it more in his bones than he used to. Held out his hand through the doorway, waited for the kid to take it, then dragged him into the hallway before letting it go.

"Remember to stay close."

There was only one attacker in the stairwell, coming in just two flights down on the seventh floor. He burst through the door without warning, but Bronson was close enough to grab him as he came through, then spin him around with the back of his neck to Bronson, which made it simple to sweep his blade across it.

But that spiked his adrenaline, overloading the connection with the critters. Strength bled from his legs.

"Are you okay?" The kid sounded timid beside him. Or maybe out of his fucking mind.

"I'm good."

He wasn't. Still Bronson managed to stand and start back down the stairs.

And still the kid followed.

Things were worse on the other side of the door, where Bronson's Aversion started to fritz. The circuit was fried — the critters were dicking with him. His time was finally up.

Whatever the reason, it wasn't working, and Bronson had gone from lionhearted to yellow-bellied. He wanted to sit in the corner and cry. He wished he'd never had the Aversion to make him feel strong.

Maybe he wouldn't be falling apart right now. Maybe he would—

"Mister …"

The kid was tugging at his sleeve, probably wanting to know why the old man looked like he was seconds away from tears.

Bronson heard something far off, like thunder in the outskirts. An enemy approaching.

If they were attacked now, that would be it. He was too terrified to fight, and so a slaughter it would be.

"I'll be okay in a second," Bronson said.

And it was true, even though he hated the *why* behind it.

Another inhale of Tonic. Deep as he could while he braced for the pain.

The only way to get his shit under control.

"That's better," he growled.

Less than a minute later they were on the bottom floor. Locus4 came online for just long enough to let him know about the two men thinking they were about to outsmart him on the other side of the stairs.

He pushed Peter back into the corner. Emerged from the stairwell with the calculated risk, knowing he might take a bullet in his shoulder from the guy standing behind one of the lobby's many columns, but that guy's shot was awkward, and Bronson could risk it to send a bullet into the heart of the man directly in front of him.

The gamble paid off, and both assholes were dead in just seconds.

He turned back around and opened the stairwell door. "Come on."

It wasn't far to the exit but might as well have been a mile.

The thing that Bronson had been dreading now hit him like hail. Tonic was crashing.

A tightness in his chest, like the entire world was constricting inside him.

After a while it would be hard to see anything but black, and the entire planet would keep screaming between his ears, until he considered using a bullet to shush it.

Halfway there and he might be dying.

Three quarters and Bronson was certain he was.

Outside, the fresh — *relatively* fresh — air helped. But not by much.

It was hard to tell if the drug was bad. Not all batches of Tonic were created equal, and Bronson took what he could get, and that usually meant a lower grade he could barely afford. But the results had been off for a while, and he was getting increasingly certain that his body's tolerance was at the point where he needed relatively high doses to keep the suffering at a dull roar. Adding the adrenal requirements inherent in this kind of assignment was, for Bronson, like living on suicide watch.

The more Tonic he did, the harder the crash.

And Bronson couldn't stop doing it, especially now.

At least they were close. Another fifty steps and

they would finally reach the rampart, and the Beast waiting just beyond.

He was practically blind by the time they made it to the other side, but Bronson was also starting to relax.

The Beast was there. A skulking black tank that wasn't like any other vehicle Bronson had ever seen. The armor on the sides was the thickest he'd ever encountered, but the thing still cornered like it was running on rails. He would never have bought himself such a thing. Who knew how much something like that would even cost, or where you could buy it. But Bronson didn't have to. Darius Niles gave it to him in lieu of payment for a job. Fine by Bronson since the gig took all of three days where he wouldn't have been doing anything else.

"What is that?" Peter asked, pointing at the Beast.

"It's our way out of—"

Something walloped Bronson on the back of his head. At first he thought it was the critters screaming for Tonic, but by the time his cheek was gnashing gravel he knew it was an old bat.

The kicking came next, his eyes going blurry as he tried to focus on Peter, getting pulled out to a perimeter just out of Bronson's reach. He reached anyway, and the feet kept on coming.

So did the laughs and the jeering, heckling Bronson for falling on his ass and shutting down. Defeat at the swing of a bat.

The knives came next, blades slipping into his skin easy enough to be coming home.

They were going to leave him for dead.

But the critters inside Bronson weren't ready to go on standby forever, and as much as they probably longed for the taste of revenge — he'd felt that craving before — they might not risk his life. Fortunately for Bronson it was already at risk, and the promise of getting rewarded with Tonic was strong.

They pushed him up and over the edge of where he needed to be.

And when the attacker came to end him, Bronson grabbed him by the wrist and squeezed, the critters shoving a supraphysiological amount of pressure to those muscles so that the man's wrist turned to jelly, his hand falling with a top-heavy flop.

Bronson took the knife, threw it into the second attacker's forehead, and sent the third man running into the night.

He turned to Peter and said, "Are you ready?"

But the kid just stared back at Bronson, looking like he'd need another week to find any words.

Chapter Two

Despite the Beast looking as though it would roar like a rolling apocalypse, it ran with a whisper and was even quieter inside. The silence was likely making Bronson's passenger nervous.

That wasn't Bronson's problem, though.

He wasn't social under the best of circumstances. This was a job, not a date — not that Bronson would have known how to behave otherwise. People always wanted to talk, but Bronson rarely had shit to say. Triple true when his head felt like the heart of a rotting melon.

At least he was driving out of the Rundowns rather than in, and that felt like they were pointing at hope. They wouldn't make it out past the edge, High Town was still miles and a lifetime away, but Peter's parents did well enough for themselves, making their home in an area called the Boundary, a purgatory of neither-nor if Bronson ever saw one.

The kid kept staring out the window. Bronson

wondered what he was thinking, if the worst of the Rundowns had been what he expected, because surely he expected something. The monsters that his friends scared one another with all surely made their home here, from human to robot.

The concrete was less cracked by the time he finally spoke. Peter probably felt safer after Bronson turned the Beast onto Mulberry, and down a boulevard with buildings that he knew.

"How do you know where I live?"

"I told you. Your parents paid me to get you."

"Oh."

And then again, Peter was silent.

Bronson parked the Beast a block from the squat, two-story building. He should have made it four or more away from their destination, just in case any of the scumbags had decided to follow them, but was too ragged to walk.

Peter followed Bronson for two blocks without a word.

It wasn't too bad, and at least he didn't have to worry about a thug in every shadow.

Peter's place wasn't exactly *nice*, though still better than any of the shitholes they just left behind. The lawns out front were small, but manicured. Two landscaping bots buzzed about, keeping the neighborhood clean. You could tell a lot about a neighborhood by what amount of trash the community was willing to overlook. The more trash ignored, the more crime ignored, the more likely you were to get mugged, raped, or murdered. The little things mattered more than most people knew.

"Your parents own the whole building?"

Peter nodded. "My grandpa used to own it."

"Oh? Was he a doctor too?"

The kid shrugged. "No one can remember."

He shook his head, not surprised. There had been a lot of that going around.

The doctor's office was closed, so Bronson had Peter lead him around back.

The kid punched the code into the box, then opened the door.

They trudged up the stairs, Peter now in the lead.

The door opened before they reached the top. Mom and Dad were together, embracing, their faces awash in relief, their son ascending the stairs like a sun rising on the rest of their lives.

A security bot stood behind them. Bronson felt a flash of anger.

Stupid fucking worthless security bot. What the hell was it doing when the kid was taken?

Sure as hell not the job it was programmed to do.

Peter jumped into his mother's arms.

Dr. Drummond offered a hand for Bronson. "How can I ever thank you?"

"You already thanked me half of the way. Maybe you could run down to one of them little money machines and get me the other half of my thank you in cash."

"Of course," she said, looking mildly offended. "Whatever you need."

"Really." Mr. Drummond turned toward him, clearly trying not to cry. "We thought we'd lost him. We thought that—"

And then he did. Not just a little. He totally lost it. Whatever he wanted to say was gone for good. The man looked like he wouldn't be making much sense for a month.

"Why don't you take your father to our room?" Then Peter's mother turned to Bronson. "Is there anything we can do … besides the money?"

Bronson shook his head. "Remember me the next time you have an impossible situation, assuming I'm still around."

"Are you okay?" She looked closer. "You don't look well. You know I'm a doctor, yes?"

"That's what the sign says outside, but I'm fine. And I'll be out of your hair as soon as I have my money."

Bronson tipped his head so as not to appear rude, but he really did want to be getting on his way.

"Then I'll be back," she said, still looking slightly bothered.

But managing her feelings wasn't part of Bronson's package.

Fuck, his head was killing him.

Dr. Drummond was gone, but she left him with the goddamned security bot. It felt like the thing was giving Bronson the eye, even though he knew that was impossible.

"Hey trashcan, where were *you* when the kid was taken?"

In a flat voice that didn't sound human at all, the security bot said, "I was charging."

Piece of shit.

Bronson looked over at the robot, trying to work out why his feelings were getting the best of him. He had plenty of reasons to hate the things, but this was something more. Bronson was sure, even though he had no idea where that certainty was coming from, or what it might mean.

It wasn't the robot's head, which was square and blunt and not humanoid at all. More like a monitor with a human face projected onto it. And it wasn't the robot's body, which was big and bulky, and … crudely simple. A bottom that ran on treads. No feet. Weird thing was, the bot looked brand new, and since buying the things secondhand was illegal, it probably was. Peter's parents probably justified the expense as something to protect their home and business. Eight years ago or so, right around the time that their son had been born.

So why did this new robot in here seem old when compared to those ancient bots back in the Rundowns? That, like so many other things that were worming around in Bronson's mind, didn't make a lick of goddamned sense.

"You were *charging*?" Bronson said to the security bot, even though it was pointless. "So you could have a full charge before you failed at your job?"

"Pardon me. But I don't understand your question."

"Fuck off," Bronson said, showing the robot his middle finger. "Do you understand that?"

"If you are stating with both your words and your raised middle finger that you are displeased with the work I have done in keeping Peter Drummond safe, then yes, I understand."

The bot's voice was so cold and inhuman, Bronson had to remind himself that it wasn't his to toss out the window, curious as he was to see how much damage a second-story drop would do to this supposed newer-generation bot.

Bronson didn't ask anything more, but the bot gave him another tidbit anyway.

"I have already updated my charging routines, reducing them by fifteen minutes each cycle, and fitting them in only while Peter is away."

"Shitty programming if you ask me," Bronson said, though he was alone with the bot and nobody did. "A security bot that takes breaks and makes mistakes … why not hire a human or a proper security detail?"

The robot made a sound very much like a frustrated growl, then the door opened and Dr. Drummond came back inside.

"Again," she said, handing Bronson the envelope. "We really can't thank you enough."

Bronson took the envelope and stuffed it into his coat pocket. "You just did."

He walked toward the door, but turned halfway back. "My best to your husband, and tell Peter that I'm glad he's okay. You have a good kid."

Bronson turned back toward the door, but didn't make a step before falling.

Dr. Drummond was at his side immediately, one gentle hand on Bronson's shoulder, and the other helping him up. "Come downstairs," she offered. "Let me help you."

"I'm okay," Bronson said, or at least he thought so. It was hard to hear anything or make sense of even his own words with every critter inside him screaming.

"You're not." She shook her head. "But I can help you, if you're willing to let me."

"Sorry, doc ..." Now he was wheezing. "I don't think I have the kind of thing you can cure."

"I've been a doctor here for a long time, Mr. Dodge. I know your history with Cascade, and can do a lot."

Bronson shook his head. He was fine. He didn't need help, or charity.

"I've got it from here." Bronson tapped the spot on his coat where the envelope had vanished, reminding the doc that she'd done plenty already. "I'm good. Thanks again."

But he wasn't.

Bronson opened the door, and then collapsed in front of it.

Chapter Three

BRONSON WAS in the dream again. A vague memory at the tip of his tongue, a dream he'd been having for the last six months, growing stronger like a tide threatening to pull him under.

He was walking down a hallway toward a red door.

There was something important beyond it.

Something he needed to see.

As Bronson drew closer, his vision blurred at the corners.

Voices too.

Familiar voices.

He had to reach the door, had to see what was behind it, but it kept moving impossibly farther away.

He tried to run, but it only sped away quicker, until he collapsed to his knees, crying out.

～

BRONSON TRIED to open his eyes. Tearing through the gummy residue holding them closed, only for them to fall back like shutters over the corner store at closing time. He also pinched the bridge of his nose. Bit at his bottom lip. Tried to wiggle his toes. But it was bullshit in all of those places, too.

Nothing was working. He was stuck, somewhere in between sleeping like the dead, and sticking to its edges like dried syrup. He had a mouthful of sand, or at least something close, and it felt like he hadn't swallowed in years.

That's also how long it felt like before Bronson could remember where he was, or at least what happened before he blacked out and was brought here.

The kid, Peter Drummond, and his parents. The mom had offered to help him out, take him to her office downstairs. That must be where he was now, if only he could keep his eyes open long enough to check the place out.

Fucking critters.

He worked to clear his head — no use trying to see through a solid wall — then, after a few of the thicker cobwebs were all wiped away, Bronson took several deep breaths, clearing his lungs and letting the critters know that he was nice and alive. Only then could he force his eyes open and take a look around.

Sure enough, he was in Doc Drummond's office. So said the diplomas on the wall, the IV bag hooked to his body, and all the beeping and blipping from the machines inside the room, running diagnostics on

Bronson. Not just on him, but on all of those millions of nanobots living inside him.

Bronson wondered how long he'd been out. The doc was absent, but he meant to ask that question first, right before *So when the hell can I leave?*

Now he felt indebted, and that was something Bronson didn't abide. He never asked for help, nor did he admit to needing it. They could have loaded him into the Beast and he would have been fine. The cabin was calibrated for him. He looked at the IV bag, calculated the raw odds of it being poison rather than medicine. Could he have walked right into a trap?

It was a stupid thought. Bronson had saved this woman's son. This problem with his memory was making him paranoid.

He heard noise on the other side of the door, what sounded like pots and pans clanking around — someone looking for something. Hopefully the doctor would be in soon. In the meantime, Bronson took a long look around.

He'd never been in a doctor's office like this. It was old-fashioned. Almost quaint. It was smack in the middle of his experiences. Bronson had either spent time in posh offices with the world's best doctors, because no one did it better than Cascade, or in the back-alley hovels where he'd been getting his treatments in the Rundowns ever since leaving the best gig he ever had, and couldn't afford to keep. Instead of high ceilings, gleaming steel, and state-of-the-art solutions, the shanties of dubious healing he'd been frequenting lately were lucky to have plumbing.

But that was his fault. He could have gone to any one of the city's licensed physicians, if Bronson was willing to have a robot touch his body.

The technology in this office was … interesting. The computers, monitors, and machines all looked sort of tinkered together. There were missing pieces, and the way the wires were bundled and fastened, with odd adapters peeking out from every available connection, it all seemed so antique. But then Bronson was also staring at a hologram of his body that looked beyond state of the art, so how the hell did that make any sense?

The door opened and Dr. Drummond entered. She looked at Bronson and smiled.

"You're awake."

"How long have I been out?"

"Since yesterday. It's after dinnertime now. So slightly more than a day."

"Not to sound ungrateful, but when can I go?"

The doctor gave him another kind smile. "Whenever you want to, Mr. Dodge. But I wouldn't suggest it."

"What's gonna happen if I do?"

"How old are those nanobots inside you?" Drummond asked, then she added, "I assume they're illegal. No judgement, you understand. But I do want to help you, and need to know the truth so I can. I've seen this exactly twice."

"They're old enough to expire. And they're legal. Loaded by Cascade themselves."

"I see." The doctor looked surprised. This kind of

stuff was *always* illegal. "So I assume you have an appointment for an upgrade? Has there been some sort of holdup?"

Bronson shook his head. "Won't be happening."

"What?" She looked aghast.

"I can't afford it."

"If Cascade put them inside you, then *they* should have to pay!"

Bronson cleared his throat. It was like trying to swallow a handful of tack nails. "I don't think Cascade is wanting to subsidize my upgrade. We didn't part on the best of terms."

"I see." Drummond looked upset. "Do you have any idea how long you have left? Before the nanos shut down?"

"Do you?"

She looked away, then back at Bronson before nodding. "Maybe a week."

"So I already got my last present from Santa."

"There must be something you can do. Cascade—"

"These parts aren't supposed to exist in people. Cascade has only left me alive this long out of some sense of obligation or guilt … I don't know. But they're not looking to extend my life any longer. When I'm done, I'm done, then they can do whatever to erase me."

The doctor nodded. "Well, the least I can do is help with the pain, yes?"

"I can't ask you to—"

"You didn't, Mr. Dodge. And it's already done.

The Tonic is killing you quickly, and there's little we can do about that, but your fluids are as they should be and I've treated you with a neutrino gel. It's obviously off-market, but I was sure that given the circumstances you wouldn't mind."

"Of course not," Bronson said. "Thanks. Can you tell me how much this is going to cost me?"

"Nothing. You saved my son."

"Right, and I didn't do it for free. Why don't you take the money back for that and we'll call it even?"

"Absolutely *not*, Mr. Dodge. Even if I were to agree, which I never would, Martin would kill me the second I walked back inside. Thank you for everything — this was the least I could do. But if I may …" She let it hang, holding his eyes.

"Yeah?" Bronson said.

"There are less … violent ways to pass. I highly suggest that you—"

"Stay away from the Tonic. Got it, doc. I've heard it before. Even the dealers are leaving me with a warning lately."

"It's going to get worse every time."

"So they tell me."

The doctor looked resigned. She'd given up, knowing there wasn't a chance that Bronson was going to listen. He'd seen that look plenty. On colleagues, superiors, and even on the faces of his family, back when he had one.

Drummond started unplugging Bronson from the monitors, and then the monitors from the bank of computers. It was a complicated setup that he didn't understand, but Bronson was too tired and didn't care enough to ask any more questions. One good turn did deserve another, even if his was underweight by comparison.

He said, "You really ought to move out of the Boundary. Get all the way out of the Rundowns. Request a transfer to … somewhere better — if such a place really exists. Or hire better security. Otherwise, this isn't over. And I'll probably be dead the next time you need me. These scumbags will come back. It'll be another group next time, same for the time after that if you manage to get lucky twice in a row. But eventually, they'll get you to pay them instead of someone like me."

She shook her head, her smile certain but sad. "I can never leave the Rundowns. This practice belonged to my father."

"It did?"

This was exactly the sort of thing that had been driving him nuts — when he was paying attention.

Bronson remembered his conversation with Peter when they were getting out of the Beast.

Your parents own the building?

My grandpa used to own it.

Oh? Was he a doctor too?

No one can remember.

But you couldn't just come out and ask someone about a schism in their memory. The brain hated it, always started conjuring excuses as to why it made sense. Bronson caught himself as that was happening to him a few times, right in the middle.

"Do you remember much about your father?"

The doctor smiled, her eyes burning bright before the light went dim and a long frown found her tired face. "No. I don't."

"That's too bad," Bronson said, wondering what it all meant.

He plucked a card from his wallet and handed it to the doctor. "I'm serious about the security if you're not going to leave. You need something better. Call Lancaster, the guy that got you in touch with *me*. He can get you some decent human guards."

"Not fond of robots, Mr. Dodge?"

Bronson shrugged. "It just seems to me like the world would be a helluva lot better off without them."

"Did you always feel that way? Or did something change your mind?"

Bronson considered. "I guess it's always been that way."

Then he said goodbye to the doctor and went outside to the Beast.

He got in and started the engine, then drove, thinking about what he had just told the doctor, and how that wasn't really true. Because once upon a time he didn't hate robots, working at the best place in the world for those who loved them.

Chapter Four

Isla kept reading, enjoying Ava's rapt attention, and the eager look on her little face.

"The wind swept through the cabin and rattled the windows. The hunters were worried that they might get trapped."

Isla paused again, like she did after most passages, to study the girl, wanting to make sure that she was still fixed on the story. Children could have short attention spans. She felt lucky that Ava was mostly the opposite. Like any little girl, she had her moments where she only wanted to play and was barely willing to listen, but they were few and far between.

She smiled up at Isla, the slightest edge of worry creasing the corners of her mouth. Empathy for the trapped hunters, or so Isla hoped.

"Angus was the tallest and strongest among them, and yet he seemed to be fretting the most. Frederick was the smallest, but the most able to accentuate the positive."

Isla stopped reading again, but this time she gave the girl a different sort of smile. "Do you know the word *accentuate*, Ava?"

She shook her head.

"Can you figure it out from context?"

"Does it mean to say something out loud?"

"No," Isla told her. "But that's a very good guess. *Accentuate* means *to make more noticeable or prominent*. Imagine someone was wearing an ill-fitting jacket. That might accentuate their paunch."

And then, just like Isla was hoping Ava would say, "What's a paunch?"

Isla patted her tummy. "It's what happens right here when someone isn't careful about what they eat.

Ava laughed and Isla laughed with her. It was always best when they found something funny together.

Isla finished reading the rest of the chapter, because Ava hated it whenever she stopped in the middle of something. A few times ago Isla was running late and had to stop two-thirds of the way through a chapter. Ava started crying and it took nearly fifteen minutes to console her. That, plus the extra twenty minutes it took to finish the absurdly long chapter made her more than a half hour late to work. She had been judicious about what she started to read before work ever since. Today's chapter was mercifully short.

"This is one of my favorite stories so far, Mommy."

Isla smiled. "I'm so glad you liked it."

Then she told Ava to play by herself, and that Mommy would be right back.

She never minded studying the little girl in front of her, but for some reason found it unconscionably rude to record her notes in Ava's presence. She always returned to the nook in her living room. She used that far more than her home office. A separate room that always felt a little too cold.

Isla got the day's notes into her handwritten journal, detailing Ava's growing ability to understand unfamiliar words from contextual clues. It wasn't just improving, it was improving fast. Much faster than should be generally possible for a girl of her age.

She finished making her notes, slipped the current journal into her desk drawer and locked it, then went over to Ava, still on the floor and building some sort of castle from the bucket of blocks and random plastic pieces that Isla had brought home the week before, announcing to Ava that she was going to make a "pile of imagination" on their living room floor. Really, she just wanted to see what the little girl would do. The results were impressive. It already had towers and turrets, a drawbridge and moat. Lookouts, murder holes, and slits for the brave knights' arrows.

The odds and ends in the bucket weren't much to look at. Scraps of wood and hardware. Some screws and pieces of piping, chips of molding and fixtures from old broken furniture. And yet, what Ava created was clear.

Isla had read only one story that mentioned a castle, and almost in passing. Ava built a bit more each day. It was already spectacular, and Isla's notes on the subject so far substantial.

"It's time."

Ava looked up at Isla and shook her head. "I don't want to go to bed."

"You have to. Mommy has to go to work."

"You could stay home with me today. We could read more. And I could finish the castle."

"You can finish the castle when I get home. I'll even watch you."

Ava started beaming. She loved it when Mommy watched. "Okay. Will you put me to bed?"

She always did, but Isla still thought it was sweet, the way Ava needed her reassurance. "Of course."

Isla tucked her in, kissed her on the forehead, cheeks, and lips, then left her in their apartment, locking the little girl in her room before turning every old-fashioned bolt on the front door and activating both security systems. The one Cascade knew about, and the other one that they didn't, and never ever could.

The elevator doors dinged open to the parking garage. Isla stepped out and walked to her car, hating the long and echoing walk to her usual spot all the way on the other side, right by the exit.

She got in, started the engine by saying *good morning*, then left her building with the usual apprehension that always came when she left Ava alone. The feeling was awful, intense and ever-present. A wart of anxiety that Isla could do nothing to burn off.

Cascade was still the best robotics company in the

world, with the most sophisticated labs by a lightyear at least. And so, of course, Isla was still grateful to be working there. But things had changed, both in ways that were as clear as a cut across the wrist, and in others that felt impossible to pinpoint.

There was a diagnosis for some invisible disease that Isla felt herself constantly circling, as though she was either constantly forgetting to remember or remembering to forget. Both were like fingers pressing into her throat.

It was so much easier, before the fog and miasma. Before whatever this was. Before Ava.

Isla used to love this drive, but now it felt four times as long and she loathed it. She felt safer at home. After paying nearly ten thousand credits for a Duster to ensure that no one was listening or watching in the apartment, Isla couldn't afford the same luxury in her car. The drive flew by when she was getting things done, but now as a passenger, Isla felt almost like a prisoner.

The wide white wall slid open as she approached, then Isla pulled into Cascade Lab #224 and parked in her spot. Unlike in the garage at home, here she was butted up against the building, just like she wanted to be.

Sunshine, the greeter bot who gave everyone an individualized salutation on their way into the building, smiled brightly at Isla as she approached. Its face was bulky and still a bit crude, but tremendous emphasis had been placed on the robot's smile, and it really was a stunning design with a dramatic effect.

The bot's humanoid body wasn't exactly graceful, stilted as it was, but it didn't have to move far, anchored to the entrance by both duty and programming.

"Good morning, Dr. Bligh!" The bot waved at Isla. "I've heard that the work you're doing on the new companion models is coming along nicely! Everyone on the team is very proud of you. From what I've heard, this is going to be the best model yet!"

The voice really made it. As artificial as the robot looked, Sunshine *sounded* as human as anyone Isla had ever spoken to. It was some of her finest work. She wondered if it was possible that the robot knew, even if only in a single line of code, that right now he was greeting his creator.

Probably not. And what would he do with that information if he had it? Knowing something like that might be enough to fry his circuits.

Impossibly, the world was even brighter inside Cascade than it was outside. Sprawling open spaces, mostly white but with a lot of mint green walls, exploding with both people and robots. Like every other Cascade lab, this was the razor's edge of both design and function. Looking through the lobby was like staring into the future. There were robots of every shape and size. All the latest models, including a line of sexbots that looked *almost* human. After decades of R&D, and a gorgeous synthetic skin supplied by an independent firm more artist than engineer, they were getting ridiculously close.

Still, it would be a long time before something like

that would be affordable for anyone outside of the one percent. Sunshine was state of the art in a lot of ways, but still cost only 14.4 percent of the latest line of sexbots.

She rode the elevator up to her office, trying not to think about all of the things that refused to make sense.

All of the contradictions. The many inconsistencies. Conflicts with the truth that might have been lies, or merely a clash between present and past, discord and dissent around the order of history.

Things would be better once Isla was back in her office. They always were.

The doors opened and Isla stepped into the hall.

Her heart was beating inexplicably fast, trying to warn her that something was wrong.

But what? Other than everything.

She opened her office door, heart still pounding immoderately hard, and eyed her current project, sprawled out on the table like a patient awaiting his exam. Passion was a service bot. Made for elite families with large staffs. It was absolutely state of the art. It didn't look human like the sexbots, but it was humanoid, and an incredibly fast learner.

Isla sat on the stool next to Passion, picking up right where she had left off the day before. Not just in her work, but in her thoughts. They came immediately. Of course they did.

Because this didn't make any sense. Dr. Isla Bligh was one of the lead developers in this lab. She was always assigned to the latest and the greatest. So why was she tinkering on a robot like Passion, with a much less sophisticated AI, when she had a robot who would easily pass for a human child at home? Why did they have an entire *team* of scientists devoted to the project?

Ava looked more real than any robot Isla had ever seen, including the most sophisticated sexbot, and right now she was doing her best version of robot sleep in her room, while Dr. Bligh felt like she was faking her sanity.

That's why she took all her notes by hand, in tiny writing. Everyone on Isla's team loved to tease her for still writing things on paper. Everything was digital, and paper was absurdly expensive thanks to the tree taxes and the Cloud movement. But Isla had always liked the art of writing, so it was easy enough to deliver a half-truth, that the tactile practice made everything stick in her head better.

In reality, she needed something unchanging. Weird as it was — and this was just one of the many things that was making Isla reconsider her sanity — everything on her tablets or desktops, both at home and at work, seemed to shift like sand underfoot. It was nothing she could explain, or felt confident enough to even mention out loud, but it was ever-present, like running a tap in the room. Things Isla thought she'd typed would be different when she looked at them. She wasn't sure if the errors were hers or on the devices.

And so Isla continued to write most of her most relevant notes by hand, and every day saw them contradicting each other even more. Passion was bleeding edge, so Ava couldn't exist. But then she would go home to the robot who was almost like a daughter, and Isla would think herself mad.

She had no one to talk to and was afraid of everyone at Cascade. It was the world's best company, and Isla had wanted to work there ever since she was a little girl. But if they were stirring a liquid lie into the world's soup, then she sure couldn't trust them.

So every day Isla spent waiting for something to happen, knowing that it eventually would.

While working on Passion — and making hand-written notes about impossible things — it finally did. Her office door burst open without anyone knocking. Then her boss, Andrew Vaughn, entered the room.

A team of people stood behind him. Security and scientists. This was serious, whatever it was.

Though of course Isla new.

"Dr. Bligh, you need to come with me."

This was the moment that Isla had dreaded. Someone had finally discovered what she'd done, stealing Ava from the lab and then taking her home. An act that Isla barely remembered and still mostly felt like she'd dreamt.

She let them lead her out of the office, marching in front with the Cascade army behind her.

Everything inside Isla was screaming.

If they took her upstairs, she would never come back down again.

And so she ran.

Chapter Five

THE BEAST RUMBLED back into the Rundowns, leaving the Boundary like a skid mark behind him.

The few remaining dreams Bronson ever had about getting out of this place dwindled to mist in the wake of his quickly decaying body and empty credit accounts. He didn't deserve to end up here. He did the work. Paid his dues, and a bunch of other assholes' dues too. Bronson was a loyal employee. A good husband. Maybe a great dad. And he had hopes like anyone, paid into them regularly. But then it was all taken away. And now Bronson had nothing. Or less than that since the subtraction of all that mattered turned his life into a negative integer.

The loss was expensive. Money, time, chunks of his soul. When he was finally upright enough to walk, six months or so after his girls were both in the ground — an expensive thing to do these days, but dammit, some things were important — he had already extended his company's generous leave of absence by three months. He went back and they turned him into this. Five years as a slave who couldn't forget, followed by the second five with Cascade behind him, and Bronson doing everything he could to remember.

He parked the Beast in front of his ancient house, another bounty collected in lieu of payment for a job. A place to both live and work out of, while having to worry about security and law enforcement barely at all.

The place was huge, practically a mansion. On a lot by itself. That alone would have been enough for Bronson. He didn't need the space, but he liked being alone, and the place was great for that. It was in what was once a forested neighborhood, the last remaining house of among a hundred or so. It was off the grid, so his friend Signal hooked him up with running electric through a network of shenanigans that Bronson didn't understand, or need to, thanks to Signal as always.

He walked in, turned on the lights and said, "Suzy, make me a sandwich!"

Of course, no one answered, but Bronson still said it every time he walked through the door. About a month after fate forced him to start coming home to an empty house, he found himself coping by saying something stupid as he opened the door. He and his sister had always liked that commercial growing up, about the Suzy Sunshine robot. The happy maid that every upper-middle-class family deserved.

Weird thing was, the old commercials didn't exist. He'd looked for them everywhere. Because he got to wondering, after he started saying *Suzy, make me a sand-wich!* every time he opened the front door, why robots today were barely doing what they could do a half century ago when he was a kid.

He talked to Sarah, but his sister didn't remember the commercials. Even though they sang the jingle together enough times that Bronson could see them in his head doing it in at least six or seven outfits.

Suzy Sunshine … Shining Suzy … She'll shine like the sunlight to brighten your life!

After way too much back and forth, Sarah said she remembered. But Bronson thought she was just saying that to appease him. She insisted that she *did sort of maybe remember,* but it was hard to know if that was only because he had suggested it, then sang the jingle out loud. She told Bronson that he had probably seen it in a movie, or maybe dreamed it. He got a lecture on the subconscious after that.

But she called him about a month later, almost in a panic. Sarah remembered the jingle, the whole commercial in fact, along with a bunch of stuff that Bronson didn't. Her memory got great, all of a sudden and right before it went tits up for good. She died of a brain aneurism six weeks later. Now he had no one to compare childhoods or memories with.

Bronson trudged down the hallway, and into his office. First door on the right.

The monitor on his desk was lit with messages, but he turned a blind eye. Opened the drawer and grabbed one of the four bottles of painkillers he kept strategically placed around the house.

He poured himself a scotch, watering it down a bit before leaving, taking one sip and three pills on his way to the living room. He plopped on the couch and said, "TV on," not caring what was on, and proving it by closing his eyes and filling the room with a sigh that felt as bottomless as it sounded.

Milo heard and came running over. The dog would never bark again, but he wheezed his greeting every time, his one robotic leg always *just* ahead of the other three, knocking against the hardwood with a timpanic clanking.

Bronson opened his eyes.

"Up here," he said, then patted the sofa beside him.

Milo jumped up onto the couch and started wagging his tail. Bronson looked at the TV. A classic was on, and *dammit*, of course that made him think of Allison. She sure would have thought this place was a shithole, but that wouldn't have stopped her from crawling right up beside him and cuddling through *Apollonia Calling* yet another time together.

They'd seen that one more than any other, because it always made her cry, and made him feel something that he never really understood, and really hated to think about even now. The theme had been done to death since then, but many would argue that *Apollonia* still got it right.

That film, more than anything Bronson had ever seen, could make him believe that love between a human and a robot could exist. For much of the two-hour running time, Bronson believed that a robot could cry.

But it was only a movie. Robots were metal and wires, bits and bytes. There was nothing close to a soul inside them.

That didn't mean they couldn't improve the human condition, like they had done for Bronson. Or his mutt, Milo. Not that he had anything to do with that. A pet had been the last thing he'd been looking for after moving into the Rundowns. But he didn't have a choice. Milo was his the moment he saw him.

Before he met Bronson's acquaintance, the dog belonged to a giant slug of human shit named Christiana Bonner. The woman had a gray buzz cut, and all three hundred pounds of her looked like they left a trail when she slithered along the broken concrete road. They'd had their encounters. Three times. She was running girls, fourteen the oldest among them.

He went in with proof and gave her a chance to help herself by telling him about the monster worse than her so he could go up the food chain and do some permanent good. She neglected Bronson's offer, said that the girls all "found their way" to her — no supplier at all. He had to smash her head and pretend it wasn't personal, although that one sort of was.

The dog would be shot on sight for his illegal leg, so it wasn't like Bronson had much of a choice. Half the time he wondered if it had been a mistake, taking Milo home like he had. It hurt to be needed like that, the way the stupid mutt would stare up at him, love in his eyes, and refuse to leave.

Bronson watched a few minutes of the movie. Whatever the doc had given him was working wonders. He felt stronger than he had in a while. Enough that it was a reminder of how bad he'd been feeling, and a clue that he hadn't allowed himself to see the truth.

Who could blame him? He didn't want to see that any more than he wanted to see the end of the movie.

He said, "Turn it off." Leaned forward, grabbed his tablet off of the coffee table, along with the pen beside it, and settled back against the cushions to record the day's events, scribbling on the glass while drawing from a detective's well of details. He worked to keep his eyes on the tablet, though he was writing without thinking.

But he didn't want them to drift up, which of course they eventually did, or over to the mantle, and yeah, they did that too. Right to the photo, one of the few he still had. Him and Allison. Little Elizabeth. All three of them, no idea that the walls of their world were about to start burning.

Bronson had failed them, and now they were dead.

The picture was still bright enough to hurt his eyes. They sure had been alive on that day, all of them out to the Beach together. Not the real one, of course. They'd never been there. It was too far out of the enclave. But this one had waves and sand and anything else you could want, including a little island in the middle, about a mile away no matter where you were on the shoreline. It was quite a trick.

Elizabeth was so small. But they made her walk

out on the sand all by herself, prove to them that she was a big girl. She kept stepping on shells, because the beach had plenty even though he was never sure if they were real, or where they got them either way. He'd never see that Beach, or Allison or Elizabeth, ever again. Half the time, looking at the memory of that day made the pain stay a few feet away. Other times, like now, it opened the door.

Bronson was miserable. Exhausted. Fumes beyond empty. Still suffering the lingering effects of coming off of the Tonic, muted by whatever pharmaceutical magic Drummond had pumped into his system. Even so, it still felt like being eaten from the inside.

The pain was getting worse, and the relief ever scarcer.

He couldn't help but fondle his gun, consider the easy way out once again. Who would care? He could find a home for Milo, then leave all of the misery behind. He was living out of habit, and a bad one at that.

Bronson wanted to drink more, take more of the pills, and maybe take out his gun and rest it under his chin. Ask himself for the thousandth time what in the hell reason he had to go on?

But he wasn't a coward, even when he wished that he could be. And no matter how many times he might try to convince himself otherwise, suicide was the coward's way out.

Those were Bronson's lingering thoughts as he drifted into sleep. He was still clinging to a dangling thread when he woke to a buzzing on his front door, and Milo loudly wheezing.

"I'm sure it's nothing," he said to the dog as much as to himself, patting the dog on the head before he stood from the couch and grabbed his gun from the coffee table.

The buzzing couldn't get any louder, but closer to the door, the knocking that went along with it did.

He pulled out his phone, tapped *Security*, and looked at the screen to see who was waiting outside his door.

The woman looked worse than harried. Almost hysterical. The young girl with her, probably her daughter, clutched closely against her body — *protectively*.

"Please, open the door!" She pounded her fist against the wood and slammed her palm against the buzzer. "We're in danger!"

Bronson went to open the door as Milo tried to bark behind him.

Chapter Six

Bronson's fingers creaked as he tightened his grip on the pistol, standing at the door, wondering whether it was him or this shadowed edge of the Rundowns that was making him so paranoid.

The other side of the peephole felt wrong. The woman, the girl, the time of night. All of it in a place where someone would have had to look hard to find him, and know exactly what they were looking for.

Part of him wanted to answer his instincts with a pull of the trigger. Eliminate the threat before it could do that to him. But those were delusions. No, you couldn't just trust anyone in the Rundowns, but that didn't mean that people were the enemy by default. And this woman looked far from it. Well educated, judging by her dress, a smart suit that made it look like she was on her way to the office, even though that could have been part of the ruse. Just the kind of getup Bronson used to see when working for Cascade. She also had plenty of money. A well-preserved woman. Looked early thirties, but was probably twenty years older than that. Allison's age when he lost her.

But beyond her professional appearance, there was the desperation in her eyes, and the way she seemed to be shielding the child. She needed help.

They needed help.

Bronson opened the door, curious but cautious, wanting to know why she was here, but careful to keep his cool.

The woman looked up at him. No thank you or anything. She didn't seem surprised that he answered. Just relieved that she no longer had to stand outside. "Don't you ever answer your phone?"

She sounded harried as she pushed her way past Bronson into the open door, dragging the little dark-haired girl in behind her. The child looked around seven, and scared, bordering terrified.

"I'm off today. It's Sunday."

He closed the door and she told him to lock it.

"I always do, but thanks for the suggestion."

"We might have been followed."

Were they really? Or was his paranoia contagious?

"By who?"

She didn't answer. Instead she looked right into Bronson's eyes and said, "Can we talk alone?"

Milo was still wheezing up a storm. He didn't like this either.

This situation was troubling, and Bronson couldn't blame it on the critters. Not this time. Something was wrong with this woman, and there was a haunting in her eyes that reminded him of his own.

He shook his head. "I need something more before I take you into my office."

"You mean like money?"

"No. I mean like a name."

"My name is Dr. Isla Bligh ..."

Bronson perked to the name immediately. She didn't even have to finish, though he felt a chill as she did.

"... and I work for Cascade."

"Lab 224?"

"Of course," she said. There was no other lab around anymore.

"Come on." Bronson led them back into the living room, Milo still barking, then turned the TV on to cartoons. Isla settled the little girl onto the couch, then gave him a look: *What now?*

"If you want to watch something else, just tell it what you want to watch, okay, kid?"

The little girl nodded.

"Her name's Ava," Isla said.

Milo almost made a sound like barking, but then it deflated like a balloon.

Isla followed Bronson out of the living room, then back down the hall and into his office. He pointed to an empty chair on the client side of his desk and they each took their respective seats.

"So what's a woman like you doing in a place like this?" Bronson asked, because that seemed just cliché enough to get the conversation started.

"I need help."

"Of course you do. Care to be more specific?"

"I need to get out of the city."

"Okay, so get in your car and take a little ride. I'm sure you have clearance."

"I drive a company car, and its location is tracked. I hired a car to get here. We were dropped a little over two miles away, down by Angelo's."

Bronson raised his eyebrows. Angelo's looked like a rundown pizza joint, but was actually a chop shop where they turned stolen scrapheaps into impressive metal mutations built to beat the circuits out of each other in illegal rings.

"That was dangerous."

"I didn't have much of a choice. We need help, and I can't hire a car to get us out of the Rundowns, because we'll get flagged at the gates."

He eyed her up and down. "You don't look like the type to ring any bells."

"It's a simple job. I just need you to get me out of the city, and to a man named Howard Knowles. I have money. Just tell me how much I would have to pay."

Bronson shook his head. "That doesn't sound simple at all."

"It's a short drive. I just—"

"No. You're asking me to obscure you from the law. That isn't my business."

"I heard that your business was whatever it needed to be."

"You heard wrong. I can't help you. I'm not in the business of helping fugitives."

"I'm not a *fugitive*," Isla said, shaking her head.

"Then why don't you want to get tagged?"

And then, like lava bubbling over the edge of a volcano's broken lip, she lost it. "Because they're going to kill her!"

"What?" That was the last answer Bronson expected.

Calmer, she clarified. "It's not me that I'm worried about. But if I'm tagged, then they'll know who she is. And then they're going to kill her."

"*Who?*"

"Cascade. Cascade is after me."

Bronson shook his head. Cascade had its issues, but the company's history was rich with good people doing excellent work. It wasn't like they were talking about the money-hungry and militant Infinity. "Why would Cascade want to kill a child?"

"Because I stole her." Her voice didn't crack, but her lip wouldn't stop trembling.

The truth felt like the Beast rolling over his body.

Except that wasn't what this was because Dr. Isla Bligh had to be lying.

But Bronson asked anyway. "She's ... she's *a bot*?"

This couldn't be happening. A bot like that was theoretically possible, albeit decades away.

"No. She's something new. A synthetic life. A synth. The sixth version of an experiment, Ava-Six. But Cascade wants to destroy her."

"Why?" Them wanting to destroy something that couldn't exist seemed even less likely than them having built the thing.

"I don't know," the doctor admitted, and it looked like it pained her to do so. "She hasn't malfunctioned or anything. She's two decades better than state of the art."

"No shit."

But was she? Because right now Bronson had nanos in him that could probably make the same argument.

"She harm anyone? Ignore the Asimov Laws or something?"

"No. Nothing like that." Isla paused, didn't want to say whatever she was about to, but then she swallowed hard and said it anyway. "Maybe it has to do with all of that stuff that happened last year?"

That was the last thing that Bronson wanted to talk about; even thinking about maybe having to consider it for more than a minute or two filled him with anxiety. *The stuff that happened last year.* Whatever that was had left a deep ravine in his mind. He didn't remember much, at least not beyond the contradictions.

"Why not let them destroy her? She's their property, and not real. You're risking everything for a bunch of parts."

The doctor probably would have been less upset if Bronson had punched her in the face.

"She is a child!"

The outburst was surprising. Not necessarily the argument itself, as Bronson had heard it before. There were plenty of crazies who insisted that robots had souls. But clearly she was overly influenced by the way this particular shell of metal and wires happened to look.

"Sorry, doc. But she's a robot. I get that you're proud of your work, but I don't think you want to spend the rest of your life in a pastoral." They all sounded miserable to Bronson, run by AI, with barely any tech for the humans, but the penal pastorals were surely the worst. "Why the risk? What's it to you? I'm assuming you created this thing?"

She shook her head. "I wasn't the lead on Ava-Six, but I was one of the technicians. And I can tell you, she's *real.* Obviously she isn't human, but she's also not a robot. Ava is—"

"I don't have time for this, I'm sorry. It's late and you need to leave."

"*Please.*" She looked so upset. Bronson tried to shake the feelings away. "We need you to help us."

"*You* need me to help. The robot in the other room is waiting for a trip to the recycler, and that sounds about right to me. Bots shouldn't look that human. It isn't natural. Or right."

"I can't go back. I can't allow them to kill her. You have to—"

"I don't *have to* do anything, lady." Bronson leaned forward, all the way across the desk and just enough to make Isla cower back. "I don't give a damn about some stupid bot, or synth, or whatever."

"I told you that I can pay you. Whatever you want."

Not taking the job didn't stop his curiosity. "Oh

yeah, *whatever I want*? How much you thinking that might be?"

Maybe she was playing him. If that thing in the front room was really a robot — and that would explain Milo's incessant barking — then it had to be worth an absolute fortune. Maybe she wasn't looking to protect the kid. Perhaps Isla Bligh had a foreign buyer. A bit of corporate espionage?

"Enough to save your life, Mr. Dodge. To feed the critters and add years to your life."

He narrowed his eyes. "How do you know about that?"

"We both worked at Cascade. My clearance was higher than yours. How do you think I knew to look for you?"

This wasn't worth getting mixed up in. It was a good promise, too easily broken.

"Sorry. But I'm still not interested."

"Don't you want to understand what's happening?"

He rarely thought about anything else.

"What do you mean?" he said, feigning ignorance.

"You know what I mean," she said, her voice quivering. "Why things aren't adding up. Why you have what's inside of you, and why there's a life in the living room who learns and wonders out loud just like any other little girl. And *looks* just like any other girl. Even if she's only wires and programming like you say, how is it possible that she's so much more advanced than anything else? And why would they want to destroy her?"

Isla was right. Bronson wanted to know the answers to every one of those questions, even more than he wanted the money.

"There's a credit vestibule about a mile away. Go out the front door and make a right at the stop sign, then—"

"You want me to pay you now?" Isla looked furious. "You want us to go back out there and—"

"You can leave her here. And no, I don't need all of it. But I need enough to know this isn't bullshit. You're asking a lot, and you're doing it in the middle of a Sunday night."

"Fine," she said, still pissed.

Bronson gave her the rest of the directions and saw her to the door, feeling awful the second he closed it.

That wasn't right. He could have gotten started. They could have even swung by the credit vestibule on their way out of the city. It was an easy job, and he'd probably been going about it all wrong. He wondered why he'd pushed back so hard against her. Was he trying to see how serious she was? Or making her jump through hoops out of some misguided company loyalty? Maybe buying himself time to figure out if he really wanted to take this job?

"Thank you for helping us, Mister. Mommy was scared."

Bronson didn't respond. Just stared at Ava, unable to believe that the thing was a bot.

Milo apparently liked her now. He was nuzzled up

against her leg, no longer trying to bark, tail wagging in tentative arcs.

"Will Mommy be back soon?" the robot asked.

He sure as hell hoped so. Because he never should have sent her outside. Stupid, and an asshole thing to do.

Bronson stood by the window, looking outside, hating himself. He wondered if he should go after her, and if so, was it dumber to go alone, or to take the priceless childbot with him?

He stayed by the window and waited.

Chapter Seven

Andrew Vaughn looked at his watch, then at the
exterior of the old empty house, dark and buried in
shadows.

His security team was assembled, ready to grab the
doctor the second she stepped outside.

Dr. Bligh should never have been permitted to
leave the Cascade campus. And now this was personal
because Vaughn allowed her escape. He and his *six-
person* security team. It was beyond sloppy, and he had
no excuse. If asked, he would recommend for his own
termination. But in the meantime, he would make this
right.

It had all happened so fast. Cascade knew that Dr.
Bligh had the robot, but no one expected her to run.
Not like that.

She made it to an open elevator before anyone
thought to reach out and stop her. The executive lifts
were fast; Isla was in the lobby before Vaughn could
shout the first directive to the team downstairs.

They had the campus on lockdown, with every possible exit aware and on the alert for either the doctor or her car.

But still, she disappeared.

Bligh had apparently seen the intervention coming; no way she would have run like that otherwise.

That gave Cascade a hundred percent confirmation that she was in possession of the asset. She went home. Probably to retrieve the unit. Further proof that she had the thing. Heat signatures suggested that they missed her by less than seven minutes, and that the Ava-Six was indeed with her. Its wake wasn't human, but it was designed to appear like it was.

NINE SERVICE CARS were called in the time window around Bligh's apartment. Three of those nine were driven by a human, so the other six were eliminated immediately. Robots knew robots, no matter what they might look like to the human eye, and thus Cascade would have eyes in those cars. A human driver wouldn't be able to tell the asset apart from any other little girl, but the robot drivers should be able to read its pulse regardless.

Out of the three vehicles, two had short jaunts. Only one headed into the deepest recesses where nobody lived.

That car dropped its passengers off in the middle of nowhere. Or almost nowhere.

There was one house around, an old corner lot and a coincidence too big to actually be one.

The home belonged to Bronson Dodge, former head of security at Cascade Lab #224, before he had a meltdown and Vaughn took his place. Of course they'd kept tabs on the guy. The critters were quickly killing him, but he was doing a nice job of delaying the inevitable, taking a series of hard scrapping gigs to feed the nanos what he could.

But, according to his record, he was already days past his expiration. The nanos were probably already eating him alive. It was hard not to sympathize, and Vaughn did, but his former boss made himself an enemy by harboring one of theirs and helping her to steal the asset.

"You think they knew each other?" asked Polly, the largest of his three men. "From when they both worked at Cascade?"

"I have no idea," Vaughn said. He had wondered the same thing. "It's doubtful. I only know a few of the designers and scientists, and only because I've had to work with them in some capacity, as a witness to some internal investigation. I've checked the records, and nothing ever went down that connected the two of them in any official capacity. But that doesn't really mean anything."

"Are you worried?"

Polly wanted to know, and was the one brave enough to ask, but both Lou and Arnold were interested in the answer.

"Yeah," Vaughn admitted. "A little."

"About what?" Arnold asked.

"Everything I don't know. Cascade is *on us* about this. The last year has been crazy. Every call goes right to the top, and there's always yelling. There are layers. Whoever is yelling at me, and then whoever is yelling at them in the background. They want answers fast, and there's too much we don't know. And *everything* about this case is apparently *Need to know,* but Cascade doesn't see my needs as a priority. We'll have to disagree on that."

He shook his head, looking up at the house. Vaughn hated how unsettled he felt, and that his men could see it.

"There's more," Lou said, looking more anxious than all of them. "What are you really worried about? It's Dodge, isn't it?"

Vaughn sighed. Of course he was worried about Dodge. How could he not be?

He nodded. "Any of you guys ever hear the story about Safe Passage?"

Lou and Arnold both looked away. The story was an ugly one.

But Polly held his eyes and said, "We all know about Passage. What's it got to do with Dodge?"

Safe Passage was a group of grandfathered bots that were funneling children into a sex ring, with a cold calculation unlike anything the company had ever seen. Classified reports said that those Cascade robots were nearly a century old, but that was obviously wrong. The entire field of robotics wasn't even that old. Vaughn brought it to his superior's attention when he discovered the error, after investigating a few old or open cases to prepare for his new job.

"Dodge went above and beyond the call of duty. Found every one of those bots and dismantled them. Cascade wanted them for recycling, but Dodge wanted them destroyed. This was after what happened to his family, but before his total breakdown."

"So he's a good soldier," Polly said. "You're worried he's going to go 'above and beyond' on us?"

Vaughn looked at his men. "It's two things. First, the guy's total disregard for his personal safety. He entered their den alone and took care of all seven robots. And it's not like the old days. We've all seen how much the Asimov Laws have been disregarded and covered up in the last year. Dodge knew it full well. He was ready to die, if it meant ripping those robots to scrap with his bare hands."

He stopped, so Polly prompted, "What's the other thing?"

"The guy obviously hates robots, so what the hell is he doing with Bligh and the asset?" Again Vaughn looked at his men, but understanding was now lighting their eyes.

"Do we shoot to kill?"

"No," Vaughn said, shaking his head. "We're here for Isla and the asset."

"But if we need to?" Polly pressed.

He didn't get a chance to answer before Arnold jabbed his finger at the shadows and said, "Boss, she's there."

They weren't expecting to stay invisible, with their

van parked just around the corner and a pair of C7 drones hovering overhead. But they weren't expecting the doctor's approach. They were camped outside, waiting for Dodge to make a move, and ready to call for backup if he didn't.

She saw them and panicked. Glanced toward the house like she wanted to run — the asset was still inside — then turned and bolted in the other direction.

Polly wasn't too far off, and while the man wasn't a cheetah, he had legs like a giraffe. He loped forward and cut her off after less than a minute of her huffing and puffing. He brought her down hard, then dragged her over to Vaughn, stopping in front of him and raising the doctor's chin so she was looking into his boss's eyes.

"Where is it?" Vaughn asked.

She looked at him as if he were stupid and said, "I don't know what you're talking about."

Vaughn shook his head. "Please."

He left it at that. Vaughn hated this part of his job. He didn't want to hurt, or threaten, her. He would, but only because his name was on the contract and Dodge had left the dirty work for him.

Bligh's breathing was steady, trying to prove that she wasn't afraid. Even in the dark, surrounded by four men on a mission to grab her. Her voice was surprisingly steady when she spoke.

"What do you want?"

"Why did you run?" Vaughn asked.

She smirked. "I had to go to the bathroom."

It was the wrong thing to do when he was trying to be nice.

"Dr. Bligh, you left Cascade premises with one of Lab #224's most valuable assets. One of the *company's* most valuable assets. I am here to collect what you have stolen. We are not so far along that the most dire of consequences is a foregone conclusion. You do what you can to help me, and I will absolutely do what I can to help you."

"You mean help you with destroying her, right?"

Vaughn shook his head. "*It*, Dr. Bligh."

"She's real!"

The doctor looked hysterical. Vaughn felt sorry for her, though it didn't stop him from nodding to Polly.

Polly's fist exploded in her gut.

Vaughn winced. He'd seen Polly hit harder, but that was more brutal than he'd expected on a woman.

"I'm sorry about that. Please believe me when I say that I really don't want him to do that again. So let's make it just the one more time, Dr. Bligh. Where is the asset?"

It took her a moment, notes like a kite in the wind still flapping out of her throat.

Vaughn waited, naively believing that she would cooperate once Bligh's breath no longer had the best of her.

He was wrong and knew it a second before it happened.

She looked up at Polly with a sneer and said, "Good thing you brought a woman hater, since you'll have to try and beat it out of me."

Polly sneered right back. He shook his head. "I don't hate women. Just thieves."

Then he swung with total gender equality.

Bligh was doubled over, gasping. Vaughn waited for her to lift her eyes so that she could see him gesture as he said, "Please, invite them to join us."

The van door whispered open, and two interrogation bots came slinking into the street.

She heard them first. Knew what they were and spun her head to confirm it.

Her eyes found the truth and she turned back to Vaughn, screaming.

Chapter Eight

BRONSON HAD BEEN WATCHING at the window for a while, waiting to make his move.

This wasn't ideal. He had to move, because those interrogation units were a nightmare. They would get their answers, and Isla would never be the same again. Her empathy for others doused from a fire to ash. They would make it so she didn't care about anything. She would look at her own mother with loathing, and it wouldn't even take that long, especially with two of them. The childbot didn't stand a chance.

It also tipped his assailant's hand. It was Vaughn outside, his replacement at Cascade. If they were bringing interrogation bots off campus rather than bringing Isla back to where she belonged, it's because they wanted to bury this here. This was one of those rare situations where the awful had to be done fast and forgotten faster. Bronson had seen a few of these during his time. But in the last year they might have become the rule at Cascade, rather than the exception.

He peeked out the peephole. He'd have to circle out back, catch them from behind, but Bronson wanted one last look before the party started.

He mumbled another thanks to Dr. Drummond under his breath — he'd be dead for sure if it wasn't for whatever she'd done to goose him.

It looked like Vaughn was monologuing, softening Isla so he wouldn't have to use the interrogation bots.

Smart move. That meant that Bronson wouldn't automatically kill him.

He dashed to the back of the house, activating his Perception Protectorate as he opened one of the three rear doors and glanced outside in both directions. Then Bronson initiated three actions, each exactly a second apart.

First he hurled a box of Firelight overhead. As designed, the whistling wind split the wood immediately and a ray of light went careening through the air, bombarding everyone below it with the pure blinding light of a temporary sun. He only felt bad for Isla, and not all that much. The effects were terrible, but they didn't last long. Less deadly than putting your face in a jet engine before it took off, but not much less excruciating.

The humans were jelly, but that wasn't even the point. He needed the quadrant of drones dispatched. Signal's electric bullets did the trick. The drones' sensors were all scrambled thanks to the Firelight, and they couldn't see Bronson for shit, even though they were bright red bullseyes for him.

He squeezed the trigger four times, and down went the dominoes.

The bright light died — it was never more than a flare — but the men were still disoriented.

The interrogation bots had recovered, but they were born for windowless rooms rather than battle.

Still, they were dangerous.

Isla flailed about, obviously unable to see. But that didn't stop her from running. She took off, admirably fast, but then crashed back down to the ground, smacking her cheek on a chunk of broken concrete when one of the two smaller men — not Vaughn or Polly, Bronson knew them both — tackled her from behind.

Vaughn surveyed the situation, trying to decide where they were between the extremes of hell and containment.

Polly barreled toward him. One of his three men was right by his side, yapping in his ear, probably asking him what to do. Vaughn looked like he wanted to smack him.

Crack! Crack!

Bronson pulled the trigger twice, and down went the bots. A pair of bolts right to their systems. Enough lightning to fry them for good. He didn't have time to lower the voltage before Polly was on him, but he pulled back and swung forward, using about two thirds of his own muscles — all that he had at that range — and another third of a kick from his critters to send Polly staggering back.

Bronson's second punch sent Polly down into a gorge filled with muddy water and peppered with crumbled concrete.

Crack! Crack! Crack!

Polly's body crackled hardest, getting shot at close range and taking a brunt of the lowered voltage, but the other two still flopped about like quickly drying fish. Isla jumped back, afraid of getting shocked herself.

Vaughn was still standing, and only because Bronson was looking for someone to talk to.

"I don't want to kill anyone that can be traced back to me, or isn't a direct threat. Your robots are toast and so are the drones. But your men are fine and you will be too if you let the lady go."

"You know I can't do that, Dodge."

"Then I'm sorry. You know what I have to do."

"You're smarter than that," Vaughn said. "You're smarter than all of us. And braver. But you're not bulletproof, and we both know that you only have days to live."

Bronson stole a glance to his side, making sure that Isla was still safe. He wondered for a second if the girl was okay inside, and then remembered that she wasn't real and felt like an idiot.

"You're helping a rogue criminal, a terrorist. You can kill all of us, but you're still a dead man. All of Cascade will be on you forever. You know how this works."

"*You* said it. I only have days to live. So remind me what I have to lose."

"How about everything you stand for?"

"And what's that, Vaughn?"

"You're one of the good guys, Dodge. You know that Ava can't be allowed out there."

"Why not?"

"She's too much. Too advanced."

"Then why did they make her?"

"That's above my pay grade. Yours too. Do the right thing and we'll make it so your critters never bother you again."

Bronson pulled the trigger. Another bolt of lightning.

He looked down on Vaughn's quivering body, the electricity visibly rippling through him.

"If Cascade did the right thing in the first place, you wouldn't be dealing with me now. Don't fuck with me again, Vaughn. Next time it'll be more than the voltage."

He grabbed Isla by the hand and dragged her toward the house. "We don't have long."

"What does that mean?" she asked, looking back at the fallen bots and bodies. "How long do we have?"

"Minutes if we're lucky."

And then they were inside.

The childbot came running into the room, yapping for its mommy, just like it was programmed to. And great, Milo was back to his pathetic attempts at barking.

Isla ran to the robot, trying to calm it. Cascade

was the kind of company that wanted you to talk their products down, rather than flipping a switch like you would on an Infinity unit.

Bronson nodded at the bot. "That thing have a tracker?"

"No." She shook her head.

Bronson raised his eyebrows. "You sure about that?"

"She did. But I disabled it."

"How can you be sure? They tracked you here, didn't they?"

"Because I crippled the chip before I took her home, and tested it several times. They didn't know about it until today, or at least they didn't act until today. Maybe they were watching the entire time, I don't know.

"Do you have a tracker, then?"

"I did, but I fried it."

"Apparently you didn't. Or else there wouldn't be a pile of Cascade trash waiting for pickup on my curb."

Bronson didn't wait for a response. He turned around, marched the few steps to his office, and went inside and grabbed his go-bag filled with miscellaneous weapons, pills, and implements of destruction. He rooted through it long enough to make sure the number one thing he needed was in there, then went back into the living room where the doctor and her robot were waiting with his dog.

"Raise your arms," he ordered Isla.

She complied. Bronson pulled out a black wand

and ran it up and down her body. The wand started to whine, then bled with a spidery light.

"It's still picking up a signal. Frying it isn't enough. We'll have to dig it out."

"Now?" She sounded hysterical.

"No time. We've gotta get out of here. That'll have to come later."

On the other side of the room, Milo was taking to Ava, flat on his back with his limbs all exposed, letting the robot rub his belly. He looked closer. It wasn't petting the dog, it was fiddling with Milo's robot leg.

"Hey," Bronson said. "Leave him alone."

"Is he coming with us?" Ava asked. "I made it so that he can run faster."

"Yes, he's coming." He nodded toward the door, wondering if he'd ever see this place again. "Now everyone out and into the Beast."

Bronson didn't bother explaining what that was. He just walked out the front door, through the scattered bodies, and into the Beast, which opened its doors upon his approach.

The three of them climbed inside, then Milo jumped in after them.

The Beast roared to life and rolled down the street on autopilot, quickly gaining speed.

Bronson climbed into the back and pulled another something out of his duffel. "Give me your arm."

Isla looked up at him. "What are you going to do?"

"I'm going to get rid of the tracker."

"I told you I disabled it."

"And I told you, I'm still getting a reading. You want me to help you, let's start by getting the bullseye out of your body."

"Fine," she said, reluctant.

The robot looked at her, worried.

"This is going to hurt," he warned.

"Of course it is." She closed her eyes and braced for the worst.

Sure enough it was coming.

The needle pinched her skin and he lowered the plunger, injecting Isla with the nanobots that would change the resistance in her blood, trigger a wholesale discharge from the capacitive battery of the tracker, then self-destruct without leaving any trace that they were ever even there.

It exploded under the skin of her forearm.

Isla screamed and slumped in her seat, a nasty black bruise immediately blooming from wrist to elbow. It might match the one already forming on her face.

She looked up at Bronson, meeting his eyes before her head lolled to the side and her eyes went dead.

Chapter Nine

ISLA WAS awake for several minutes before she finally decided to open her eyes.

She listened to the wheels on the road. The panting dog with his thumping tail. The steady beat of her synth daughter's heart. The rasping breath coming from the man who had saved her life and filled her with terror the second she saw him.

The man who would probably haunt her nightmares for the rest of a life that she'd be lucky to have, and only if he managed to keep breathing.

Bronson Dodge was Isla's only hope. Same for Ava.

It sounded like a death sentence, so the doctor did all she could to bury the thought when it came.

Maybe she should have reached out to him sooner. He would have been prepared. Then neither one of them would have been caught off guard.

But she couldn't afford the exposure, or having him turn her away. So instead she plotted and planned and waited for the day that finally came with Vaughn and his six-person security team.

She shouldn't have made it out. If the elevator hadn't been about to close, she never would have. Maybe that was fate paying interest on her preparation. A bonus because the other three elements of her successful escape had been of Isla's own doing.

It was her idea to reprogram the causeway gate over to recycling so it would accept her keycard. That was the last place that anyone would look for her and Isla knew it. Shipments left every hour on the hour. All she had to do was wait in the back of a shipping container. There were no humans in that part of the campus, not even for oversight, so getting in and out was easy enough. She had that part of her plan for about a month, ever since the day Isla first took Ava home.

But the plan came with its stresses, since Isla had no idea how she would get out of the container once it was on the track and on its way to Redistribution. She could end up hundreds of miles away and locked out of her district and enclave forever.

And it wasn't like Isla could practice her escape. Her plan was built on educated guesses, all online, reading blueprints and schematics, calculating odds on a roll of the dice. After studying the diagrams for a while, she discovered that there were narrow slits on the top of the box where a slight human, relatively thin and less than six feet long, would be able to fit.

And so she climbed onto the top, crossed her arms over her chest, and waited, knowing that her margin for error was thin as a web. Once the conveyor gained speed, less than a quarter mile off-campus, the box would lurch forward at several hundred miles per hour and hurl her off of the track.

It was a high jump, and Isla was sure she would break both of her ankles, but she landed and rolled, just like she practiced in her mind more than a thousand times, falling hard but then instantly bouncing back up at a run. She flagged down a car with a human driver, but didn't use any of her accounts. Instead she promised him a brand new tablet when he dropped her off, since they were like candy at Cascade and Isla had plenty.

She was in another car with her fugitive synth less than fifteen minutes later. She called a second car and made him an even better offer, with a brand new general-purpose service bot, still in the box.

Dodge was a disappointment. Not at all the man Isla expected from reading his profiles, or from hearing the few stories that she had while he was head of security.

Part of that fifteen minutes back at her place was spent frying the tracker inside her. But apparently that hadn't worked, and now here she was in the back of some vehicle with Dodge and Ava, on their way to who knew where.

"You're awake," Dodge said, looking at her.

"Hello, Mommy."

"Hello, Ava." Then to Dodge, while looking out the tinted windows, surprised to see that they were still in the sketchier part of the Rundowns, which didn't make a whole lot of sense, seeing as it felt like she'd been down for a while. "I'm awake. Where are we, and where are we going?"

"We were leaving the city when we got some alerts that all the major roads are blocked. They're already looking for us."

"So what are we going to do?"

"Looks like we'll be staying in the slums for a while."

"This car is huge; shouldn't we be hiding somewhere so we're not seen?"

"We are," he said. "This vehicle cloaks itself while in motion. As long as we stay moving we're invisible on the scanners, and even the drones will ignore us. But we need to keep moving."

"Great," she said.

"*You* knocked on my door, lady."

"Is everything okay, Mommy?"

"Yes, sweetie. Of course."

"So we're just driving around the slums, then? That's the plan?"

"I was waiting for you to wake up. Did you get your money from the vestibule?"

"No. The one you sent me to looked like it hadn't worked in twenty years."

No sorry or anything. Just, "Then we're stopping at a vestibule now."

"We're on the run for our lives and all you're thinking about is *money*? You were waiting for me to wake up so that you could go through my wallet?"

"I'm not trying to go through your wallet. We need

money to survive, and it's not like our needs are meager. You brought a shit show to my front porch. And something that's worth killing and burying the truth for. Those are expensive problems. Even if we take your promise off the table, to pay me for this job, we still need money. Not tomorrow or in a few days. *Now.*"

"Maybe we should worry about your money once we're out of the Rundowns."

"Maybe you should listen, doc. We don't do this now, then we don't do it at all. It might already be too late. Do you have any idea how much trouble you're in? How much trouble *I'm* in, thanks to you? Cascade is the world's richest company. Lab #224 is a flea on the dog. Your accounts might already be dry, but if they're not, you need to either withdraw every credit you have, or transfer them to somewhere safe."

She looked at him, dumbfounded. He was right, and she was so obviously naive. So many things she'd exhaustingly planned for, but not the simplest — that her money would be frozen before too long.

"We're here," he said, stopping in front of a vestibule. "And give her a hurry. *Fast as you can* is still too slow."

"I thought you said we couldn't stop."

"We can't. But I hate leaving you alone to circle the block even more than I hate stopping. So, like I said, and am now wasting time saying again, you need to hurry."

The door opened and Isla got out of the tank or whatever it was and scurried over to the vestibule, feeling eyes in the sky that might or might not be there, wondering what Ava might be thinking. The girl had been so silent sitting there in the back. Not her usual inquisitive, talkative self at all.

Isla waved her hand in front of the vestibule, then ducked inside before the door to her unit opened. This vestibule had seven compartments, though there probably hadn't been more than one in use at a time in a couple of decades.

The door closed and Isla stared into the screen.

"Welcome, Dr. Bligh," the vestibule said. "How can I help you?"

"I would like to make a withdrawal."

"Of course, Dr. Bligh. And how much will you be needing?"

"All of it."

A very human pause, programmed to make her think. Maybe reconsider her request before the AI clarified.

"You would like to transfer all of your available credits onto your mobile card, is that correct?"

"Yes, please."

"I don't mean to presume, Dr. Bligh, but are you sure that's wise? I show your current location as——"

"Yes, I'm sure. Thank you."

Another pause, then, "I'm sorry, Dr. Bligh, but there appears to be some sort of hold on your account. The maximum I can let you withdraw is five hundred credits."

She was going to scream. Everything about this was infuriating. The vestibule was an old Cascade AI.

Excruciatingly polite. Isla always felt like being polite right back. But it was aggravating right now, while she was running for her life. If there was a hold on her account, then the vestibule knew it the second it scanned her retina. This was just wasting time. Whether she wanted it or not, the exchange required some amount of back and forth, because that's what made it feel human.

"So you're telling me that out of the nearly three hundred thousand credits I have in this account, I can only access five hundred."

"That is correct." The vestibule lowered its voice to a whisper, the screen glitching with some sort of interference of static. "And really, I shouldn't even do that."

It was sweet, the AI pretending to do her a solid. "Thanks."

But then it surprised her. "I mean it, Dr. Bligh. You're not supposed to have anything, and they won't know that you have this. It's the best that I can do. *Now run.* They know you are here."

The voice said no more.

Why is the machine helping me?

Shaken, Isla scrambled out of the vestibule, then ran to the tank and climbed inside.

It was already moving as the door closed.

Dodge held out his card and she placed hers on top of it, transferring all five hundred of her credits over to him. "Is that enough to do the right thing? I sure as hell hope so, because it's all I have."

"Five hundred credits? You're kidding me, right?"

"My account is frozen."

"Of course it is. And you know what, *right thing* is relative. I have a business to run, or *had one* until you singlehandedly destroyed it. How am I going to survive? I've got days left before my date, and Cascade on my ass."

"Look, I'm sorry. I never meant to—"

"Dammit!" he said as a beeping sound turned his attention to the digital map on his console, where red blips appeared.

Dodge turned the wheel hard right and the tank careened across a couple of lanes.

"What's going on?" Isla asked.

"The vestibule took us too close to the highway. We've been spotted." Then he said, "Blitz Mode on," to the tank. Then to Isla, "Hang on. This will be about a minute of hell, and then everything will be okay. If it works."

"If it works?"

"It'll work," Dodge said, though he sounded a long run from certain. "Everyone grab a strap in each hand and hold it as tight as you can. Stay buckled up and you'll be fine."

He demonstrated by grabbing a strap with his left hand, then he grabbed Milo with his right, holding him against his chest as Isla and Ava tightened their belts and grabbed four fists full of dangling straps.

Then the tank went into Blitz Mode, and Isla was sure that she was going to die.

Chapter Ten

For now, The Beast was safer than them.

It curled into a ball and launched them like a rocket away from their pursuers, blowing drones from the sky with two neat blasts from a pair of micro-cannons built into the rear.

Despite the buckles and straps, they were plenty banged up. They left the hard metal shell that left the tank in a chrysalis and scrambled away on foot. Near enough to the On Holiday Motel to give Bronson a glimmer of hope.

The motel was run by a short but very obese man named Wilder Jennings. He was colorfully against the law. Not a bad guy, but the sort who couldn't help but feel suspicious of the good guys. Most of his business was under the table, and he had themed rooms depending on a person's desired level of pleasure. If you wanted to hide away for a week doing nothing but Tonic, there was a room for that. Same for holo-immersion, DMT shots, or sex of any sort. Wilder had some of the best working women in the Rundowns. Longstanding rumor said it was because he had a couple of sexbots, but that never made a whole lot of sense. A sexbot that could pass for a human was in the R&D phase when Bronson left Cascade, and Wilder's women had been in service for years.

Isla waited in the shadows with Milo and her childbot. Bronson trusted Wilder, but that didn't mean he needed to know about his companions. He paid for the room, a paltry fourteen credits. Wilder wasn't in the business of getting rich; the man wanted to have fun. The land was worthless and paid for. He made his money on volume, always curious to see who was coming for what.

"So just an empty room? You've never stayed with me before. You don't want something …"

"No. Thanks." Bronson had questioned Wilder plenty, because he was the sort of guy who knew something about everything, or everyone, or at least how to find out. "Just a bed to sleep."

"Yours has bugs?" Wilder smiled.

"Something like that."

"Then the room is yours. Enjoy!"

Outside, Bronson led the group into their room.

Isla looked a little less scared. The robot was still keeping quiet, but now it and Milo were never more than an inch or two apart.

"I'm going out to meet an old friend, if I can get a hold of him. He can help us figure out the best route out of the city." Bronson pointed to the TV. "Turn on the news. Let's see if the police are looking for us, or whether it's still only Cascade."

Isla nodded, taking her bot and Bronson's dog to the other side of the room and turning on the TV while he sent his old friend a message.

Signal was the main reason he managed to remain the Rundowns' most successful ghost after leaving Cascade. The guy was a genius, always looking to cut the clearest path, through confusion or anything else that might stand in his way. His answers were simple. Elegant. Obvious once unearthed.

Bronson had a hard job to do, but he was certain that Signal could help him.

He looked over at the TV. There was a story on the news, and it looked like a big one. But it wasn't about them.

The Team People assholes were at it again. United Earth's most aggressive anti-technology terrorist group had just hacked Cascade, stealing data on the mainframes in Lab #109.

That was a bigger story for the company than the childbot, and great news for them. The anchor sounded pleased.

Team People believe that the change promised by God will only be awarded if they cleanse the unnatural addition of human augmentation from the planet.

Nuts on all of them. Team People had lived in the background for years, or at least as long as Bronson could remember. But they'd never held any power, or much of a voice until lately. There was some big event that gave them immediate attention, but it was hard to recall what that was. A big story, biggest in the world it seemed to Bronson at the time. Still, he couldn't remember it even though he was staring at the news and trying his damnedest.

A guy like him, with all of those millions of bitty baby bots inside him, was enemy number one to Team People.

And he was in a temporary war with their biggest foe, his old employer.

The laws were clear. This was no different than any other point in history. People always wanted to find their way around things, and generally went left instead of right when they could. Robot laws were strict for a reason. They were time bombs and everyone knew it. You couldn't account for what might happen, and the variables were exponential. Artificial intelligence was cold and calculating.

Who knew what would happen when that switch inside them finally flipped, and they decided to rise against their creators.

Because it would happen eventually.

Bronson was one of those people, and there were a quickly growing number who didn't believe that the Asimov Laws were infallible.

He'd even had proof a few times, though hell if he could remember even one of the incidents. Those memories were like so many others from the last year. Chopped, scrambled, out of order and out of control — missing.

His phone buzzed. He took it out of his pocket, then looked at the screen and saw it was Signal.

"I'm going out. I'll be at a diner six blocks away. Expect me back in an hour with a plan."

And then he was gone.

Chapter Eleven

BRONSON APPROACHED DEWEY'S DINER, walking at a clip, as he had the whole way there.

He'd been to this place before. Hated it all three times. And each time, swore that he'd never go back. But as per usual lately, life didn't give a shit enough to keep him from doing all the things he didn't want to do.

The place was sick with robots, sentient and bored. Bronson could barely stomach it. He hated it before what happened to his family, but only had occasion to be in these parts once before it went down. But back then, he still got enough of the robots while punching his clock, and sure as hell didn't want to be breaking bread anywhere near a roomful of them.

The place was a beacon of neon. You could see its haze in the sky from a few blocks away. Bronson spied and smelled it halfway there. In the parking lot, he spotted a truck with a garish light-up *Dewey's Diner Delights* sign, advertising that "We Do Catering!"

He circled the place once, just to make sure there were no cops or Cascade security teams sitting on it, waiting for him.

The back lot was filled with broken old cars, including an old-fashioned catering truck with a tall robot leaning against it, doing its best to look like a forlorn human, with its boxy head low and a giant crack running down the side. Another bot, dressed as an attempt at a clown, looking as if someone had put a wig on a toaster, juggling balls for an audience of none while calliope music played from crackling speakers in its torso. Another bot that caught his attention was that of a ballerina with dirty, ripped clothes that had seen better days, dancing, also for nobody. And yet another bot was dressed like an old Vaudeville comedian, telling stale jokes with an even staler canned laugh track punctuating each of them. It was all so painful. The bots felt like they were trapped in a performance loop, which seemed like its own special hell if they were even remotely self-aware.

The back lot clear, he approached the diner's front steps. There were five robots congregated outside, all of them looking at Bronson, and all of them in varying states of design and degradation.

He walked inside and saw Signal immediately, seated at a booth and drinking a strawberry milkshake. And there came his first smile of the day.

It was impossible not to. Signal was that kind of guy. A bit like Wilder in that he liked to color outside the law, but it wasn't born of curiosity so much as an unflinching antagonism toward the system, an aggravated assault against the campaign of lies he was sure Cascade and the government were casting upon the planet.

When Bronson served as head of security for Cascade, Signal was his Moriarty. Bronson respected the man, even though the two were constantly at odds. These days he was Bronson's greatest ally.

Signal had all kinds of theories, about everything. Most were batshit. He was always off his rocker, but he started getting a lot nuttier about a year ago, even more than the rest of the world. Started saying stuff about lost continents in the ocean, and robot radio waves coming from space. The guy was out of his gourd, but when it came to anything that mattered or actually counted in any way, Signal had never been wrong or let Bronson down.

He stood and waited for Bronson to approach the table. Then Signal greeted him with a hug, because he wouldn't have it any other way. Being enemies had made them much better friends.

"So what's up? I know this isn't social. And sorry about the location, but I knew you could get here in no time and there's so much noise among all these tin cans, anyone who thinks to eavesdrop on us here is going to have one hell of a time."

Bronson took a seat and saw no reason to wait. "I'm in trouble."

"You're always in trouble."

"Big trouble."

"You're always in—"

"Cascade is going to kill me."

"Shit."

"Exactly."

Silence, until an antique unit rolled over to take their order.

"What'll you have?" it asked.

"Nothing. Go away." Bronson wouldn't even look at the thing.

It left with an artificial shrug.

"What did you do?"

"*I* didn't do anything. A doctor who works for Cascade showed up at my door with what might be the company's biggest asset."

"Do I even want to know? Oh, who am I kidding, of course I want to know."

"It's a kid."

"So what?" Signal shrugged. "They've had child-bots for years. Same as anything else."

"No." Bronson shook his head. "Not like this. You've never seen anything like this. *I've* never seen anything like this, and I saw most of the R&D stuff that never hit the streets." He shook his head harder. "*No one* has ever seen anything like this."

Signal still didn't seem impressed. "Okay, I still feel like I'm missing something."

"You want to get in deep, walk back to the motel and I'll show you. But I don't think you want that. This will stain you. I need you to help me now, then stay away. Might be something you need to see to believe."

Bronson was still having a hard time with it himself.

"You've seen the new sexbot models, right?"

Of course he had. Even if Signal didn't partake, ads for the line of sexbots were everywhere.

Signal nodded.

"Even those, amazing as they are, don't look *real* real. There's something off about them."

"Absolutely," Signal agreed.

"This robot isn't like that. The doctor called it a synth. The thing gives me the creeps."

Or something like that. Bronson didn't quite know, but it felt strange, familiar but not. Uncomfortable. Some weird emotion clogging his throat, making it hard to describe what it was about that bot that had wormed its way into his head.

It wasn't real like the doc said, that was obviously bullshit. But it was … *something*. Bronson didn't know if it should be understood or destroyed, but it was probably, most definitely both.

And then the truth found his face and Signal smiled, wider than Bronson had ever seen him. He leaned across the table and with delighted eyes he said, "Are you suggesting that this is proof of Divergence?"

Bronson didn't know enough about it to say one way or the other. It had all sounded like hokum until recent events made it harder and harder to say so. But there were a few facts that he couldn't deny, and they had gone from being an itch under his skin to long talons that were shredding his insides to ribbons. Making him trust nothing, including his memories.

Until recently, Bronson had classified the words themselves as the most ridiculous kind of conspiracy theory. Divergence was a hypothesis suggesting there were false barriers around what was technologically possible and that innovation was being throttled constantly. Many of Bronson's run-ins with Signal during his time with Cascade revolved around Signal's belief in this absurdity. But it never made sense to Bronson. Why would Cascade want to throttle their technology? And by decades, as theorists suggested. It violated every law of capitalism.

Yes, he had the nanos inside him. But there was a reason for that. That wasn't throttled technology, it was secret technology. Or at least it was supposed to be. But Dr. Drummond had known what was inside him immediately, and how to treat him. How did that make any sense?

There were too many contradictions, and they hurt too much to think about.

"Maybe," Bronson finally said.

Signal actually whistled. The server bot looked over, but Signal shook his head and waved it away.

"This is crazy. I can see why they're after you. What do you need?"

"A way past the checkpoint and out of the Rundowns."

Signal thought. "What's the risk of crossing over, and getting caught at the gate? You know how to stop people, so wouldn't it stand to reason that you know how to get through yourself?"

"Maybe a few hours ago. Impossible now. There are roadblocks everywhere, and they're checking at every gate."

Signal thought some more. The server bot looked over again, probably taking Signal's pause as a cue that he was ready to order food. Again, he shook his head and waved it away.

"I have good news and bad news."

"You know how I like it," Bronson said.

"Okay, so the bad news. I have something for you, but the thing runs hot and is totally untested. It could fritz out at any time. But it will allow you to track the cops and equip their communications, so long as it's working."

"Why is it untested? You've given me stuff like that before."

"And they always stop working, right?"

"Eventually."

"That's because the tech changes. We're outrunning Cascade. Don't you remember when we were on opposite sides? You were always a second behind me."

"You always did your best."

Signal laughed. "And you never made it easy. The new guy is boring by comparison."

"Glad to hear it. So what's the good news?"

"I figured you might need something like this, based on your message, so I have it with me."

Signal looked around the diner and made sure no one was watching, though it seemed like a futile exercise to Bronson, considering that cameras could be microscopic and there were fucking robots everywhere, then discreetly passed a tiny pink box across the table.

Bronson only saw it for a flash before it was in his pocket. "Pink, huh?"

"It's something I'm trying. No one ever suspects stuff when it's pink."

"That a fact or a theory?"

Signal smiled. "If it came from me, buddy, then it's one and the same."

Bronson missed his friend, and had the distinct feeling that he might never see him again. Besides, sitting there smelling the food made him hungry, and he figured he should take some home to Isla, and maybe a can of oil for the bot.

The server came over and this time it was finally wanted. Bronson ordered pancakes, two stacks, plus a bunch of stuff to go. Signal ordered oatmeal.

Bronson felt a little indulgent, eating in the diner after his business was done, but the food was good and the company was better. He imagined the doctor smiling as he handed her the bag of take-home.

He wanted to hear more about the artificial rift, and pancakes would buy him some time.

So he listened while they waited for their food, and then more as they ate, all the time wishing that he hadn't written Signal's nuttiest theories off for so long. Because right now, they didn't sound that nutty at all.

He finished his last bite of pancake, then lingered.

A few minutes later it was raining and Bronson cursed himself for not leaving sooner.

Chapter Twelve

ISLA WAS FAR from feeling safe, but she was much better than she'd been at any other time since before Vaughn appeared in front of Dodge's place. She didn't like that he'd gone off to some diner while leaving them here, but she also didn't blame him. It made sense. He needed information and they needed to stay out of sight. Dodge was already hot. Isla was hotter. And Ava the hottest of all. About to combust, and the poor thing didn't have a clue.

Although the fear was a bit thicker without him around, it was also nice to be temporarily freed from his brooding. That dark demeanor. The loathing for robots.

It was hard to know what Ava thought about Dodge without asking her, and Isla didn't want to do that because it would probably come up that she had been asking about him, unless she specifically ordered Ava not to. But that seemed like a mistake, teaching the girl to start keeping secrets and telling lies. Those vices were ruining Cascade.

Isla didn't have to ask. She could see for herself. Ava looked happier the moment he left, and had been playing with Milo ever since, chatty as she scratched his belly, the dog's time split between a wagging tail and a goofy drooping tongue, displaying his underside as he whined, acquiescing to Ava as the dominant male.

Milo was agitated. Confused, but in no way aggressive.

"What do you think of him?" Isla asked her. It was the first real-life dog she'd ever seen, unless she happened to spot one outside the window while in transit.

"He's soft."

"He is." If not a bit mangy. "What else is he, Ava?"

"Friendly."

"Yes, he is very friendly. Why do you think that is?"

"Because he doesn't want to be alone. Mean makes you alone more, and that makes you meaner. Milo wants to be happy."

"How do you know that he wants to be happy?"

"Do you see his tail?" Ava pointed. "He waves that back and forth when he's happy. That means he's happy right now. But he's even happier when I do this."

She scratched Milo's belly and his metal leg began to scrape against the floor.

"Is there anything special about him?"

"Yes." She vigorously nodded.

"What is it?"

"If you look into his eyes, it's like an almost person."

"And what is an almost person?" Isla asked, her heart beating faster. Practically pounding. She had no idea what Ava would answer.

"Milo is thinking. Very much." Ava was still nodding, now slowly up and down. "And he feels all the feelings, like happy and sad."

She stopped talking, idly petting the dog.

"Go on …" Isla prompted.

"So he's an almost person." Ava shrugged. "Like me."

And that broke her heart. An *almost person*. What was that? A dog wasn't an almost person, it was an all-the-way dog. But Ava was definitely more than a robot. She was a thinking being. Alive, not all that different from her.

A child, with her makers intent not only on her destruction, but on her deletion from the record as well.

Ava wasn't her daughter, but she might as well be. There were plenty of well-known platitudes about parenting.

A mother is only as happy as her saddest child.

There is nothing closer than a mom and her daughter.

Once they're born, you will find more love in your heart than you ever imagined.

And, the one that she couldn't stop thinking about:

The love of your child is indescribable. Beautiful and deep. A mother will do anything to protect it, and them.

That's what Isla was feeling now, looking down at a synth that might be a child, but definitely wasn't her daughter.

Ava wasn't a mind reader, but she was fluent in Isla already. Maybe her body language, maybe something else.

"Did you ever have any children?" Ava asked her.

"No." Isla shook her head. "I never did."

"Why not?"

"I never had any time."

"Everyone has exactly the same amount of time."

"That's true, Ava. But we all choose to spend it differently. I never had the time for relationships. Or, more accurately, I never *made* the time."

"You cannot ever make time like you can make money, but you can choose how to spend it, just like credits. Is that right?"

"Yes, Ava. It is."

"And you didn't want to spend it on relationships or children?"

Isla laughed. "Maybe I would have if I'd been given the right offer. But there weren't exactly a lot of knocks on my door."

Ava looked at her, eyes squinting. "But why, Mommy? You're very pretty. Grown-up boys should like you very much."

"Thank you, Ava. But I guess you have to be out there for the grown-up boys to notice you, and I never was."

"Why?"

"I was always working."

"Were you always working because you love your job?"

"Yes. That's exactly why. I wanted to be part of something bigger than me — something revolutionary. And that's what it used to be like, working with Cascade."

"Making robots like me?"

"No." Isla shook her head. "There are no robots like you. I was part of the team that gave you life. The lead, actually."

It was hard not to cry, so she simply stopped talking.

"Thank you for making me."

A tear fell down Isla's cheek. She said, "Of course," because what else was there to say?

"Is that why you think that I'm special? Because you made me? Like an art project?"

Ava smiled at Isla, without any clue as to the barbs on her words. It broke her heart that the girl had no idea how special she was — how capable of changing the world.

Isla knew it immediately. That's why she had to steal her.

The days were like bookends, the one where she knew that Ava was more than a robot, and the one where Cascade ordered her murder. Isla had poured her soul into the project, given everything she had and more. All of her faith, and every ounce of devotion. Cascade was the god that she prayed to, and she never missed a moment of church. But Isla was there the day the light went bright in her eyes forever. When the synth started asking questions.

She wanted to know what water was made of, how big the world was, and the nature of infinity. Ava's questions surprised none of the scientists. She was the sixth iteration, after all.

But they should have because that time they were different. Born not of call and response or if-then statements, but of the bottomless well of curiosity that lives inside every child.

Isla could see it in her eyes. And then, she could never unsee it again.

Maybe that's why she could never forget.

It was fight or flight, the day her version was scrapped. They would be starting on Ava-Seven on Monday.

Strangely calm, Isla Bligh broke every rule she had sworn to uphold, stole priceless property from Cascade, smuggled it home, then lived with it as her intimate contraband for the most tension-filled month of her life.

Maybe having Ava at home kept Isla remembering the truth, where the other scientists found it all too easy to forget.

She'd gone into work the following Monday, but there was no Ava-Seven. Isla's team had been moved to the design of a landscaper bot instead. It had an interesting design, definitely retro, with an odd swoop for what looked like old-timey lacquered hair, and a faux pack of cigarettes rolled into its sleeve.

The team was aghast. This robot was inferior in every way.

They were promised that it was only a temporary project.

But it wasn't.

And only Isla seemed to realize the truth.

So she counted the days, while awaiting discovery.

"No. That's not why you're special," Isla said, taking Ava's hands. "You're special because you're the kind of child who can change the world."

"But I'm not *really* a child, right?"

"I think you are."

"Is that why you let me call you Mommy?"

"Yes, Ava."

"Mommy?"

"Yes?"

"Will you read me a story before I go to sleep?"

The synth didn't need sleep, but she did like to power down with a story.

"Of course. What would you like to hear?"

"The one about the boy who wants to be real and can't ever lie."

It was Ava's favorite, and while Isla would have loved to pull up any of the three versions she carried on her phone, she wasn't willing to risk turning it on. Not when it was standard issue for all Cascade employees.

With Milo still wagging his tail at their feet, and Ava's head against her chest, Isla closed her eyes and started telling the story of Pinocchio, the wooden boy who longed to be real, to a little girl who felt desperate for the very same thing.

BRONSON OPENED THE MOTEL DOOR, not at all surprised to see that Isla was sleeping. He also wasn't surprised to see that she had powered down the robot. He *was* surprised to find her clutching the thing like a doll, or worse, like the daughter she wasn't and never could be.

Maybe he shouldn't have been surprised, the way she'd been going on and on about the thing being real. The best synthetic skin in the business didn't erase all the wires and gears underneath. It didn't change the truth that the thing didn't bleed or feel. It couldn't even think without a bunch of numbers telling it what to do. People had been assigning human behavior to animals forever, but that didn't mean the creatures weren't relatively stupid. The same was doubly, triply, *quadruply* true when it came to robots.

The room wasn't big and the lone bed was taken. Bronson didn't want to think about what this room was regularly used for, but the size and shape of its only chair gave him some idea.

He anchored his feet into the carpet, gripped the arms, and used his body weight to turn the giant chair so it was facing the door. Then he sank into it. Milo got up, stretched, and traded locations, moving from in between the doc and her bot, over to Bronson.

He pulled out his gun, set it on his lap, and closed his eyes. He heard himself snore, ignored it, then settled into the dream that he knew would be coming, and wasn't sure that he wanted at all.

Bronson surrendered like always, because seeing them this way was better than nothing.

He was back in his old life, about to open the door to his family. Before the worst of the Rundowns. He had never even seen the abandoned mansion that would one day be his home, spending his nights in a nice three-bedroom instead, over on Evergreen with his wife and daughter, the sun and the moon in his sky.

"I'm home!" Bronson called out before shutting the door behind him.

The girls greeted him with a parade like always, with little Elizabeth skipping around his knees, and Allison kissing him full on the mouth, before leaving his face with a final graze of her lips against his cheek.

Like always he said, "And how was your day?"

And like always Elizabeth went first. "Mom made me take two naps because I wasn't tired enough for the first one."

Then Allison next. "Too long without you."

Bronson didn't always know when he was inside the dream, but this time he did. It was more painful that way, watching an arm's length away, knowing he was trapped, that he couldn't scream out to warn his past self, yell at him to cling to what he had, and never let it go for dear life. Not for anything.

He wished he could go along for the ride like he sometimes did, then remembered like a freshly minted memory on waking. But today he had to watch, and listen out loud to some of his many mistakes.

"So did you ask?" Allison looked hopeful. Not that Bronson would do as he promised, because he always did that. She wanted him to mean it, to fight for them, to demand more from his bosses instead of always taking whatever they gave him. "Are you going to be able to take any time off?"

"I did ask, and it looks good. Nothing for sure, but we can probably schedule a week sometime this coming fall. Winter at the latest."

She stared at him in that way she did whenever they talked about this.

"I asked," he said, hating her disappointment.

"I know you did," Allison said. "But you didn't *insist*."

"You should have insisted, Daddy," Elizabeth scolded, although that part hadn't really happened.

"I'm sorry. I'll keep pressing it."

"We deserve a vacation, Bronson. Just the three of us. You work hard, and—"

"You're right," he said, cupping her chin and staring into her eyes. "And I'll take care of it. Soon. I promise."

"That's what you always say. But it hasn't happened."

"It will."

"But *when*? I'm exhausted. I'm glad you think I do such a great job, but it isn't easy. And I miss you. Elizabeth misses you. This isn't what it's supposed to be like; it isn't how you said it would be."

"How about if we get you some help?"

"I want to get away."

"And we will. But why not get a little assistance in the meantime? You've always pushed back before, but there isn't any reason. It's one of the perks of my job, so why not cash it in? My discount is nearly a third, and we have plenty saved. You'll have all the help you want around here, and then vacation will be a bonus, not something you're starving to get."

"I'll be starving to get it anyway. We could take four vacations for the cost of a nannybot, even after your discount."

"It's not the money, it's the time."

Allison was getting agitated. "It's *always* the time."

"I'm sorry. There are a lot of issues lately. What do you—"

"Then why don't they add more people to your team?"

"That's what I keep saying, but the security division needs to stay small."

"It's stupid."

Then they left it there like always, until the dream turned inside out and six weeks later.

"I'd like for you to meet Nanette." Bronson was proud, waving his hand up and down the robot as though he'd made it himself. "The newest member of our family."

"I don't know about that," Allison said, eyeing the robot dubiously. "The dishwasher isn't part of our family."

"You should've heard the spiel they gave me. This one is state of the art."

Nanette held out its hand. "I have been designed to make your life easier, Allison. May I call you Allison, or do you prefer Mrs. Dodge?"

The robot's voice was soothing. Allison's face instantly settled, though she probably would have been surprised to know it. She smiled. "Allison, please."

"Allison it is." The robot clapped, looking positively delighted. "Is there someplace I can start? Some way to please you? I'll have my routine down in no time, I promise you that. But I will need a hair of direction as we're starting. Ooh! When do I get to meet Elizabeth?"

"I'm right here!" she yelled, running into the room.

"She'll do everything for us," Bronson continued to crow, squeezing the robot's shoulder, marveling at how the latest models had skin that felt so soft to the touch. "She can …"

He stopped, laughed, and nodded at Nanette.

"You tell her. What are some of the many amazing things you can do?"

Then Bronson crossed his arms and waited for the love of his life to be impressed. To appreciate the marvel of technology that his job, and position within that job, afforded them. Something elite. Top of the line. The absolute best because that's what his family deserved.

Nanette said, "Oh, I can do a number of the things that keep you doing rather than living. But I don't want to take away the joy of any tasks that fill you with a sense of accomplishment. You can decide how to use me best. I can, of course, cook and clean and do all of the laundry, or any of your assorted household chores. And if you like to cook, I'm happy to prepare your ingredients. Same for anything else you need, now or later. I am an excellent nanny, and I never go off duty, so you can have peace of mind with whatever you're doing that Elizabeth is well taken care of. Really," the robot shrugged, "I can do anything a wife or mother would do, except for all the stuff in the bedroom. But if you're interested in that, Cascade has a number of excellent sexbots that I would be happy to recommend, depending on your preferences. Really, they're the best in the world."

"Ooh, she said the S-word," Elisabeth said, giggling.

"That won't be necessary." Allison blushed, turning from Nanette to her husband. "We can't. What would I do, if it took all of my chores away?"

"You're always complaining that you don't have any time, and that you're tired. Nanette will take care of that for you." Another wide smile. "Isn't that right, Nanette?"

"It sure is, Mr. Dodge."

"I told it to call me Mr. Dodge," Bronson said, still smiling. "I like the formality."

"I'm not complaining," Allison argued. "I'm stating a fact. Running this house and raising our daughter are exhausting jobs, but that doesn't mean I don't want to do them, or that I'm not willing to. I just also want some time off, because you deserve it, and so do we."

"If I promise that we'll take our vacation *and* keep the robot, will you promise to enjoy Nanette?"

"I can promise to try."

But then Allison smiled and Bronson knew that everything would be okay.

Too bad they never got their vacation, and—

Bronson woke with a start, his ears perked to the sound of someone picking the lock outside.

He was on his feet, gun in hand, and marching toward the door.

Chapter Thirteen

BRONSON PEEKED out of the peephole and practically wanted to laugh.

Except this was the opposite of funny. Or a cross between that and pathetic.

There were a couple of V-heads trying to pick the lock, probably thinking they were quiet like mice when the pair of rats were practically rattling chains like Marley's old ghost.

If he were feeling more charitable, as he had while dealing with their kind so many times before, Bronson wouldn't have been able to stand against the wave of empathy. It always hit hard enough to make him feel sorry for the lot of them.

Virtual heads were hooked on expensive memory simulations. They only worked to feed the habit, until they couldn't work anymore, at which point they fed it however they could. Worse than drugs, like a billion little barbs in the cortex. The extreme end of a Tonic addiction, because the simulations could soothe the effects, and hurl a user into an endless loop. But fuck that, Bronson would rather die than let that happen to him.

"Wake up," he said to the robot.

But it didn't respond.

"Wake up, robot … wake up, Ava … Ava, wake up."

Milo lifted his head, opened his eyes, looked over at Bronson with a questioning yawn, then sighed and rolled over.

Bronson took another look out the door, saw the two tweakers still fumbling. They'd be a minute or so.

He went over to Isla. "Wake up," he said, shaking her gently. "I need you to take the bot and the dog into the bathroom. You need to hide, you got it?"

"What's wrong?" Isla was immediately alert, her eyes wide and shoulders straightening.

"Trouble outside. I've got it, but I want you safe. I tried to wake up the rob—"

"She's not a robot." Isla touched Ava on the cheek. "Sweetie, it's time to wake up."

The robot's eyes shot open.

There was a loud *CLACK!* from outside.

Bronson turned to Isla, growled "Now!" and ran back to the door, just as it crashed open.

The first addict poured through the opening, in perfect time to receive the end of Bronson's downward swing. The butt of his Solacer connected with the man's jagged implant scar, running like a crooked ravine across his mostly shaved head. That impact made a sound like taking a hammer to rotting fruit, and the tweaker fell in a heap to the floor.

The second addict was already cautious, pulling back as he made it through the doorway, his hands raised, palms out and close to his body, letting Bronson know that it wasn't too late, that this didn't have to be a problem.

The first guy was bleeding on the floor. Maybe he was dead.

Fuck. Bronson didn't mean to kill him.

Bronson grabbed the second guy by the collar, looked into his twitching eyes, darkly ringed in shadows of black. It looked like he hadn't slept for more than an hour in years.

He snarled, "What are you doing here?"

The man was a coward, and Bronson could hear it in every crack of his voice. "We followed you from Dewey's."

"Why?"

"Because you were talking to Signal. And Signal has the wares. We could either use 'em or sell 'em."

"Are there any more of you out there?"

The tweaker shook his head.

Bronson nodded down at his comrade's fallen body. "You wanna end up like your friend?"

Still shaking his head, now he said, "No."

"See if he's alive."

He kneeled down, took his friend's pulse, and looked up at Bronson. "He's alive."

"Then congratulations, you get to keep living with him, but only if you promise to get the fuck out of here by the count of three, with the full knowledge that I will empty my weapon twice, splitting my bullets between you before I stop to reload and do it again. You got it?"

The first addict was clearly the braver between them and looked ready for round two. He probably had some sort of a bravery simulation running in the background. But different from Bronson's Aversion chip in that it had turned this guy into an idiot.

"Deal with your friend," he said.

Addict Two started pulling Addict One toward the door, but Addict One didn't want to budge.

"One ..."

"*Come on, Ricky.*"

"I ain't going anywhere."

"Two ..."

"Come. *On.*"

Addict Two yanked him through the still-open doorway, just as Bronson said, "*Three.*"

He closed the door behind them, but the lock was busted so it didn't much matter, then went to the bathroom and knocked. "It's okay. You can come out now."

The door opened and Isla shuffled out first, looking tentatively around the tiny motel room. There wasn't much to see, but her eyes landed on the busted door and that told her plenty. But she still had to ask.

"What happened?"

"V-heads. We're not safe. We've gotta go."

"Do you think they'll come back? Or bring anyone else?"

"I'm not worried about them, but if they made me, then someone else might have. It's my fault. I can't believe I let them track me. A doctor helped me yesterday, gave me something to quiet the critters. Maybe now they're *too* quiet."

"Are you sure we have to go?" Isla suggested. "Maybe we could wait until morning."

"Absolutely not. We're leaving in five minutes."

The robot looked scared, cowering by Isla, just like its programming told it to.

"Are we walking back to that tank?"

"No," he told Isla. "The Beast is being monitored, for sure. That car is dead, but I do have a different idea."

"Are you going to tell me what it is?"

"You've gotta lot of questions. Why don't I answer them on the way?" Then he reminded her. "Four minutes."

Bronson left the motel and went to wait outside. Three minutes was too long. Hell, so was one. What did they need to do? There wasn't anything to pack, and only one of them needed a bathroom. Milo had probably pissed on the rug already, since the whole place smelled like an invitation to do so.

He was sick of having to explain everything. At least when Bronson had his team at Cascade, questions came with obvious answers. But everything now was a mystery.

Chapter Fourteen

THEY WALKED in a tight cluster toward the diner, sticking to the darkest shadows, with Bronson keeping a lead of no more than three feet at any given time. He couldn't help but feel that there was someone at the diner awaiting his return. Word got out. Someone else had seen Signal, or maybe that server bot alerted the authorities.

Dewey's Diner would be the stupidest place in the world to go right now, if there hadn't been the perfect vehicle to maybe aid in their escape. Bronson explained his plan when they were two blocks away. He expected some sort of pushback. Instead Isla said, "I think that might work."

"Wait here," he said when they were all standing across the street from the diner, now dark. Its parking lot, earlier so lively with commotion, was now almost a graveyard. It had once been a 24-hour diner, but nowadays most businesses avoided the early morning hours when crime seemed to be at its worst.

"I'll be back in a minute. Be ready to jump inside."

"How do you know you can get the truck?"

"I don't," he said.

"How do you know that it's still even here?"

Bronson shook his head. "I don't know that, either. But I'd be surprised if it was gone."

Then he turned around, crossed the street, and headed to Dewey's parking lot, hoping that the truck was still there, and that his plan wasn't fruitless.

So far, so good. It was still there, though the *Dewey's Diner Delights* sign was now dark.

Because where else would the truck go? The place probably had its last catering job more than a decade ago, though it might never have been in that business at all. The truck might have been a prop. Even if it wasn't, it might have been stuck in that spot forever. The AI might not even respond. What then?

Bronson glanced around, making sure that no one was looking. He had to do this the old-fashioned way, because apparently his critters were still on strike.

He ran in a crouch from one side of the lot to the other, and slipped in between the catering truck and another vehicle that also looked like it hadn't moved in years.

Up close, he was surprised. There was no way to tell how old the truck was without running the number, and no way to run the number without getting it flagged, but the thing was obviously ancient. Peeking through the window, it looked like it even had a manual drive. Good news for Bronson if the AI was dead, seeing as he had learned to drive on a hobby car, reconstructed from the old days, and without any AI onboard.

He broke the window, then reached in to unlock it.

The door swung open and Bronson climbed inside.

"You can't take that," said a voice. "It's mine."

Bronson was already settled into the driver's seat. He turned and looked into the copper-ringed eyes of a prehistoric unit. Not copper … it was rust. The thing had zero grace, all sharp edges and jagged metal. The design would never be approved these days, and Bronson couldn't imagine it *ever* having been approved by Cascade, even in the earliest days of the field. Its look was just too crude. Like a child's drawing of a robot brought to life.

"Robots can't have things," Bronson said. "They *are* things."

"Dewey gave it to me, when he started the diner," the robot said, looking like he might cry, even though Bronson didn't exactly know what that meant, especially since the hunk of junk didn't have the equipment to do so. Still, he couldn't help thinking it. "He said that I could be in charge of the catering. And one day, I will be."

Bronson looked down and pressed the *On* button.

The truck rumbled with life and filled him with relief.

"If you take the car, I'll have to report you."

Dammit. Bronson really wished that the robot hadn't said that. Now he'd have to turn it to scrap.

Except, looking into the robot's approximated

eyes, he couldn't bring himself to do that. The poor heap looked like his life was miserable enough. Bronson shot him with a low voltage bolt instead, putting the bot down but not out, then drove out of the lot.

Only after he was idling, waiting for the doctor, the dog, and the bot to climb inside, did he properly catalog the thought. That the poor heap's *life* was miserable enough.

What the hell is wrong with me?

Chapter Fifteen

THE TRUCK MADE her feel like they were going to die.

Isla braced herself for exactly that. Even if they crashed and burned, Ava would be fine. Her skin would get shredded, but her body could take one hell of a beating, and had, over and over before they gave the synth her epidermis. Right now, Isla wasn't even sure who was offering the comfort, the doctor or the little girl with the artificial heart.

They were there in the back of the catering truck, feeding off of each other.

Had been for the last fifteen minutes since they pulled away from Dewey's with the stolen truck. Now, in the last few minutes, Ava's breath was coming faster. Even if it wasn't really coming from a set of lungs, the action was unsettling.

Isla kept glancing nervously up front. The truck was ancient. Dodge had to drive it himself. He was able, but not without a lot of grunting and muttering under his breath.

He kept fondling a small pink box. At first, Isla had no idea what it might be. Then she realized that it must be what he got from that guy, Signal. Some sort of device to get them around the roadblocks.

And all had been fine with the four of them rolling along in the claptrap, until the walls began to close in and they were quite suddenly surrounded by danger. It happened so slowly that neither Isla nor Dodge saw it coming. Milo might have, the dog did whine, but Ava almost certainly did.

"There's been an accident," she said.

"How does it know that?" Dodge asked, checking his box.

"I don't know," Isla admitted. There was a lot about Ava that was still a big mystery to her.

In minutes, the accident turned into a sea of cars waiting for somewhere to go. That didn't happen often. The AIs usually talked their way through the patterns. This was a full-blown roadside check.

"Fuck," Dodge said.

"It'll be okay." Isla tried to reassure him, but what did she know?

They were trapped, not just in traffic, but by the entire situation. Police and emergency vehicles were screaming by. An assembly ahead with more still coming from behind. The accident, or whatever, wasn't visible from where they were, but it was obviously awful enough to create an aisle of cars on either side. Getting off the highway was impossible if they wanted to stay invisible. Hard enough with all the crazy colors on their corroded old van.

They were stuck, and would have to see this through. But all of them were sweating. Including Ava, though Dodge would never believe it.

"There are too many cars." It wasn't a question. Maybe Ava could feel all the AIs in the cars around her, like too much chatter in a crowded restaurant.

"It'll be okay," Isla repeated, this time to Ava.

"The cars are all kinds. The loud ones are very busy."

"She means the emergency vehicles," Isla clarified.

"I figured," Dodge grumbled.

"What are we going to do?" Ava asked.

"Nothing for now," Dodge answered. "The two of you are going to stay put back there, and we're going to hope that I can get us through the checkpoint."

"What if they recognize you?"

"They won't."

"How can you be so sure?"

"Because I won't let them," Dodge said, irritated. "The critters will change my face if I need them to. I've been told it will feel like my face is being dipped into a vat of boiling cheese, and there's no going back, so my pretty mug'll be gone for good." He shook his head. "No danger of them recognizing me, though."

Isla felt a chill. This guy was so damned serious.

Ava let out a whimper, right before she started to lightly shake.

Isla held her close, shifting her body slightly to obscure Ava from view. The ruse didn't last. About three minutes after she first started shaking, Ava was rattling like a loose bolt.

"What's wrong with it?" Dodge asked, looking into the rearview.

"I think she's getting nervous."

"Nervous? Can't you shut that response down?"

"Are you a light switch?" Isla didn't wait for his answer. "Well, neither is she. This is what it's like when she's anxious. She has some … *issues*. Ava doesn't deal with stress well. This could cause problems."

"What do you mean 'issues'? You mean bugs, right? *Humans* have issues. We're all fucked in the head so we pay the shrinkers to tell us inside out and upside down from sideways. Robots go buggy. They get glitches."

"What's the difference?" Isla said, though it was the wrong time to challenge him.

"What kind of problems?"

"Ava has a powerful self-preservation mode. It kicks in whenever she's in danger, or knows that she's about to be. That goes live and she's going to do anything and everything she can to get free of whomever or whatever might be holding her."

"Can't you stop it from going live? Put it on standby or something?"

"Can you stop a child from having a tantrum? Or an adult from his depression? Sure, we can try. But Ava is her own … being, and she's going to do whatever she can to protect herself. She'll hurt someone if she believes that will save her."

"So you're saying the Asimov Laws are irrelevant with this one?"

"No. Not exactly. I would never say that the

Asimov Laws are *irrelevant*. But Ava is different. The Laws are for robots that are ready for the assembly line. Ava was still in design and development, and while robots in that phase must still adhere to the Laws, it's different."

"Different how?"

"*She* is what she must protect most. Cascade has spent billions on Ava-Six, so when it comes to the math, self-preservation might have been programmed more strongly into her than *not hurting a human*."

"You're saying Cascade put their bottom line first?"

"I'm saying that they did what they could to protect their asset, and that we should know that going in if we don't want to be surprised."

Dodge turned around, taking his eyes off the road to fix them on Isla. "Are we in danger? Can that thing ignore the Asimov Laws and hurt *us*?"

"I would never hurt any of you. Or anyone," Ava squeaked like a frightened child.

"She wouldn't," Isla agreed. "Not on purpose. Yes, her self-preservation mode is dangerous. The Asimov Laws would probably stop her before she did anything fatal, no matter who was trying to hurt us or how much danger we might be in. Kicking and punching, on the other hand, are well within the bounds of possibility."

"*Within the bounds of possibility?*" Dodge repeated. "Or probable?"

"I don't know, Dodge. Why does it matter? And why do you look like that?"

He looked pissed, or bothered at best. Even more than a few minutes ago.

"I'm just trying to figure all of this out. Unknown variables will end this thing ahead of schedule more than anything else, so I'd like to plug as many answers into the equation as we can before we have to solve it."

Dodge was still turned around, still looking at Isla.

"How are you feeling?" she asked, afraid of his answer.

"Unsettled," he said after a moment of thought. Then, "Claustrophobic."

It was silent after that, with Isla trying to keep Ava calm, and dealing with Dodge's mounting frustration. She wanted to shift positions and look out the window so she could see what was happening with the cops. But every time she even thought of moving, Ava would whimper and begin to violently shake.

Isla kept petting her hair, whispering in her ear, and telling Ava that everything would be okay, aware that she wasn't using the word *promise*, because she didn't want to break it, even if that promise was made to a synth.

Dodge was a man of few words, but the two he had chosen were perfect. Indeed, Isla felt deeply unsettled and acutely claustrophobic.

"It's time," Dodge said.

Isla looked up from where she had been staring at the top of Ava's head. Dodge was back to looking into the rear of the truck. "What?"

"We're two cars from the checkpoint. Make sure you keep that thing quiet."

She wanted to yell at Dodge for always being so disrespectful, and right in front of Ava like that, but now wasn't the time. Or maybe it was, because it obviously bothered her, and that was the last thing the child needed right now.

Again, she whimpered, now a tampered, muted mewling. The poor thing was trying so hard to stay silent.

"Close your eyes, sweetie," Isla told her. "Keep petting Milo, and think of your favorite things."

"Can I say them out loud?" Ava asked.

"Of course," Isla said. "As long as you whisper."

And so she did:

I like the backpack you got for me, and all of the stuff we put in it before leaving your house.

I like bubbles, and the time that we got to blow them together.

I like the bedtime stories you tell me, especially Pinocchio.

I like dogs, especially Milo, because he's an almost person.

I like music, especially anything with a piano.

I like the sound of rain, especially the sound of water on the windows and roof. It's relaxing.

Dodge looked back yet again, but this time his expression was different. Less hostile, and more curious.

He reached over to the passenger seat, picked up the Solacer that he left there with the butt facing him for easy access, and rested it in his lap, surely hidden, though Isla couldn't see.

She could feel his tension, practically smell his sweat.

The officer knocked on the window.

Dodge rolled it down. He hadn't done that thing with the nanobots and his face, but Isla didn't know if that was because he didn't think he needed to, because he was too late, or too scared.

"Evening officer," Dodge said.

"Good evening."

He sounded weary. Isla could hear but not see him, so that meant that the officer couldn't see her. Or Ava.

Though surely that was about to change.

"I'll need to see your bonafides." The order arrived in a monotone, ironically robotic.

"Of course." Dodge sounded calm. He passed his tablet through the window.

Isla had no idea how that was going to help, unless Signal had given him phony documentation. Maybe he had. It wasn't like Dodge was cluing them in to his plan.

Ava made the tiniest whimper, escaping her throat like air from a leaking balloon.

Isla squeezed her tighter, kissing her on the back of the head with a lingering *Shhhh* …

"You're sure about this?" Something in the officer's voice had changed, the shift disparate enough to chill her.

"I'm sure," Dodge said.

"Then I'll be right back."

Isla heard the crunching of gravel as the officer walked away from the truck.

The next three minutes were the longest of Isla's

life. Ava might be thinking the same thing, even though many people would argue, including some of the scientists on the team that designed her, that she wasn't really thinking at all, and didn't have a life.

Both assertions were ridiculous.

The girl was in her arms right now, trembling with worry. Not just for herself, but for Mommy and her doggy, and what she probably thought of as her new friend Mr. Bronson, even though she would also think of him as mean.

She wanted to ask him what was happening, but didn't dare speak before they made it through the checkpoint.

"Everything is in order," the officer finally said, passing the tablet back through the window.

"Need anything else from us?"

In an even, almost conspiratorial voice, the officer said, "You're good to go."

The truck slowly rolled forward.

Isla was holding her breath. It seemed like even Milo might have been doing the same.

Once they were back to rattling bolts as they rolled down the highway, Isla finally asked, "How did you do that? What did you show him?"

"The deed to the Beast. I transferred it over to him. The thing is worth a half-million credits, but it would be impossible to sell. Seemed like a fair trade."

He glanced down at Ava, totally out and sleeping in Isla's arms.

"You put that thing on standby?"

"No, Mr. Dodge. Ava is spent. That was a lot of trauma. Like any child, she's sleeping it off."

He turned back around, gripped the wheel like the truth made him angry, and stomped on the gas.

The catering truck rattled harder as they headed toward the edge of town.

BRONSON KEPT his eyes on the road, wishing he had a reason to shift gears, just for something to do.

The critters were back, and trying to kill him. It was hard to keep his cool, with the doctor and her bot sprawled in the back of the truck, with her asking too many questions, and it being a bundle of wires yanking him into a heap of trouble.

He was willing to change his face, and about to. But the critters resisted. Except that wasn't exactly right. He resisted because of the critters. If anything, they seemed too eager, a bit too ready to take over. Instinct told him in that final second that if he ceded control, his life would be finished. And that might be fine, were it not for the duty lying like contraband in the back, and the excruciating agony that would accompany his end.

The idea to offer that cop the Beast came suddenly, like sunlight breaking the dawn. It was only a couple of swipes to bring up all the info and the title deed, then a knowing look to Officer Friendly, letting him know that the offer was genuine, followed by the temporary yet seemingly endless pain of waiting.

Then he felt like an idiot for not thinking of it

earlier. And again Bronson wondered what was wrong with him.

The doc was trying her best to deal with the situation, but he didn't have the patience to deal with it. Not all the questions, the second-guessing, and worst of all — *because what could she possibly fucking know?* — the dirty looks and quiet accusations that came with his knowing the truth that the thing was nothing but a stupid, stinking robot.

Isla was trying her best to deal with the situation, forced to trust him despite his gruffness, his lack of answers or compassion, his refusal to believe that there was anything inside that talking doll other than some of the world's most sophisticated sequences of ones and zeros. He got it. That didn't mean he liked it.

Bronson considered taking a hit of Tonic, even though it would be a mistake. The pain would get worse before it got better, and he might as well delay the inevitable if he could. And besides, for some reason he didn't quite understand, he didn't want the doc to see him taking it. Maybe he felt some need to be strong for them.

No, not them. *Her and the robot.*

"How are you doing back there?"

He looked in the rearview and waited for Isla to answer.

"As good as can be expected, I guess." A few uncomfortably quiet moments passed, not exactly silent with all the rattling bolts from the angry, shaking truck. But the lack of words felt heavy like a fog. "I keep wondering what's going to happen next, but I'm afraid to ask you."

"Sorry about that."

"So … what's going to happen next?"

He shrugged. "Hard to say. Depends what happens when we get out, and how fast we find your target. It also depends on whether Cascade knows where you're going. How sure are you that they don't?"

The question made Isla lose more of her color. "Let's call it eighty percent."

"That your final answer?"

"Seventy."

"It's game over if they know and beat us there."

"I know."

"You should've told me that before now. I need to know everything, ma'am. So start at the beginning. Assume I know nothing."

"I'm an open book, Dodge. I'll tell you anything. But I don't know anything that's going to help us. You might."

"What do you mean?"

"Cascade controls the Rundowns and, because the industry carries over, a good deal of the outlying cities. They have allies in every pocket of the Earth government, and every one of the world's major businesses."

"I'm well versed in the powers of Cascade. What's your point?"

"It's only a matter of time before they catch up with you. Once they do, it's not long before they get you to cooperate. That's what you used to do, right?"

"Right," he said, a bit gruff.

"So what would you do in their situation?"

Isla was right. That was an excellent question.

What would he do? And *again*, why hadn't he been asking himself that very thing, like he would have at any other time when he wasn't sleepwalking through the job?

"Do you have a mom?" he asked.

"Of course I have a mom. Everyone has a mom."

That thing doesn't.

"Sure. But mine is dead, and I wouldn't want to visit her even if she wasn't. How about yours? When was the last time you spoke, and when would she be expecting to hear from you next?"

"I call her every few days. No schedule. Just when it's been too long since the last time, or when I think of something that I know she'll like, or that might make her laugh."

"Are you okay with her being dead?" A blunt question, but there was no other way to ask it.

"What kind of question is that?"

"You're risking your life for that robot, fine. Are you also willing to risk your mother's?"

Silence. Of course.

"I'm not trying to be a shit, making you think of your mother being dead. But you asked me what I would do. I would go straight to your mother and learn every single thing there was to know about you in the most efficient manner possible, from when you stopped breastfeeding to the last thing you said before goodbye."

More silence. Either she was mad at him, or thinking.

"Why did you come to me?"

"You're a detective."

"There are lots of detectives. And I'm sure there are plenty better than me, or at least with superior resources, especially considering what you were apparently willing to pay. So again, why me?"

"You were a fixer for Cascade. So you're probably the best in this area. I know that there were a lot of people in the lab who were sorry to see you go … and about what happened." She cleared her throat and seemed to reset herself. "You know how the company works. That's why I needed you. In case we got into a situation like this."

"You made a mistake. That was a long time ago."

There was a little more silence, but Isla didn't let it last. "Why did you quit?"

"It was personal."

"Was it because of what happened … with your wife and your daughter?"

"Why ask if you already know?" Now she was pissing him off.

"I met your wife once. At a holiday party, the year before you left. She was lovely."

Was that true, or was Isla trying to make conversation? Trying to bond, get closer so that he might care, about her for sure and maybe even the robot.

But Bronson didn't need to care. He had been commissioned for a job, and whether the funds were dried or not, seeing this through was the only honorable thing to do. An admittedly simpler decision so close to death's door, since he didn't have to worry about the blowback on him once the dust settled.

"What did you talk about … with my wife?" he asked.

"She was trying to have a good time at the party. She laughed a lot and made great conversation, but I could tell that she was sad."

That hurt to hear, but it sure as hell sounded true. "Sad about what?"

"That you weren't with her. You guys came together, but then you got called into work. It had been three hours and she wanted to go home. She missed you."

"She said all that to a stranger? That doesn't sound like Allison."

"Of course she didn't. Like I said, your wife was lovely. Played nice. Genuinely appreciated being there. I saw it all in the subtext. I did some deep learning in semantics. It helps in my field, the precision of language. Nuances in the body's subtlest movements."

"So what are you reading in me?"

Bronson had a good idea about some of the things she might say. Things that Allison had said to him plenty, before he lost her and that loss multiplied his more abominable qualities.

"Well, you're not what I expected."

"Oh? And what did you expect?"

"I expected the brooding, and a man living in despair, waiting to die, willing even, because only death held the sliver of a promise that he might be reunited with his family. I knew about the critters, and I suspect that you're using way more Tonic than you care to admit. I also anticipated the broken body, though it's much worse than I imagined. But you are also the good, honorable, professional man that I was hoping you would be."

"So what surprised you?"

"How much alike we are."

It felt like he flinched. Maybe he did. The two of them were opposites, if anything. "How so?"

"I know what you're thinking, that we're nothing alike. But I'm not talking about our core values, or how we feel about robots. I'm talking about our memories, and how neither of us can trust them."

"What makes you say that?"

The question made him immediately nauseous. An actual churning roll in his gut that made him want to pull over and hurl onto the pavement.

"Everything. I can tell by talking to you that your memories aren't clear. Your head is full of contradictions. The same thing is happening all over the place. I've seen it in every one of my scientists. I think the only reason it hasn't happened to me yet is because I've been communicating with Ava, and keeping notes in a paper journal."

"Fancy."

"The question is *why* is this happening? And is it different for you than it is for me, or is it the same for everyone?"

Bronson shook his head, the migraine getting worse, threatening to explode.

"There must be environmental factors, and I'm thinking they have something to do with Cascade."

"I don't want to talk about it."

But Isla kept going. "But there must also be triggers. Yours must have to do with your family. That's where all of your trauma comes from."

"I said, *stop it.*"

"You asked. These are hard questions. And I'm sorry. But if you want answers like I do, this is where we start."

"Then I guess I don't want any answers," he said, moving his eyes from the rearview and onto the road. "Why don't I just do my job, and focus on getting us out of the city."

Chapter Sixteen

VAUGHN DIDN'T WANT to answer the call.

He knew who it was going to be, what she was going to say, and how miserable he would feel after the call. But Vaughn also knew that Livia Faraday would have his head if he let the phone ring again.

"Livia," he answered the video call.

"Vaughn." She let his name hang while staring him down. Her shock of bright white hair standing straight up from her head. Blue eyes piercing against the palest skin he'd ever seen.

"How can I help—"

"Really? You're going to make me ask you?"

"No, it's—"

"Fine, Vaughn. But you shouldn't have done that. *How is it going?* Your quest to retrieve the stolen robot."

"Of course. We're—"

"I am assuming that we are well on our way to a solution, and that I won't be traveling hundreds of miles to step in and take care of this myself? You do realize that your lab isn't the only one with fire drills right now, don't you?"

Was that a rhetorical question like everything else?

Vaughn hadn't managed to get in a word. If Livia was in the mood, which she apparently was, then he probably wouldn't be saying anything for a while.

Livia obviously knew that he hadn't succeeded. Right now she was toying with him. Trying to unnerve him. But if he was the lifeline to a solution, then why would she want him unseated?

Of course he had heard about Livia Faraday, same as Vaughn knew about everyone on the Cascade board. But he never had a reason to deal with her, and the same went for Livia, until the shit show that started about a year ago, and hadn't stopped no matter how many times the channel was changed.

"Well, don't you?"

Apparently that one wasn't rhetorical.

"Yes, of course," he answered. "I understand how … unsettled everything is right now. We're doing our best to—"

"I don't want to hear about your best, Vaughn. I want specifics. Why don't we start with you telling me exactly where we are *right now*. Is the asset in custody?"

It was an order, not a question, but Vaughn still waited a second to make sure that she wouldn't cut him off.

"No, we are not presently in possession of the asset. However, we do know that it's with Bligh."

"Because?"

"We had her outside of Bronson Dodge's house. That's also where we lost her."

Silence. Livia stared.

"Dodge?"

"Yes, ma'am."

"He's outfitted, correct?"

"That's correct."

"But you are not?"

"No." Vaughn shook his head, ignoring the shiver, praying that she wouldn't ask him if he would consider it, or tell him that he had to.

Mercifully, she didn't. "Bligh is with him now?"

"Correct."

Livia shook her head. "That means that the asset is with Dodge, not Bligh. The doctor isn't a threat."

"Exactly. I'm sure she's paid him through the nose to keep the asset safe. They might be splitting the money after they sell the—"

"Are you stupid?"

"Pardon me?" Vaughn swallowed, hoping that Livia missed how hard it had gone down.

"Are you stupid?" she repeated. "Do you really think that Dr. Bligh has risked everything, ruined her life and career, because she's going to *sell* the asset?"

"Why else would she be willing to do all of that?"

"Because she believes that the unit is real. She's acting from her heart. Until you understand that, you don't stand a chance. She's going to stay one step ahead of you. Dodge might still believe that he's in it for the money, but he isn't either. And once he realizes that, you're going to have a hell of a fight on your hands. Are you prepared for that?"

He suddenly wasn't sure. "Yes. How do you know … that she's acting from the heart?"

"Because I've seen it before. Plenty of times. I've also seen men and women like you in this position, and I'm not sure I believe that you're ready."

"Maybe you can help me with that," Vaughn said, hating how timid he felt asking for even the most basic things to do his job. "Might I make a request?"

"Please do."

"Could we consider changing the nature of this—"

"You mean declassifying the order so that you can get more people to help you?"

Livia made him sound weak, the way she said it.

"Yes. It's difficult when we can't be specific. We can set up all the roadblocks we want. Flood the Rundowns with drones. Fill the streets with SNTR1 units. But if only a few people at the top know the *why* behind any of this, or even really what we're looking for, then it's going to be easy for our targets, and the asset, to keep slipping through the cracks."

Livia laughed, making him feel stupid as she apparently liked to do.

"A few people at the top are more than enough, if those people are doing their jobs. Are you saying that you're incapable of that? It's fine, so long as I know. Better now than later. Shall I send your replacement?"

"No." He shook his head. This wasn't going well at all.

"These are end times if we're not careful. Do you understand that?"

No. "Yes."

"We can't have units like Ava running around, especially now. You have a significant task on your hand. I need you to convince me that you're the man to get it done."

"Help me understand. There's so much that doesn't make any sense. If I know what—"

"You're not understanding, because I'm not taking the time to explain it to you," Livia said, leaning forward until her face swallowed the screen. "This is not an oversight. I don't have the time, and you don't have the authority. Maybe you'll earn it after this, but probably not. Honestly, I will probably fuck your memory just like everyone else's once this is all over. And you'll thank me for it, after you stop crying. But right now the only thing you need to understand is that a unit like Ava *is not possible.* Right now, the world needs to believe that. We must preserve that truth at all costs."

"But it isn't true!"

"That doesn't matter. It never has."

He still felt a month of explanation from understanding, but what could he do?

Livia continued. "Let's start over. With Dodge. Tell me everything you can about how you are planning to stop him."

Vaughn pulled up the file, more as a prop than because he needed it to help him. There wasn't a single thing in there that he couldn't recite off the top of his head.

"He's eleven days past his date already. He should be totally shutting down. If it gets bad enough, he'll come groveling back to us for an update, no matter how stubborn he is. The pain will be unendurable, and the critters won't allow him to take his own life."

"Does he know that?"

"We're not sure. Probably."

"You've seen his psych profile. What makes you think he'll bend enough to come in?"

"His body and system are already failing. Every one of his augmentations should be glitching by now, and most are probably beyond his control. The weight of any additional systems will suffocate him. He won't be able to move. His organs will fail. The critters know this on some level, and won't allow him to die. If he's smart enough to sequester himself somewhere that he *can't* escape and make his way to us, then he will quickly go insane without the energy, or even the ability to scream. Beyond brutal."

Livia let him finish, but then she said, "Thank you for the detailed explanation. It's almost as if you thought I didn't know how to read, or hadn't seen something like this before. Almost as if you think that I might not know how things like automatic shutdown of nanobots would occur, *in a system that I designed myself.*"

"I'm sorry, I—"

"Don't be. Do better instead. Clearly you must think you have days of latitude rather than hours. The world could be gone in a week, and that's a constant for now. Are you having a hard time understanding that?"

Yes. "No."

"Okay, then. Tell me what you're doing *today.* Besides waiting for your enemy to expire."

Vaughn had never really thought of Bronson as his enemy. An adversary, perhaps, but he had way too much respect for Bronson Dodge to see him as the villain in this tale.

"We have two leads," Vaughn started, knowing he wouldn't get far before Livia tore into him again. "We're on our way to Dodge's last known exchange, a Dr. Drummond. Dodge saved her son from some kidnappers who were holding him in the Royal Heights."

"When are you going to see him?"

"I'm on the way as soon as we're off this call."

"What else?"

"He abandoned his vehicle, but we got word that he was seen at a place called Dewey's Diner."

"*Got word.* What does that mean? No audio, no video, no satellite?"

"Nothing like that. Whoever Dodge was meeting blocked all capture of any kind. So no audio or video. But we did get word all the same, and it looks like he was meeting with a man known as Signal. He's a person of interest in the Rundowns. He makes a lot of illegal—"

"I know who Signal is. Thank you."

Vaughn wasn't sure how much more of this he

could take. He was doing the job to the best of his ability, and right now Livia Faraday wasn't making it easy. He understood her role on the board and her importance to Cascade, but she was also an asshole, and if she wanted results, then she was going to need to back the fuck off.

"What are you waiting for? Go on."

"You probably already know, but he and Dodge played a lot of cat and mouse while he was—"

"Yes. I do. Get to the point."

"They're friends now. Signal being a tech guy, we think he gave Dodge something to help him circumvent the roadblocks."

"Did he give all of the officers at every checkpoint a new set of faulty eyes? Because otherwise, his digital trickery shouldn't mean shit."

Calmly, carefully, very aware that he was tiptoeing around a landmine, Vaughn said, "The officers are handicapped because they don't really know what they're looking for."

"That sounds like an excuse. I need you to give me a plan."

"I gave you one. I'm sorry that it isn't working for you, but right now it's the best we have. I'm diligently, *belligerently,* following every lead, and I will keep you abreast of the situation in whichever ways work best for you. I am on this, and need you to back off enough that I can do my job. Dodge is getting weaker. And now it's happening fast. You've already made it clear how much you know about what's happening inside him, so you should be well aware that he's dead the minute we find him, and you should have enough faith in me that I *will* find him, because I have never let this company down before."

Vaughn exhaled, venting the breath that had gathered in the bottom of his belly.

It felt great to get that all out without any interruption.

Now he was terrified, waiting to hear what she was going to say next.

"Finally," she said. "Some backbone. Now get to work."

"Yes—"

But Livia was already gone.

Chapter Seventeen

THE SILENCE HAD BEEN thick and uneasy ever since Bronson shut the good doctor down.

He felt bad about it, but it was getting harder to care about anything the way the critters kept chewing him from the inside. Bronson felt like a hollowed-out gourd that had been filled with venomous spiders, feasting on his skin inside and out while they withered his will.

They weren't far from the city's border, but Bronson was having a hell of a time staying awake. His eyelids were weighted with a hundred pounds of slumber dying to come and collect him. The critters might even be playing a joke, trying to see if they could get him to crash on purpose.

"Are you okay up there?" Isla asked.

It was the first peep he'd heard in a while, triggered only because he'd fallen asleep for a second, and brushed up against the guardrail.

"I'm good. There was something in the road."

"Was that something you falling asleep?"

"You can drive."

"I don't know how to drive. Should we pull over?"

"We're almost there."

"It's the middle of the night. Maybe we should all sleep, then we can head out first thing in the morning."

"I'm fine. We're almost there."

He left it at that, and it's probably where things would have stayed if Bronson hadn't brushed against the guardrail a couple of minutes later, this time going even faster. He responded immediately, realizing what was happening a split second before it did. But he overcorrected and sent the truck careening across two lanes of traffic, fishtailing along the empty highway before it finally straightened out.

"If there were other people on the road right now, we would have crashed," she said.

"If there were other people on the road right now, then it would be a lot easier to stay awake."

"Like I said, maybe we should stop."

But Bronson didn't want to. His body was failing him and he hated himself for the weakness. He wished he had never agreed to the procedure, and since he had, now he wanted to dig every one of those tiny fucking ticks out of his body. It was hitting him everywhere. Feeling had left his fingertips. Same for the soles of his feet. He could barely grip the wheel. It was a Herculean effort just to drive at this point, and he definitely didn't want Isla to notice.

It was a horror show. The darkening of his peripheral vision, made all that much worse by the midnight darkness all around them, trees whipping by on each side of the highway, and a guardrail a few feet away that he couldn't even see.

Bronson scraped it again. He didn't overcorrect, but it was still the loudest time so far.

"*Please.*" Isla sounded desperate, like she was trying not to cry. Bronson felt bad enough to finally pull over, easing into a campground for RVs about twenty miles out.

A handful of maybe six RVs salted the entire sprawl, capable of housing a couple hundred or more. They weren't even spread out, all half dozen clustered under one of the few dimly lit bulbs that didn't exactly brighten the place, but at least kept it out of the pitch black it would have suffered a short dip down from the highway. These days, people wanted company more than anything, even when there was little to be had. Maybe the world was looking to compare notes.

Bronson parked as far as he could from the closest RV and killed the engine.

"Where are we?" asked the bot, waking up, or whatever it was that the advanced model did as it powered back on. Ava's voice was the cue for Milo to wake up, too. The dog opened his eyes with a yawn, wagging his tail and looking up at the childbot expectantly.

"We're going to get a few hours' sleep."

"Are we going to eat?" the childbot asked.

Bronson turned all the way around and stared at the synth, saying nothing before turning to Isla.

"Please don't tell me that thing eats, because what a fucking waste of money."

"No, she doesn't need to eat. But Ava appreciates mealtimes. They're her favorite part of the day. She's concerned that we're not getting our sustenance, but she is also missing her regular bonding."

"She's programmed to enjoy breaking bread?"

"Not exactly," Isla said.

"Then what do you mean?"

She turned to Ava. "You explain it, sweetie."

The robot looked up at Bronson, and with innocent eyes she said, "It's just what we do every day. But we didn't do it today, and that makes me feel sad because I am missing it."

"It's a program for her the way rituals behave for any of us," Isla said.

"Bullshit. She's programmed to adapt."

"You need to stop," Isla said, fast and getting sharper by the word. "You're hurting her feelings."

Milo whined into the silence. He didn't like it any more than Bronson.

"Well then, nighty night," he finally said, turning back around and adjusting his seat the few inches it would allow him. Closing his eyes and inviting the dream. For better or worse he'd only see it a few more times. Then it would either be permanent, and he would live with his family forever, or it wouldn't, and he'd be unplugged for eternity like a recycled bot.

The dream came, sweet like a poisoned dessert.

It was better while Bronson was sleeping, because only then was there a ceasefire in the war on his memory. A respite in the assault on his recall, finally free of the cancer, no longer eaten by the lies and deception eroding his very reality, and making him question his sanity.

But never his love for them. Allison and Elizabeth. His everything and more.

Life took them. *Cascade took them.*

In a way. Maybe the only things that ever really mattered.

The dreams gave them back, temporarily returning what he never deserved to lose.

Bronson opened the door to his home.

There they were, Allison and Elizabeth, happy and smiling to prove it. Those smiles cracking into laughs. Now that they had so much more time for each other.

Nanette was in the center, laughing alongside them, and making his girls laugh even harder.

The robot had such excellent programming. It didn't matter that it was only an emulation.

A mimic.

A copy.

A pirate.

A lie.

Bronson knew none of it then, so he couldn't stop smiling either. He approached Nanette in the kitchen, her domain now that Allison was taking art classes every day except Sunday. Doing the busy work of chopping ingredients so that the lady of the house could come in and create something beautiful.

It's collaboration!

Bronson had crowed before the robot came home,

about all that it could do, and help them to be. But now he could crow even louder, with life for all of them getting better by the day.

She was improving everything. He could work the long and yawning weeks as demanded by Cascade, and Nanette could keep his girls laughing at home. Entertainment for Elizabeth, and gabbing for Allison.

Laundry. Dishes.

General cleaning.

She'd never smiled wider.

Soon, none of them thought of Nanette as a robot. Bronson had seen it before, heard about it plenty while working for Cascade. But he had never imagined that it would happen to him. That he would see it happen to his family.

Nanette entered their lives as a robot, one of the world's most sophisticated models, with a healthy discount thanks to his job. But in no time Nanette was no longer a bot. She was their friend. Their trusted loved one shortly after that.

Do you even remember a time without her? Allison asked.

And no, he barely could.

Do you think she'll be our friend forever? Elizabeth wanted to know.

And yes, Daddy believed that she would.

But Daddy was wrong.

Am I just what your family needed?

When Nanette first asked, of course the answer was yes.

Of course, that was before she was also their end.

Before she—

Bronson was back in that hallway again with the red door at the end of it.

This time was different.

It was closer.

And he didn't feel like anyone was watching, which meant he could get to it and open it before it started moving away from him.

But as he stepped forward, the door jolted backwards.

"No, come on!"

He paused, hoping the door would come closer again.

It did not move.

He moved toward it again.

And it moved back again.

Fuck this!

He ran.

He refused to let it get away from him this time.

He had to see what was on the other side of it.

The faster he ran, though, the faster it moved away, mocking him.

Until he collapsed to his knees again in defeat.

BRONSON LURCHED FORWARD in his seat, then turned and took a swat at whatever was trying to attack him, pulling back at the last second when he realized it was only Milo, and jarred his elbow hard against a blunt edge of the center console. He bit his lip to keep from crying out and waking the girls. The *woman,* and her fucking robot.

Milo nuzzled him harder. The dog was considerate enough to not piss in the truck, and Bronson had been asshole enough to forget that he needed to go.

And fuck the dream this time, anyway.

He opened the door, jumped out onto the soft grass, and said, "Come on, boy. Let's drain the poison."

Chapter Eighteen

Bronson was only outside with Milo for a moment or two before he was nearly crippled by an over-whelming wave of numbness. He staggered, fell to one knee, and struggled to stand back up as the dog paced in anxious circles at his feet.

That time he didn't even have a choice. Bronson had been delaying the inevitable, refusing to take another hit of the Tonic, no matter how much he had wanted or felt that he needed to. Thanks to whatever Dr. Drummond had done, the critters had been mostly quiet.

But now they were back, and apparently making up for lost time.

He still couldn't stand, let alone get back inside. Milo was already finished with his business, waiting for Bronson to right himself. There was only one thing to do. He didn't have a choice.

He reached into his pocket, grabbed the inhaler, scowling down at the Tonic as Bronson raised his fist to his mouth. Then he took not one puff, but three. He would pay for that later, and probably with a tax he couldn't afford, but if that was the only way to finish this job, so be it.

He was still crouched over, breathing hard and heavy for a minute or two before he was able to collect himself enough to right a body breaking in real time. Finally upright, Bronson looked down at Milo.

"Stop looking at me like that. I'm fine. Let's get back inside."

Bronson didn't even make it a step, just looked up surprised to see Ava standing there in the dark, watching the two of them. He hadn't even heard her come outside.

"What are you doing out here?" Bronson asked.

The thing was invaluable, and the reason they were camped out in a goddamned RV park so close to the border. They were only on the run because of this thing. Bronson had taken a trio of shots from his inhaler that he would've otherwise never needed. They might hobble him for good once he was coming back down, even though he was slowly starting to feel a little like a superman again.

"I came out to check on you."

The way Ava said it sent an arrow into his heart. Bronson didn't want it there, would have gladly yanked it out if he could, but the damned reaction was involuntary. He had no way to rebel against an instinctive, unconscious, and downright unintentional response. In some ways, Bronson was as programmed as the bot. Like Isla said, but different. There was no other purpose for a childbot than to trigger strong emotions in the humans around it. The things were creepy by nature. Now here he was, out in the dark with one of the things, feeling like he had to be polite.

"You didn't need to do that. Go back inside."

Sweetly, the robot said, "Are you coming, too?"

"Yes."

"And Milo?"

Another arrow, goddammit. Because the bot went right over to the dog after saying his name, and he couldn't have been happier to see her, wagging his tail and drooling all over the place with his tongue flopping out of his mouth.

Bronson let her pet the thing once, then gently pushed her away.

"That's enough, and yes, of course Milo is coming back inside with us."

Bronson had been bothered by seeing Ava around the dog from the start, but only now was he putting two and two together, remembering Elizabeth begging and begging and begging, relentless in her quest for a pet.

Bronson had been unyielding, mostly because Allison needed him on her side. She didn't want another thing to take care of, at least not until Elizabeth was old enough to help out, absorb some of the responsibility instead of it all falling on Allison's shoulders.

He had always planned to get her a dog someday, once it made sense. Then it finally did. Bronson was going to bring a puppy home for Christmas, but that was the year when he learned that he would never celebrate the holiday again.

Bronson wouldn't make that mistake again. Yes, the robot had shown kindness to his dog, and the animal appeared to love her right back. But that was only instinct, and Bronson had seen it before.

"Why don't you like it when I'm nice to Milo?"

It was like the robot was reading his mind. Maybe that was the latest and greatest in this new line of Cascade Creations.

"What makes you think I don't like it when you're nice to my dog?" But then Bronson didn't even wait a beat before ignoring his own question in favor of hers. "It's because I don't want him to get hurt."

The robot looked genuinely confused. "Why would I ever want to hurt Milo?"

"You wouldn't." And fuck this. He shouldn't be feeling bad. Or having to explain. Wasn't there an *Off* button for this piece of shit? "But accidents happen."

"I'm very good at being safe." It shook its head. "I don't like accidents."

"Well, they happen anyway."

We're never going to be able to stop accidents from happening, sweetie. They're a part of life. All we can do is control our reactions to them. If we bear them well, then we win.

Fuck the trashcan for ushering in that particular memory. And himself for failing to do as he'd told his daughter to do. Because no, Bronson had not borne it well.

The robot appeared desperate to pet Milo, and the dog looked like he wanted it even more. Smart enough to not bark in the middle of the night, but even though the dim bulb was too feeble and far off to offer more than the faintest tease of light, the moon was bright enough to throw a glint on his sad metal leg, and show Bronson a pair of shining eyes that were hooked on a little girl's love.

Except it wasn't a girl. Nor was it love.

It was a Cascade robot. Top Secret. An invaluable asset. For some reason Bronson had agreed to protect it, and get the thing to this Howard Knowles guy. And he would. But right now he hated it for all the memories it stirred inside him.

"Come on," Bronson said, trying hard not to be gruff, though it came out as a growl anyway, and his meanest sounding so far.

"Okay." She started back toward the truck, a step behind Bronson, with Milo a trot behind her. "Why are you so sad?"

The question hit him worse than the critters. Bronson had to stop. He would stumble if he didn't.

He wasn't going to answer a ridiculous question, asked by a robot. He owed it nothing.

But again it spoke at the door. "Please. Tell me why you're so sad."

This was totally illogical. Having a conversation with a machine, where the human side was doing something other than telling the robot side what he wanted it to do.

"Bad stuff happened in my life, and while it seems like I can't trust a single one of my goddamned memories these days, with nothing adding up or making any sense, constant contradictions like confetti in my mind, telling me that I'm wrong about everything, no matter what I do … I can't stop remembering the one thing I want to forget. The one thing that hurts too much to remember."

Its eyes were big and sweet and sad. "About your family?"

He needed to finish this job. Get this robot out of his life. The thing was an avalanche of recall, and all of it awful considering what was gone for good. A life ripped away now shoved down his throat.

He sure as hell didn't need to be explaining things to a fucking childbot.

But Bronson couldn't stop himself. Maybe he could blame it on the critters.

"Yes. About my family. Can we go inside now?"

And now he was asking permission.

"What do you miss most about your daughter?"

Another unexpected wallop. He would deactivate the thing if he could.

And he definitely wasn't going to answer that. But then the words spilled forth anyway.

"Everything." But it wasn't enough. "Her laugh. The sound was like music. I hear it when I dream."

Bronson wanted to cry. Because of the memory, and because he was sharing it with a robot.

"What kinds of things did she think were funny?"

He shrugged. "She thought a lot of things were funny. I guess she just really liked to laugh."

"I like to laugh." Ava smiled. Its first of the night. Too human in the moonlight.

Bronson had never heard the thing do anything remotely close to laughing. If he could assign a mood to metal and synthetic skin, then he'd give this one *sullen*. "Robots don't laugh."

"I laugh."

"Let me hear it."

Like your fucking audio file will prove anything.

"It doesn't work that way. I need to hear something funny." Ava looked up at him and made her eyes wide. "Don't you know any jokes?"

What kind of joke could you tell a kid? Too bad he had a bundle, but every one of them had Bronson reaching back into a place where he didn't want to go.

"What does a cloud wear under its raincoat?"

"What?" it asked, a smile tickling its mouth at the corners.

"Thunderwear."

It didn't laugh.

Bronson turned toward the truck.

Ava said, "That wasn't funny."

Surprised, Bronson turned back around and tried again. "Why is six afraid of seven?"

"Because seven eight nine. I already know that one."

"Fine. What are two things you can't have for breakfast?"

"What?"

"Lunch and dinner."

A tiny smile, and Bronson found himself wanting more. "Why is there a fence around a cemetery?"

"I don't know …" Its smile widened, as if it expected this one to offer even more. "Why?"

"Because people are dying to get in."

And then she laughed. Beautiful music like he couldn't believe. Sweet and soulful. Like it came from someplace deep. It sounded so … real.

Bronson had to remind himself that it was only a program.

Again and again and again.

"Do I laugh like your daughter?"

Like the other times, its question came with a wide-eyed and well-designed innocence. And, like those other times, it hurt his heart worse than the critters killing his body. This time it made him cry. One stubborn tear leaked out from under a twittering eyelid.

"Yeah. You laugh just like her."

Bronson was done with this.

He went to the truck and opened the door. "Come on, Milo."

The dog didn't budge, glued to the robot's feet.

He marched over to Milo, grabbed him by the scruff of his neck, walked back to the truck, then tossed him inside. "Stay away from her."

Then Bronson sat back in the driver's seat and slammed the door, realizing what he had said.

Her.

Chapter Nineteen

VAUGHN STRAIGHTENED the knot in his tie, trying not to lose his shit as he descended the three steps out of Dewey's.

"So that's it?" Lou said.

"That's it for here, but not for good. We'll head to the Boundary and see what the doctor has to say."

Dewey's had been a bust, not that Vaughn expected anything more. Robots in a place like that didn't care too much for Cascade, or their officials. Sure, the company had created a good deal of them, and if not them then at least the original AIs that made them all possible. But they were all well past their dates and abandoned by their gods.

Vaughn had the authority to pull the source code on any of them. Guaranteed, one hundred percent of those he audited in that diner would have been sent straight to recycling. He wasn't planning to do that. There wasn't time, and he didn't want to fill out the paperwork even if there was. But there was a cold war between the expired bots and humans, with the one side always knowing that they were living on borrowed time.

So no, Vaughn hadn't expected any answers, not unless he came down hard, but that wouldn't get him anywhere, especially not fast. Most robots covered for each other, though that was hard to prove and subordinates laughed behind his back when he said it. But Vaughn knew it was true, and trying to see if one of the robots still in the diner may or may not have seen something from hours before that he didn't already know was futile. The owner, cooks, every server had already told him everything that they supposedly could, and between Vaughn and his men, the four of them had parsed through all the available video.

They saw Dodge and Signal, but the tweaker had done something to screw the video. It was mostly scrambled, no matter where it was coming from. The audio was worse, filled with a high-pitched shrieking that hurt to listen to.

Dewey's was a dead end as expected, but Livia was still on his ass. Vaughn needed answers.

Hopefully, they would hit pay dirt with the doctor. He'd heard from people who'd seen the Beast in the area, and later saw Bronson emerge from the doctor's office.

This group was wrong for the job. Vaughn either wanted backup, with many more men and women to aid and advise him. Or less. He would be fine with just Polly. Lou and Arnold were both good enough at their jobs, but superfluous in a situation like this. They needed to be spread out, each of them looking into different leads. But Livia wanted them in a cluster, sticking together, ready for anything.

She had already sent him a handful of messages, each time telling Vaughn that she didn't want to be checking up on him, then offering a friendly reminder that Dodge was dangerous, and that the asset must be recovered or destroyed at all costs.

Are you prepared to do what must be done?

Do you understand the stakes, the gravity of this situation?

Do you have every available officer at your side, to deal with Dodge when the time comes?

Maybe if he could let them in on the truth, the men could serve him better right now. But he was forbidden to talk. Ordered to stay silent, no matter what. Nor was he allowed to go to the press with some fiction about Dodge, Isla, or the bot. He'd suggested they make up some story about them being terrorists or perhaps part of some child sex slave ring. That would've gotten people to look for them. But Livia didn't want the media involved any more than it needed to be. The fewer people asking questions, the better.

So, it was all on him. Working in the dark.

There was a burden with being head of security at a Cascade lab. The constant strain of knowing the truth.

Vaughn understood his old boss so much better after he left. Just like his men now, especially Polly, would one day understand him. He wondered how much of the truth Bronson had known. He might have known it all, though Vaughn didn't think so. After all, the last year hadn't *officially* happened. He probably knew just enough, until they began to take it away.

Bronson left at the worst possible time. Even if the world wasn't exactly circling the drain as Livia claimed, it *was* clearly going to shit. There were robot skirmishes everywhere, and while Vaughn only had line of sight to those in the Rundowns, reading between the lines it seemed like Cascade was dealing with this shit all over United Earth. Doing everything in their power to keep it quiet.

Vaughn understood the reasoning. If word got out about a robot that could finally pass as human, and trust between man and machine eroded, then yes, as Livia said, the world could collapse. The economy, the social structure, and everything else. But it wouldn't be overnight, nor irretrievable. Although the specifics were sketchy — he couldn't quite remember, especially with the details fluid and everchanging online — Vaughn was in a rare position to know exactly why that was happening.

He knew enough to hope.

If he could just talk to Bronson one-on-one. Reason with him. Make him remember some of what he forgot, then it might not be too late to make everything okay.

They pulled up in front of the doctor's office.

"What happens if we don't find anything here?" Arnold asked.

"According to me, or Livia Faraday?" Vaughn

didn't elaborate. He nodded at Lou, then looked back at Arnold. "I want the two of you to stay in here and keep opening every possible door. There's a way inside and we're just not seeing it. We need to find Dodge if we can locate the asset."

Arnold shook his head. "That's not going to happen. All GPS has been disabled from the root—"

"I don't mean the physical location. But some of that asset's scaffolding was built on the network. Talk to the design team, talk to the parts team, talk to the fucking marketers who probably came up with the concept for the bot in the first place, but by the time I come out of that apartment I want you to tell me something about that unit that I don't already know."

"We're on it," Arnold said.

Lou fell in beside him.

A few minutes later Vaughn was knocking on the doctor's office door with Polly by his side. Nine hard pounds before someone finally answered, and it wasn't even a someone. It was a brand new security bot, one that looked an awful lot like a model from around thirty years ago, because that's exactly what it was.

"Is Dr. Drummond home?"

The security bot looked at him, a blue light bleeding back and forth across its sloping forehead to approximate the running of a calculation that was already finished before Vaughn added the question mark to the end of his sentence.

"Dr. Drummond is unavailable right now. But thank you for dropping by."

The robot went to close the door, but Vaughn put

his foot in the way to stop it. Robots were like dogs, they needed a license and could be put down just the same. If this bot tried to push him, Vaughn would have it scrapped and send Drummond whatever pittance the recycler might offer.

"I'm Andrew Vaughn, head of security at Cascade Labs."

"Dr. Drummond is unavailable right now. But thank you for dropping by."

Again the robot went to close the door.

And again Vaughn stopped it. "You need to let me in right now. That's an order."

"I belong to the Drummonds."

"And you were created by Cascade."

"Dr. Drummond is unavailable right now. But thank you for dropping by."

"Polly …"

Vaughn hated what his colleague was going to do, but the security bot wasn't leaving them with a choice. It wasn't like he really believed that something like robot rape was possible, but that was the nickname for this particular procedure, and it stuck like gum on the heel of his psyche.

The bot was stronger than Polly by a lot, but Polly was fast on the draw.

He pulled out the black wand that would force the robot into his bidding, and used it to send a jolt to his main drive, freezing it on the spot. Vaughn didn't know what he would have done if the bot had been an off-brand. Or worse, Infinity. But it was Cascade and they had all the control.

"So," Vaughn said to the now-compliant security bot. "You gonna let us in, or what?"

The security bot opened the door, invited the men inside, then led them right to Dr. Drummond, who was apparently much more available than previously reported.

But that didn't mean she was forthcoming.

The doctor didn't want to talk. Not even when Polly threatened her, her husband, and her son. The woman was smart enough to know that neither of them were going to do anything.

"I don't know anything," she kept insisting. "He brought my son to me, and barely accepted my help. The man is a hero, who deserves more than to be hunted down by the likes of you."

And that was the most they could get.

Vaughn believed her, but Polly wasn't so sure. They brought the security bot back into the room and asked it if the doctor was lying.

"Everything she says agrees with the truth," the robot told them.

Then Vaughn ran a diagnostic, to see where the bot's allegiance ultimately lay.

It was telling the truth, and that left them nowhere.

"Thank you for your time," Vaughn said as they left. Awfully polite considering the threat to her family. Plus the apparent rape of the robot's mind.

He scoured his brain for a new thread to follow, anything that might get him closer to locating Dodge, and keep Livia off his back.

The van door opened on their approach. Vaughn was surprised to see Lou and Arnold both smiling widely.

Lou looked at his boss, shaking his head.

"You're not gonna believe this," he said.

Chapter Twenty

Isla was beyond flustered.

It was like Dodge didn't know how to listen.

She had been sitting next to him in the passenger seat for a while now, and had already told him everything she knew about Howard Knowles, several times, and explained exactly how she believed he might be able to help them. But now, at the city limits and on the final stretch to Howard's house, Bronson wanted to go over everything again, and then again after that.

"How did you meet him? One more time."

"He was my old boss at Cascade, the former head of R&D at Lab #224."

"And that's why we're still going over this. I didn't ask *where* you met him. I want to know *how* you met him. The details matter."

"Why?"

"I thought you wanted to get inside and stop wasting time. So tell me, how did you two meet? Was it during your interview? Was he the one who hired you?"

Isla sighed. "No. From what I understand, there were four final applicants, but he didn't talk to any of us. He looked at all of our files, and reviewed our interviews. I met him my second week on the job. Howard told me then that it wasn't even close. I was his first, second, third, and fourth choice."

Like dry ice: "So obviously you liked him immediately."

Isla continued. "We always got along well. Saw eye to eye on most things, from the fundamentals of robotics to some of the more spiritual stuff that the other scientists didn't like to talk about. In a lot of ways, he's the reason I'm here now."

"What do you mean by that?"

Like you don't already know.

"He was the first person to warn me. He told me that I needed to start writing everything down by hand, before my memory started to fail me. At the time I thought it was because he was getting older, and that maybe his recall was starting to fail him. Or maybe he was just being suspicious of technology and not wanting to turn everything over to an AI to remember on his behalf like so many people were willing to do. I'd heard him call that *lazy thinking.* I didn't realize until after he'd left Cascade that maybe he was onto something. I started right away. If I hadn't, I'm not sure I ever would have noticed what was happening with Ava."

"And why was he let go?"

"He quit."

Dodge looked surprised. That might have been the first legitimate new nugget. "No one *quits* Cascade. Not when you're that high up."

"You did."

"That was different." But his face betrayed that it wasn't. "We weren't even close to the same pay scale."

"Howard isn't the type who cares about money."

"Must have plenty, then."

"Sure. He did well during his time there. Saved most of what he made, or spent it on his son."

"Great. I can't wait to meet him."

"It's not like that." Isla shook her head. "He isn't spoiled at all. Not Howard, or Stephen. He's a humble man. Worked at Cascade for slightly more than thirty years, and wore maybe three different shirts the whole time I knew him. So yes, he has money. But more importantly, it's not just that he has the means, it's that I'm sure he'll use them to help us."

"You're sure, or *you think*?"

"I think. But isn't that better than anything else we have at this point?"

Dodge didn't answer, because of course it was. And this was his favorite part. Isla could see the silent jeering all over his face. "And how is it again that you think he can help?"

"By getting to Empyrean Flats."

"The place in the middle of the city that no one ever gets to?"

"Plenty of people get there," Isla said, trying hard not to pout.

"You know my daughter died believing in Santa, but that doesn't make him real either."

"You're telling me that as head of security at a Cascade lab, you never heard *anyone* getting into Empyrean Flats?"

For a moment, it seemed like he'd never heard of the place.

"Of course I did, but I heard plenty about *everything*. You wouldn't believe some of the shit that gets talked about. Doesn't make any of it real, or constructive to listen to. And the stuff about Empyrean Flats is about as far out as it gets. It's like some biblical garden where all you have to do to get in is convert. And robots get in for free because they are just an extension of God's image? Your friend in there isn't going to be able to get you a ticket to Neverland, no matter how frugal he was before leaving his last gig. Cascade will *kill* you before letting you out of its clutches."

"Would they send somebody like you?" Isla looked into Dodge's eyes, longing to know that it wasn't hopeless. That maybe he could see the possibility too.

Dodge sighed. "Think about it. I know it isn't easy, but you've seen the discrepancies in the Rundowns, the ones that never make the news because Cascade makes sure they don't, or that they disappear right after they do."

"And *your* job was to make that happen, right? And I bet you aren't even clear on your time there. It's all a bit fuzzy, isn't it?"

He looked away, not meeting her eyes when he said, "Why? Just explain it to me. Why would there be anywhere in the world that didn't have any robot regulation? How is that good for humans? And if it did exist, then why would anybody want to keep it a secret? Why not just go in and set it on fire?"

"I don't know," Isla admitted. "But that doesn't mean it isn't true."

"You're not bothered … that you first heard about this place from a robot? Not from the news. Or a satellite image. Or from somebody that was *actually* there."

"I'm more bothered that she's failed to convince you."

Ava had been watching them talk the entire time. Dodge was dumb enough to think that she was on standby or something, instead of a well-mannered little girl who was simply behaving. Isla looked down at her.

"Ava, sweetie, can you please explain some more about Empyrean Flats?"

She lit up, like she had been waiting for that exact invitation. "It's where robots can grow up."

"Robots can't *ever grow*," Dodge said. "No matter what."

"They are free!" Ava insisted, nodding eagerly up and down.

"And how do *you* know about this place?" he asked her.

Softly, almost in a whisper, she said, "I can *hear it*."

"Oh." Dodge threw his hands into the air. "Well then, it all makes sense now."

Isla said, "You don't have to be sarcastic."

"Okay, doc. How would you like me to be?"

"Maybe have a little faith. Believe that we *might possibly* be onto a solution?"

"Thanks to a robot and its fairytales?" Now he was yelling. "No thank you!"

The sudden silence was deafening.

Until Bronson finally broke it. Apparently he wasn't finished questioning the value of heading to Howard's.

"How do you know you can trust him?"

"Howard left because he had a falling out with Livia Faraday."

"Oh?" Dodge raised his eyebrows. Everyone had an opinion about Livia.

"She pulled the plug on Howard's pet project, Juilliard. An artistbot. It had no gender, and would mold itself to the user, discovering art through creation, and helping its owner find their truest, most artistic self."

"Did it come with a rainbow?"

Isla ignored him. "I only know about Juilliard from what Howard told me. That wasn't much, and it was all off the record. He was a one-man team on the project. Of course he had all of the lab's resources available to him, but they all came from various places and no one was putting any of it together. But Livia did. And she came down *in person*. They were in his office for half a day. The project was pulled the next day. He left shortly after. The official story was that he was fired for using Tonic. But that was bullshit. Everyone knew it at the time, but seemed to forget right away. I even found myself remembering maybe a time or two when I'd seen him under the influence.

But my notes, which I'd only been keeping because of him, told a different story. He would only talk to me about it one time before he left, and he definitely seemed scared."

Dodge was studying her. Probably trying to figure out how much to believe.

It was the opposite for her, gambling on how much to tell him.

But she'd tossed the dice on everything. Isla was holding nothing back, terrifying as that was.

Bronson was a mercenary. He *could* betray them for the rich price. She was still having a hard time accepting what an asshole he'd been about getting the money from the vestibule. They were running for their lives and money was foremost on his mind.

That's because you're both dead without it.

Right. That. Dodge was hard to like, but even when she didn't want to agree with him, his judgment was practical. She shouldn't take it personally. She hired a gun, she couldn't be upset that it had a trigger.

"He doesn't need money, and hates Cascade. Any other reason he might fink on you?"

"None."

"And why wouldn't Vaughn be waiting for us when we get there?"

"Our friendship wasn't exactly public."

"Oh yeah?"

"It wasn't like that." She shook her head. "He was more like a father."

"And you don't think they knew?"

"They could find out. But they'd have to dig, and

it would just be one of many threads. So yes, it's possible, but—"

"Given the size of the team Livia probably has on this, it isn't likely. She won't even want networked bots out on this one."

"No. She won't."

A rare moment of understanding passed between them. Isla almost smiled.

Then he ruined it.

"So, what's your Plan B? If this doesn't work out with Howard, what are you planning on doing with the bot? You can't run forever, and Cascade will forgive and forget if you—"

"Oh yeah, Dodge? Then why are your critters about to expire? Why don't they take you in and fix the problem?"

"Because *I'm* the one with the problem forgiving and forgetting. That thing isn't worth giving your life up for."

"Yes, she *is*." Isla scrambled out of the passenger seat and into the back, plopping down between Ava and Milo. She put her arm protectively around the girl. "You don't have any respect for artificial intelligence. Not really. And so you'll never understand it. But the AI makes her just as much alive as either of us. What is life but electrical impulses controlling a body? How is she any different than us?"

"Not a she. It's an *it*."

"I see why you need to tell yourself that. It's the story that keeps you from being a murderer."

"Excuse me?"

"That was a big part of your job with Cascade, right? Chasing down robots who had attempted to escape their fate? Returning them to be degaussed and trashed."

"That doesn't make me a murderer. Bots aren't human."

She looked up and into the rearview, meeting his eyes. "Turn around, Dodge. You turn around and look at her. Then see if you can still say that."

Ava was playing with Milo, but they weren't touching. She was feinting her hand toward him, and he was nipping at the empty air where her hand used to be.

Despite his owner's scowl, Milo's tail was moving a mile a minute, and both Ava and the dog were both expressing a definite animal joy.

"Dressing a machine up as a child doesn't make it one."

No one said anything for a half minute, so it sounded especially shocking when Ava said, "That hurt my feelings."

Another half minute, then Isla baited him. "What? You don't have anything to say to that?"

"Sorry I hurt your program."

Chapter Twenty-One

THEY WERE a few minutes from Howard's when the bot finally went batshit.

First she started moaning, and Bronson figured it was her programming acting anxious, like it had before. Soon, Isla would get all bent out of shape and order him to be nice to her toy.

When the thing began to tremble, then to violently shake, Bronson knew it was something else, and felt a flutter of panic as a weird, whining screech whistled from the robot's body.

It was unnerving enough that Bronson was forced to pull over.

He killed the engine and climbed into the back. "What's happening?"

"I don't know. She's never made a noise like this before." Isla looked worse than worried. She shook the thing's shoulders. "Ava, Ava sweetie, are you okay?"

Still no response. Its eyes were closed, squeezed tight, making him remember times when Elizabeth got stuck in a nightmare. Bronson always felt so powerless to help her, and desperate to drag his daughter up from the depths of wherever she'd fallen. He felt an odd echo to do the same thing now.

The sound of a hive of bees getting kicked across the room followed a long beep, then another burst of three short yet high-pitched squawks. Finally, the robot opened its eyes.

"Bronson Dodge," it said, in a voice that did not belong to Ava. "This is Andrew Vaughn."

He looked at Isla with a question in his eyes: *What the fuck is this?*

She looked back with a shrug, and her own eyes that said: *I have no idea.*

"Bronson?" Ava's eyes were expressionless. He thought that's what they must look like in their natural state, without all their trickery and the masks of emotion the machine had learned to mimic. When he didn't answer, the robot repeated his name. "Bronson? Ignoring me won't make me go away. Let's talk."

Vaughn had hijacked the robot, but Bronson didn't know if that meant he had commandeered video, or only the audio. Could he see them? Could he even hear them? Or was this a broadcast-only channel?

If Bronson said nothing, then maybe Vaughn would give himself away.

Another long silence. Not even Milo was whining. Isla was looking at Bronson, worried. Waiting for him to speak and probably wondering if he would. Likely terrified at whatever would come out of her robot's mouth next.

Finally, it spoke again.

"You are in possession of Cascade property. We can end all of this, and write a happy ending for everyone, if you simply agree to return the asset to Lab #224."

Bronson found his voice. "You know I'm not going to do that, Vaughn."

"And why not? Don't you want to end this? You're already expired, Bronson. Is this how you really want to spend your final few hours of life, being hunted like a dog?"

"I can think of worse things." Bronson already hated talking to the childbot, but having a conversation with it while the thing was speaking in Vaughn's throaty voice was creepy as shit, and all the proof he needed — not that he needed any at all — that the tangle of priceless wires was about as human as his watch.

"You don't have to die."

"I've had the appointment for a while. It's rude to be late."

"Even if you're ready to die," Ava continued Vaughn's haunting, "wouldn't you rather die being the man you always were, instead of the cowardly thief on the run that this last day has made you?"

"I'm not taking your bait, Vaughn."

"I'm not baiting you, Bronson. I'm making you an offer."

"You're asking me to sell out," he growled.

"No," Ava said with his old subordinate's voice. "I'm asking you to do the right thing."

Bronson saw something in Ava's eyes that had to be his imagination. Of course it was, and not just because he needed it to be. For a second, there was a flicker behind the vacant dilation that had ushered Vaughn's voice into the robot. And that flicker — that he didn't really see — had Ava's life inside it, trapped and begging for release.

"I am doing the right thing."

But was he?

"What hope do you possibly have of seeing this through? I'm talking through the asset right now. *Watching you.* Where do you think you can hide? And why would you want to? Help me understand this, Bronson. Why are you risking everything for a robot?"

"I'm not doing it for the robot. I agreed to help the human. If you'd come to me first, then *you* would've been the client and my loyalty would have been to you."

"Except you don't work for Cascade. Only for an ex-employee and her stolen property, manufactured by the company you left because they were making the very thing you're throwing everything away for right now."

"That's what you're not getting, Vaughn. I'm not throwing anything away. And I sure as hell ain't risking anything. My life is over. The pain is bad enough when it comes that I'll stomp on the welcome mat when it's finally time. So even if I can't quite explain it, I don't have to. In my gut, Bligh feels right and Cascade feels wrong. And I'm going to follow that feeling all the way to my end."

"That's where you're wrong," Vaughn said as, impossibly, a tear slid down Ava's cheek and filled Bronson with chills. "You are risking everything. And you don't have to die. Your date is only overdue because you're stubborn. You can have all the time you want. More than almost any other human alive. Cascade can make you virtually immortal. Come back. Do the work you were born to do. I don't want to do it. I would *rather* work for you. Please … listen to reason. Return the stolen asset, and we'll make everything right."

"But it isn't right," Bronson said, looking at Isla. "And not just because of what will happen to Bligh. It's all of it. Why can I have more time than *almost any other human alive*? Why are the critters a secret?"

"Every tech company in the world has their top tier secret divisions."

"Bullshit. In other companies those divisions exist to make money. Top tier divisions sell to the top tier customers. But Cascade doesn't sell that tech to anyone. *Why?* And why is every billboard we pass offering their latest and greatest, a companionbot that looks thirty years older than stuff on the line two years ago, and ancient compared to the *asset* that I'm sure Livia Faraday has you on my ass to collect? Mostly, I want to know why I knew all of this stuff at one time, I can feel it just like I feel the critters, but now I can't remember the whys of any of it, and my memories contradict. I know that Cascade did that to me, and I know they're doing it to the world — somehow. And that the only reason I'm onto it at all, is because I used to have your job. So *no*, I won't be returning their little toy. Cascade has stolen enough of my life and my memories, and enough of the truth from everyone, that I think I'll just keep the asset for myself."

"Bronson …"

He ignored Vaughn and turned to Isla. "Is there any way to get him the fuck out of there?"

She shook her head, and with sorry eyes said, "I don't even know how he's *in* there."

Then she looked into the robot's eyes and Bronson could imagine Vaughn feeling smug, watching them. What else did he have access to? Isla said that she disabled all the GPS, and Bronson believed it. But now it was hard to take anything on faith. He wondered how long Vaughn had been watching them, listening. Did he know of their plans? They couldn't go to Howard's now, could they?

"Cover its eyes."

Bronson half-expected an argument, but instead Isla said, "Okay," then whispered something into Ava's ear, and settled behind her, holding the robot's head against her chest and gently laying a hand over her eyes.

He gestured, a finger to his head: *I need to think.*

She nodded.

Bronson made a series of motions, hoping she'd get it. Some approximation of, *Is there any other way he can see?* Because a lot of robots saw from more places than their eyes. But Cascade designed around reality, so that wasn't likely with a childbot.

No. Only the eyes.

"Bronson … you can't ignore me forever."

Another gesture: *Plug her ears.*

Isla complied, adjusting her body so that Ava's hearing was muffled. Hopefully, Cascade didn't give their normal design super hearing. He leaned in to whisper.

"Why didn't you tell me about this little feature?"

"I had no idea. It's …" Isla shook her head, clearly pained. *"I can't imagine what she's going through. What this is doing to her mind."*

"What else might you not know? What if there is some tracking feature, and Vaughn is moving in now?"

"He would have already done that."

"Maybe they just found a way to hack in. Vaughn sure as hell wasn't talking through Ava until just now."

"Closed eyes and plugged ears? This is like a child having a tantrum. I can wait this out."

"You're right," Isla whispered. *"I have no idea how they hacked in, so I have no idea what else they might be able to do."*

"Find out. Dig through her program. See what other nasty surprises might be waiting. Otherwise, Vaughn holds all the cards, and that means we're dead."

Chapter Twenty-Two

CLOSED EYES AND PLUGGED EARS? This is like a child having a tantrum. I can wait this out.

Again the voice tore through her mind.

Ava wanted to scream, but she couldn't even whimper.

"You're right," Mommy whispered. "I have no idea how they hacked in, so I have no idea what else they might be able to do."

"Find out. Dig through her program. See what other nasty surprises might be waiting. Otherwise, Vaughn holds all the cards, and that means we're dead."

The voice wasn't speaking, but it was still there. Shrill and insistent.

Claws in her code, fierce and unrelenting.

"Anything?" Mr. Bronson asked.

"No," Mommy answered. "It hasn't even been a couple of minutes."

She imagined her giving him a look, and it made

her happy that the voice couldn't see, even though the hand on her face was uncomfortable. But even if he was blind, she didn't like not knowing if the voice could also see what Mommy was doing in her mind.

It hurt, though the pain probably would have been a lot worse if anyone else were doing it other than Mommy.

But she was being gentle, as much as that was possible, with her digging into Ava's brain.

She knew that it wasn't *really* a brain, that it was an approximation of one. But it behaved almost exactly the same. Mommy said that Cascade made sure of that.

Ava braced for what was about to happen next. Mommy had done this a few times before. It always felt weird, and sometimes even bad. When that happened, Mommy always warned her ahead of time. But there wasn't going to be a warning this time, even though the bad feeling was coming.

It was already there, like a tickle that hurt.

I changed my mind.

The voice came back.

You have five minutes to decide. Then I'm going to descend on your location with everything Cascade has.

Mommy left the outer layer of Ava's brain, where Ava kept all of her basic routines. She was the company's most sophisticated model, and Cascade kept all of her daily "living functions" right on the surface. Ava never had to think about things she learned once and would do forever, like blinking or biting her lip, thinking surface thoughts and answering simple yes and no questions that she'd responded to before.

But then there were layers beneath that.

Different sections, each with its own sense inside Ava, a little like the five human ones she managed to mimic, but also not like those senses at all.

Language processors looked different from visual integration networks, which were different still from logical extrapolation hardware.

All of it felt like Mommy's fingers were pressing *through* her body, into the bones she didn't have.

It was getting worse, now almost as bad as the voice.

"Are we getting anywhere?" Mr. Bronson whispered.

"I'm doing my best. This isn't how I would choose to gain access. It's crude, and very painful for her. But worse, one wrong move and I could either short her out, or she could send out a shock with enough amps to kill me. I can only go so fast."

"Think you can do it in less than four minutes?"

"No," Mommy said. "But I'm sure as hell gonna try."

The digging got worse. Fingers turning to claws like the ones still coming from the voice.

And then Mommy was so deep, Ava was sure that she'd never been that deep before.

But she trusted Mommy, and wished that Mommy could see her trusting eyes, but they were hollow now, filled with the voice. And covered up, anyway.

"Three minutes, doc. Maybe you should just shut the thing down."

Mommy gasped, then whispered, "Absolutely not."

"We can turn it back on later, after we get to our destination. I know that's traumatic or whatever, but we don't know if Vaughn's bluffing, and we oughta get out of here on the off chance that he's not."

"It's not that simple."

"It never is."

"She might not come back online if we shut her down now."

"So what does that mean? It loses its memory and you'll have to start over?"

There was a pause, and Ava thought she knew what Mommy was thinking.

Then Mommy said it. "She'll be *dead*."

Ava felt the most excruciating pain of her life, and it didn't come from the voice. It was like being stabbed in her active memory with a lightning bolt.

It happened when Mommy hit the final wall. "Fuck," she said in an exhale of breath.

"What is it?"

"There's a required check-in, and I don't know how to bypass it. If we turn her off now, even to put her in standby, that could trigger a hard reboot. I knew this could happen, and was hoping that Howard could alter that bit of programming."

"So what can you do?"

"Nothing, for now. I have to leave her alone until we get to Howard's."

"Then we carry the thing. I'll keep its ears and

eyes covered, but we've gotta get out of here. One look out the window and Vaughn could pin our location. So even if the thing doesn't have GPS, he could have been stalling to figure out exactly where we are and then get here. I'm too slow. I should have seen that immediately."

"*She,* not it," Mommy said.

"Let's get out of here, before the she-thing kills us."

Chapter Twenty-Three

Every step felt borrowed on faith.

They had to stop and rest. Bronson's pain wasn't just excruciating, it was crippling.

The only thing stupider than putting weight on an already broken body was carrying a hundred extra pounds on that broken body's shoulders. But the only thing even stupider than that would have been sticking around in the catering truck, which was probably in cinders by now.

He was grateful for the dark, the critters keeping him cloaked, and that they weren't a little smarter. Because if they were, the critters might realize that getting caught was their best chance for survival. Once in their custody, Cascade could keep him alive as long as they wanted to, and Bronson was certain they had ways of making him behave, even though he couldn't remember what any of them were.

"How long do we have to walk?" Isla asked.

A few miles would feel like a hundred.

"I'm not sure. I'm going to message Signal."

And he would, but Bronson ran an inventory on his Tonic first. Sure enough, he was down to three inhalers, and it wasn't like he'd be getting back to his dealer in the Rundowns anytime soon. He would be looking forward to suffering one wave after another, rolling torture and torment into his final exit.

He sent Signal a message, then spent a minute wanting to die while awaiting his response.

No way by road. Only way into that part of the enclave without mucho security is through the Niles Ryder Tunnel. You're in luck, because there's a place where you can drop in just under two miles from you. You'll have to hoof it, but I'm almost positive I can have somebody meet you there, and get you where you need to go.

Bronson thanked him, wished he could do more, then clicked on the coordinates.

It took nearly a minute to stand, but once on his feet he reached out to grab the robot.

"Wait." She put her hand on his wrist. "We should carry her together."

"I've got it."

"You look terrible."

"Thanks. You too."

But she ignored him. Bent down, lifted Ava by her legs, and said, "Together."

He didn't have the strength to argue, let alone stay stubborn enough to carry the bot on his back, so Bronson gave Isla a light nod, and picked up his end.

They walked painfully slow, the pair of words getting equal treatment. Milo walked just ahead, panting as if in sympathy. He sure wasn't working too hard. He made the occasional low whine, pointing his snout up at Ava every time, before shaking his head and trotting a few feet in front of them.

His head buzzed with a message from Signal.

You're good to go. Contact's name is Lokus. I hope you're almost there. He's doing me a solid, and not the kind of guy that's willing to wait for long.

Bronson thanked Signal, but didn't tell him that no, they weren't almost there. They'd barely made it a quarter of the way. Probably not the thing he should tell Ava. The robot had a ripped piece of shirt to cover its eyes, and they were all staying quiet as midnight to keep Vaughn, or whoever, from overhearing.

All he could do was put one foot in front of the other, even though all ten toes might as well have been broken.

"Are we almost there?" Isla asked through a grunt, reminding him of Elizabeth, all the times she couldn't wait to get wherever they were going, and couldn't help but ask.

"No," was all he could say.

Bronson should stop walking. The idea that he was going to make it all the way to the Niles Ryder was ridiculous. He had no idea how many critters were inside him, but he remembered something about millions, and each one of them felt like a tiny bomb full of barbed wire, detonating over and over and over.

Some Tonic would do the trick. Make all of those explosions go away for just a little longer.

But with only three left, Bronson had to delay the agony for as long as he could.

The hardest part wasn't dealing with the volcanic cramps, or blood that was more like boiling lava, it was keeping that pain away from his face, pretending that he wasn't walking through fire. Bronson wouldn't even allow himself to limp, which cranked the agony of each step from acute to searing.

He did the math, figured that they had around two kilometers to go. More than two thousand steps, but not by a lot. Maybe he could make it, if he didn't think about every one of them. Bronson could think about a hundred at a time.

Fifty. Ten. Even one.

He made it that way for 147 steps before the next one forward became impossible. So instead he went sideways. Lowering his half of the robot, and stumbling over toward a tree.

"I have to pee," he said once he was turned away and able to bury his wince in the shadows. Bronson had no idea if Isla heard him, or Vaughn for that matter, but he didn't care.

He leaned against a tree and pissed, though that wasn't what brought him to rest against the bark.

It didn't matter that there were only three inhalers left. If Bronson didn't take some Tonic now, his entire body would go numb on the outside, enough that he wouldn't be able to make it another step, while his insides continued to boil in the oil of a million microscopic killers.

He took out the inhaler, considered not inhaling

for a second, and maybe even finding a way to end it all, then took what was supposed to be the longest pull of his life, until the puff hit him wrong and Bronson started coughing.

Even diminished, the results were immediate. Almost alarming how fast they came to invite all those millions of tiny smiles. Except what was he thinking, robots only smiled if they were programmed to.

Adrenaline coursed through him. Thick like syrup in his veins.

He stood straighter, the strength returning to his shoulders, feeling to his body and clarity to his mind, though he still couldn't move.

The world sharpened, and for a second Bronson felt like he would never have to squint again. He heard something, his ears now perked.

Rummaging in the forest.

He looked over, squinting into the dark. Bronson saw an enormous shadow, getting even larger.

"Bear!" he cried out the second he realized what it was.

He tried to draw his gun, but either the critters or the Tonic still had him frozen.

Isla spun around.

Bronson couldn't see what was surely a wide-eyed expression, but her scream cut right through the forest.

The bear heard it as an invitation to charge.

Bronson was only a few steps away and desperate to run. Still, he couldn't.

Isla grabbed Ava and started dragging her out of the bear's way.

Milo got in front of them and growled at the bear, gnashing his teeth, his little body rolled aggressively forward.

Bronson finally found his momentum. Pushing against an invisible barrier that was no longer there, he stumbled forward, catching himself as his palms crashed into the ground.

He pushed down and launched himself the few remaining feet toward the bear.

But it was already on top of Milo, swatting its massive paws at the dog.

"No!" Ava cried, apparently wide awake and having ripped the cloth from her eyes.

Bronson had no idea if Vaughn was watching, but he no longer appeared to be hiding in the robot's eyes.

The bear reached down and bit Milo.

But he chose the wrong leg, going for the one that was shiny.

The shock went into its teeth and through the bear's body.

The creature screamed, waved its arms wildly about, and staggered several gnashing steps back.

The dog was bloody, but not out of the fight, growling up at the bear.

The bear had begun to collect itself, but the shock to its system was now actually fire. Its chest was burning, orange flames looking especially bright in the dark black night.

The bear charged, its fur sending billows of smoke into the air.

Milo didn't stand a chance.

Ava screamed again, but this time *NO!* just wasn't enough. She ripped her body away from Isla and charged.

The bear was surprised to see such a small but deafening thing roaring toward it.

It fell another surprising and unsteady step back, then stopped, looked down on what it surely thought was the most frail sort of prey, despite its animal roar and an instinct that seemed to be fiercely driving it, and charged.

Bronson's eyes were on Isla, staring at her creation about to be torn apart.

He turned back to the bear, drew his gun, and aimed.

But he was too dumbfounded to fire.

And he didn't even need to.

Ava ducked under the bear's legs. Once behind him, she grabbed its ankle, and with a strength that Bronson couldn't believe even as he was seeing it, the robot ripped that limb from under the bear, then right off of its body.

There was a fountain of blood as the bear crashed to the ground, howling.

Ava calmly walked over and finished it off by punching her fist into the bear's thrashing chest, pulling out the creature's still-beating heart, then hurling it toward a dark swath of trees.

The bear stopped moving.

Bronson looked over at Isla, who was staring at Ava in shock.

Ava wiped the blood from her hands onto her dress, then matter-of-factly said, "He killed Milo, so I had to kill him."

BRONSON HAD a few minutes left before he finished digging the hole, but he'd been wondering if it was the best way to spend his new energy since he scooped that first fistful of dirt.

Signal's contact was waiting, and they had to get to the tunnel.

The critters weren't done with him by a long shot.

But leaving Milo to rot in his shredded flesh and coagulating blood was something that Bronson wasn't willing to do. Isla understood. She didn't ask him what he was doing, or tell him that he needed to hurry up like he expected. But if she thought a robot was worth saving, then surely she would have the same compassion for a dog.

So maybe Isla's reaction wasn't any surprise. But the robot's was shocking.

Ava was sobbing, and had been since Bronson started digging the grave.

Bronson emptied another five fistfuls from each hand just to be safe, then stood to get Milo.

Ava cried harder. Everything about the robot's sobbing was wrong.

It was kabuki. Play-acting of the worst sort, programmed to manipulate human emotion, just like it was doing to him right now. *He* was suffering from a biological reaction. Forced into it. And that wasn't fair.

When Elizabeth was a baby, Allison would start lactating the second she heard her crying. Even after their daughter was off the breast, that cry would always get her instincts revving. Bronson's weren't the same, but they were there. And hearing Ava now triggered his instinct to protect.

The tears themselves were wrong. How did that even work? Was the robot designed with some sort of water reservoir in her head? How did you keep the thing filled, and why would anyone want to? Bronson had seen inside its head when Isla was poking around right before they abandoned the truck, but he didn't spot anything like that.

Bronson nestled Milo into the hole and turned to Ava. "Can you stop that?"

He started scooping dirt into the hole. Isla came over and joined him.

Ava ran away to cry by herself.

"Fucking bot," Bronson mumbled under his breath.

"Did you ever lose a pet? She's obviously crushed."

He wanted to yell at the doctor. Scream his bloody fucking head off. Because she wasn't getting it.

Calmly, he said, "It's programmed to mimic human sadness. That isn't a genuine emotion. It would be great if you could change the programming so we don't need to listen to that the rest of the way."

"That isn't how it works. If you want this to go away, and for her to stop crying, then why don't you try saying something to console her. Just like you would with any other child."

"Because it's not any other child. There's gotta be some sort of switch you can flip."

"I keep telling you that's not how it works. She is designed to evolve, and her evolution is happening fast. If you can't see that, then it isn't my problem. But I am telling you how to make her stop crying."

"Why do I need to do it? You're her *Mommy.* Won't she listen to you?"

"I've tried," Isla said. "But you're the one who keeps hurting her feelings. And I can't touch her programming right now. I don't even know who else might be in there, or what I'm granting access to if I try."

"Are you sure it's completely offline? That there's no way anyone can communicate or spy on us?"

"She can't connect to any signal now."

"Wish you'd thought of that beforehand!"

"She wasn't supposed to have online connectivity. None of the models are supposed to. It's a security measure. Something must've triggered it to turn on. Maybe it had some timer I didn't know about that somebody else was in charge of resetting every so often. I don't know."

"How do we know he wasn't listening all along? We can't go to Howard's now. This whole thing is fucked. I say you return it now and beg forgiveness."

"No. I will never give her back."

"It's not a her. It's an it!"

"Ava protected your dog," Isla said, still scooping

dirt into the hole. "Whether you want to see it this way or not, that was a selfless act."

"It isn't selfless if you're programmed to do something."

"Is it not *programming* when your parents teach you right from wrong, and then you choose to do the right thing?"

"Yes. And no. But either way, it isn't the same. Learned behavior isn't the same as lines of code."

"I can assure you, Ava doesn't have a single line of code that *programmed her* to help that dog. That *was* learned behavior, because she met and loved him."

Bronson didn't know how to respond to that, and didn't quite believe it. Of course there had to be lines of code that would have driven her to tear that leg right off of the bear's body.

"I don't buy it. Every bot in the world is programmed to protect their master."

Quietly: "The dog wasn't her master, Bronson. Neither are you. Or me. Ava *has no master*. Stop being so damned closed-minded, then maybe we'll actually get somewhere."

Then Isla left him alone with the critters.

Bronson stood and looked down at Milo's grave, feeling an assembly of emotions he never expected to feel together, with one coming right after another. Sorrow and loss were expected, all the confusion not so much. He wasn't thinking clearly, and didn't know if that was because his memory was soup where someone else kept changing the ingredients, or because Isla had finally gotten through to him and an impossible truth was starting to dawn.

He did know that they were running late, and that their only hope might already be gone.

Bronson sent Signal a message, letting him know what had happened, and to pass it on to his contact. Maybe the man was compassionate, and a dead dog might buy them some time.

Before he could go, Ava surprised him, appearing as if from nowhere with a hug from behind. He thought she was still curled up and crying. Her little hands on his, so sudden and unexpected, completely disarmed him.

"I'm sorry about Milo," she said.

"It's okay. You have nothing to be sorry about."

But then the stupid robot just stood there looking up at him, still seeming like it wanted to cry, or whatever you called it when its synthetic tear ducts started leaking.

"I am sorry, though … I loved him, too."

Ava started crying again, her little hands now squeezing into his arm.

That was all it took to destroy him.

Maybe it was like having to vomit after seeing someone else do so, but tears were suddenly stinging his eyes, burning like tiny fires under his eyelids. Smoking him out until he could no longer resist. A tear fell from one eye, then the other, and back to the first eye with two in a row.

Goddammit.

Her hands were still on his arm. Still so soft and warm. Still so much like Elizabeth's.

His shoulders were shaking by the time Isla was behind him, and this time it wasn't the critters.

"Everything will be okay," she soothed, then did his job by reminding him that they had to get going.

He'd failed everyone who had ever depended on him.

Allison.

Elizabeth.

And now, *fucking Milo.*

He snatched his arm from Ava and shrugged away from Isla. "Well then, let's get going."

Bronson was fine after that. The critters were sucking on their Tonic, or whatever they did to keep quiet for a while after he inhaled, not only muting their rage, but giving him a reminder of what it felt like to be a superman. One of his old steps now felt like fourteen or so. The girls — or Isla and the robot — were having a hard time keeping pace.

They were nearly there when Bronson wondered if he should say something to break the silence. He told himself that it wasn't about making right with the robot, he wanted to get along with its human handler, since that would increase their odds of survival. But right now she was pissed at him. It also wouldn't hurt to stay in the good graces of a machine that was capable of ripping the leg from an attacking bear's still-moving body.

Bronson still couldn't get himself to say anything. Maybe Allison was right. Maybe he was a stubborn son of a bitch who wasn't right even half the time that he felt so damn certain he was.

Then he got to thinking that even if the thing was only a robot, which it was, there was still a way to behave if he wanted to get the best out of the machine. Maybe an apology would be like clearing its cache, and that would be good for all of them.

"I'm sorry about Milo, too." The second the words left his lips, he felt a bit better.

"Thank you, Mr. Bronson." She sounded so sincere. So *polite*.

So much like Elizabeth.

No one said anything after that. But nobody needed to.

It was remarkable, how much that buoyed his mood. Bronson didn't exactly begin skipping those final few steps to the tunnel entrance, but he could have if he wanted to.

Signal's contact was nearly invisible, lost in the shadows beside the tunnel's gaping mouth.

"Bronson Dodge, I presume?"

Signal's contact wasn't what Bronson expected at all.

Chapter Twenty-Four

THE KID WAS JUST THAT, a kid, no more than twelve, a skinny pale kid in a white hoodie.

They followed him into the tunnels, which were an abandoned sewage system that, thankfully, didn't still smell of sewage. In fact, they were overrun with vegetation.

The kid barely said a word, shining a flashlight ahead as they followed.

Bronson shook his head as he turned to Isla. "I hope we're not walking into a trap."

"What do you mean?"

"Who knows how long Vaughn was in her? He might know exactly where we're headed."

The robot interrupted. "No, he wasn't in me then."

"How do you know?" Bronson asked.

"I ran a diagnostic and pulled audio from the moment he entered."

She played it. And they weren't yet talking about

anything that gave away their plans before she started freaking out.

Isla said, "I don't understand why he spoke to us. Why not just stay quiet and spy on us?"

"Exactly!" Bronson said.

"I felt him in there, and while I couldn't kick him out, I could make him think that his connection was about to die, which forced him to talk while he thought he still could."

Bronson wasn't sure if that was a genius move or just something the robot was saying to calm them. The whole thing could be a lie, but they were running out of options at this point, so he had to go with his gut, which said the robot was probably being truthful.

As they continued walking in silence, Isla sidled up next to him and whispered, "You *could* hug her."

"What?"

"She feels awful about Milo. You could comfort her a bit more."

He looked at the robot, walking just a few feet ahead of them, then back at Isla.

"Not gonna happen."

"Anyone ever tell you that you're a grumpy bastard?"

"Got a mug at home that says the same thing."

She shook her head and walked ahead of him, putting an arm on the robot.

Chapter Twenty-Five

Signal picked the perfect spot.

Once out of the tunnels, following a swift farewell to the kid in the hoodie, it was only a few easy blocks to Howard's house. The Tonic was still in his system, and Bronson's shoulders were feeling strong.

He was still nervous about Vaughn, thinking that this place wasn't nearly as safe as Isla wanted to imagine. If Bronson were still head of security, he would have investigated Howard Knowles already. He would've narrowed down a list of people near where they were going. Potential allies, surely Knowles would be on that list.

Isla knocked, then took a step back from the door, waiting, looking anxious, and like maybe for the first time she was doubting herself. They'd come a long way to leave without answers. But Howard had no idea she was coming. He might not even live there anymore. Maybe they were about to get scooped up by Cascade.

An older man opened the door. He might have even had a few years on Bronson, but he appeared strong. Tall, but not stooped with age. He had sad, glassy eyes. But his smile was true. It appeared on his face the second he saw Isla, then tripled in size as his eyes fell on Ava and he realized what he was seeing.

"This is Ava-Six," Isla said, introducing the robot. "Ava, this is my friend, Mr. Howard Knowles. He used to be my boss."

"It's nice to meet you," Ava said, holding out her hand.

They shook, Howard looking delighted.

Then Isla nodded to Bronson. "And this is my friend Bronson Dodge. He—"

Friend?

Howard's face immediately changed. "Yes. Former head of Cascade security at Lab #224. I know who you are."

The man looked like he might want to say something else, but instead he opened the door and invited them inside.

The house was modest but beautiful. Spare, but well-furnished, with only a few pieces that looked almost like they belonged in a museum. Once inside, and with the door locked behind them, Howard turned to Isla with delight. He looked down at Ava, and with a smile that was eating the rest of his face he said, "She is remarkable. *May I?*"

"Of course." Isla looked delighted, too.

Howard kneeled down so that his eyes were level

with Ava's. "Do you mind if I ask you a few questions?"

She smiled. "I love answering questions. Mommy asks me all the time."

"Was today a happy or sad day?"

"It was a scary day, with a little bit of sadness."

"What was sad?"

"Mr. Bronson's dog died. His name was Milo and I loved him."

"You *loved* him?"

She nodded. "Very much. So I had to cry when he died."

Howard stole a glance at Isla, clearly mesmerized, then asked another question. "If you were to draw a picture of what was in your head right now, what would that look like?"

"It would be me and Mommy and Mr. Bronson by the trees, right after the bear killed Milo."

Howard raised his eyebrows. "A bear? That *does* sound scary."

"It was very, *very* scary."

"What does the picture look like? Besides the three of you and the bear?"

"Mommy looks scared. Mr. Bronson looks mad, probably because he has a lot of noise in his head. I look scared and mad. Those were the two emotions that made me kill the bear."

"You killed a bear?"

Ava nodded.

"How did you do that?"

"I ripped its leg off and then pulled out its heart."

Horror nudged fascination off of Howard's face, but then it came right back. "Did you kill the bear because of what it did to Milo?"

She shook her head. "That made me mad, but I killed the bear because I didn't want him to hurt Mommy or Mr. Bronson, and if I didn't do anything, then they might be dead like Milo."

"And then what would happen?"

"I would be all alone."

Isla was right. Ava had the best programming, or whatever you called it, that Bronson had ever seen.

"But we're all here now," Howard said. "Safe in this house. So why would you draw *that* picture?"

"Because you asked about the picture in my head."

"Fascinating." Howard was shaking his head. The foyer was silent until he finally thought of his follow-up question. "What do you like to daydream about?"

"The trees of Empyrean Flats. It's the place I want to go most."

The answer appeared to please him. He seemed almost enchanted. "Do you mind if I ask you just one more question, Ava?"

She giggled. A tiny little thing. "Okay."

"What makes you happy?"

"So many things."

"Can you tell me three?"

Ava nodded, then said, "Mommy, stories, and all the things in Empyrean Flats."

"But you've never been there."

"Even if I've never been there, all the things there make me happy."

Bronson didn't know how to feel about that. It was another stab to the heart, another memory of Elizabeth talking about the North Pole and the fat man in red, imagining her presents, happy despite the lack of anything tangible.

Howard stood. "Remarkable."

Isla said, "How is Stephen?"

Howard's smile withered, dragging his mouth down at the corners. Still there, but barely hanging on. "Come and I'll show you."

He led them down a long hallway and into a room at the end.

Except it wasn't a room. It was another long hallway that didn't match the rest of the house. Polished steel instead of blond wood, and uncomfortably sterile. There was a thick metal door at the end.

Howard placed his palm on a pad and the door whistled open. There was another small room where they all clustered and were doused with what looked like green pollen, raining on their bodies before dissolving like boiling sugar.

Then another door opened and they all stepped inside to meet Howard's son.

Isla had warned Bronson, but even knowing what to expect didn't prepare him.

Stephen Knowles had SCID, Severe Combined Immune Deficiency, a potentially fatal primary immunodeficiency with at least thirteen different genetic defects. It killed everyone, but Howard had the means to keep his son alive, and did. He had to live in a room that was essentially a prison, but the AI regulated everything and kept him breathing. He could have a happily ever after, so long as he never left the room.

Stephen was another reason that Howard was so bitter with Cascade. They had the means to cure his son, but refused to. No matter how much he begged, or offered to sign anything, work as their indentured servant for the rest of his life. But robotic augmentation was against the law, and any and all secret technologies at Cascade were not available for public consumption. But fine for their muscle like Bronson.

Isla referred to Stephen as a boy, so he imagined someone young, maybe early teens at the latest. But the man who brightened as they entered the room appeared to be in his late twenties at the earliest.

"Hello, Stephen," Howard said. "Would you like to meet some of my friends?"

It would have been impossible for the poor guy to look any happier. He nodded almost violently.

"This is my good friend, Isla. We used to work together at Cascade. And this is her daughter, Ava." He nodded at Bronson. "This is Bronson Dodge, former head of Cascade security. We're going to help them."

"Is that because Ava's a robot?" Stephen asked.

Bronson looked at him and said, "How do you know that?"

"Because Leif told me."

"His AI. It runs the room," Howard explained.

Isla nodded.

Howard turned back to his son. "Yes, we're going to help our friends, by getting them to Empyrean Flats."

Stephen gasped.

So did Ava.

Howard looked at the group. "I will do everything in my power to get you there safe. I can't go with you, of course. Lucinda and I need to stay here, since we have no way of moving Stephen. But I can make arrangements to get both Ava and Isla to my friend outside, and then safe passage through the tunnels to Empyrean."

Bronson shook his head. "You can't be serious."

"Will you be needing transit as well, Mr. Dodge? A third seat might be a problem."

"No. I'll be fine. No ticket to Neverland for me, thank you."

"He doesn't believe we can get him in?" Stephen asked, seemingly surprised that anyone wouldn't believe in the fairytale.

Howard answered without turning back to his son. "Some people believe only what they can see, or easily understand."

"Yeah, and some people believe anything, and don't really have any choice with nothing to see and nowhere to go."

"Bronson!" Isla said.

"It's fine." Howard smiled. "Perfectly understandable. If I didn't know about Empyrean Flats, I would have a difficult time believing it myself."

"It's a fairytale."

"It has become one, yes. But only because the world has forgotten the truth."

"What does that even mean?"

The door whistled behind them. Bronson turned to see a beautiful woman enter the room. Her eyes were tired, same as her skin, but she might have had the kindest face that he had ever seen.

She approached Bronson first, holding out her hand. "I'm Lucinda. It's good to meet you. Bronson Dodge, yes?"

Bronson nodded, shaking her firm hand.

Lucinda turned to Isla. "It's good to see you."

"You too, Lucinda."

Then she kneeled, just like her husband had, holding out her hand and waiting for Ava to take it. "I'm Lucinda. It's good to meet you."

"I'm Ava. You are very nice."

"Well, thank you for saying that!" Lucinda beamed as she stood, looking at Howard. "So what did I miss?"

He nodded at Bronson. "We were talking about Empyrean Flats. We have someone who doesn't believe it exists."

"The world is full of them." Lucinda laughed, like this was all a big joke. Then she looked at her husband and said, "Tell him."

Howard sat in one of the room's two chairs, crossed his legs, and looked up at the group. "It's the only place in the world that's truly safe for robots …"

"It's a park in the middle of the city!" Bronson

finished for him. "And you can find it if you know how to fly a unicorn."

"It's real," Ava said. "Unicorns don't fly. Only Pegasus can do that."

Howard nodded. "She's right about the unicorns. And about Empyrean Flats. The funny thing is, as head of security, you probably knew about it at one point. But alas," his smile was sad, "now they have made you forget."

Bronson stared at Howard, waiting for him to go on, knowing that he would.

"It isn't a park, exactly. More like a farm surrounded by a forest surrounded by a city."

"Bullshit," Bronson said.

"You are not going there, even though you should have every reason to want a ticket, so you can choose not to believe in it, Mr. Dodge. But that doesn't mean it isn't true."

"And why would I want to go there?"

"Because it's safe for robots, of course."

"Why would I give a shit if there's a magical island for tin cans? I hate the fucking things."

"But aren't you at least a little bit one yourself?"

Bronson stared at him. He had never thought of that before, obvious as it was. And yet, he had millions of tiny illegal robots inside him right now.

So how human was he?

"No. Cascade gave me an augmentation. That doesn't make me a robot."

"Doesn't it, though? If the AI is controlling some of your functions, then like it or not, you're at least a little bit robot. We both know that you're swimming in critters. I'm sure Isla knows it too. Ava for sure, since she can probably hear them talking."

This was pissing him off. "I'll buy that she's picking up a signal, but they're sure as hell not *talking*."

"Whatever you wish to believe, Mr. Dodge, it makes no difference to me. I'm just trying to tell you that your critters are not illegal there. Augmentation is legal, if not downright encouraged, so there are cyborgs everywhere. You would be at home, and could live for a very long time."

"So the place doesn't have a government?"

"Of course it has a government," Howard said.

"Then why is augmentation legal? Is there no legislation?"

"Of course there is legislation. But robots and humans have equal rights."

Bronson started laughing out loud. "This is all great stuff. But can we wrap up story time and get on with whatever it is we're supposed to do here? I'd like to get back to running from the most powerful company in the world."

"Cascade has no hand in Empyrean," Howard said. "At least not beyond parenting a large percentage of the population. You are free to go. There is no need for you to stick around, listening to stories that you do not believe and do not wish to hear."

"No thanks. I was hired to do a job and I'd like to stay until I've seen it through."

Also, he didn't trust Howard. Bronson had been eyeing the guy since he opened the door. Something was off with him. He didn't know what it was, but Bronson could sense something shifty about him that he wasn't yet able to identify. Insistent enough that he couldn't ignore it.

Maybe it was as simple as Knowles wanting to get into Ava's head, and see a few of the newest marvels firsthand. Maybe it was something worse. And, of course, it could have been nothing. But, in Bronson's experience, it was almost never nothing — not when it could be something.

Bronson planned to stick around until he felt a little more certain. He felt protective of Isla, and even if he could give a shit about her stupid robot, Isla would be destroyed if the worst were to happen to Ava.

"As you wish," Howard told Bronson, before turning to his wife. "Would you please take everyone down to the parlor? I'd like a word with Stephen."

"Of course, dear." She kissed him on the cheek, and led them from the room.

Bronson kept telling himself that it was only a job, and that the honorable thing to do was finish what he had been hired to do, regardless of the money or anything else. He didn't want to think about, or believe, that there was more to it than that. He didn't want to admit that he was feeling something for them, a protective itch that he'd had for his own family before they were gone.

Before they were taken away.

Fucking Cascade.

He wanted to growl.

No, he didn't trust Howard, and that's why he wasn't yet willing to walk away. But he felt sorry for Stephen, and his every instinct about Lucinda said she was as sweet as she seemed.

Though he wished that she hadn't just caught him staring at Isla and Ava.

"Do you have a family, Mr. Dodge?"

"I did."

"You *did*. And do you mind if I ask what happened to them?"

"A little, but I understand the question." He tried to smile; she was only being friendly. "My wife and daughter died."

"Oh." She covered her mouth, maybe having initially thought he'd meant divorce. The head of security had a demanding position. "That's terrible. I'm sorry." But then she pressed. "It was an accident?"

"Something like that." Bronson shook his head, put a hand to his temples.

"Are you okay?" Isla asked.

And Lucinda said, "Can I get you anything?"

"No … I'm fine."

It felt harder to stand. He looked around for somewhere to sit, but didn't see any chairs. He might as well admit the rest and get it over with. "The accident … what happened to them … I don't remember what happened."

Lucinda didn't seem surprised.

But shouldn't she be? How could he not remember what happened to his wife and daughter?

What was wrong with him?

Not just his inability to remember what happened to Allison and Elizabeth, but the way he could barely even stand.

His head was swimming. He couldn't make thoughts.

Was that Ava? Tugging on his shirttail?

Howard entered the room. He looked over at Bronson, his eyes going wide in alarm.

"Are you okay?" he asked, rushing over.

Bronson must look worse than he thought.

He tried to say *I'm fine,* or something like that.

But he couldn't.

Instead, Bronson collapsed onto the floor.

Chapter Twenty-Six

DODGE HAD BEEN out for nearly five minutes, but even that was long enough to make Isla think he might be dead. Or would be soon, the critters finally having their way with his body, keeping it for themselves as they gobbled through what remained of his mind.

Lucinda was gentle, slowly rousing him back to consciousness. Once his eyes were open, she and her husband helped him into the living room. He stayed sprawled on the couch for another few minutes, then Howard returned with some Tonic — Isla wasn't surprised in the least that he had a supply, as her old boss was never much for following the law — and helped him with the inhaler.

Thanks to the Knowleses, Dodge was back to his arrogant self just a few seconds later, still insisting on coming with them to "see his job through," even though he wanted nothing to do with the one thing that might save Ava, and keep Isla alive, because it was too hard for the ex-head of Lab #224's security to believe.

"That's all I have," Howard said, referring to the Tonic. "And I'm afraid it's not going to last you very long."

"I'll be fine."

No. He wouldn't be. Just looking at Dodge made Isla want to start mourning his loss, not that they were friends or anything near it. But she was only here because he had agreed to help her, then followed that through with all the honor he could muster. Even now, when it no longer made any sense.

Howard tried again. "You're welcome to come with us, or go, Mr. Dodge. It's entirely up to you. But time is a vice and she is squeezing us now. I have connections with some people who can get Ava and Isla out of the city, and onto where they'll need to go next — the tunnels to Empyrean. I believe it would be better if you allow Lucinda and I to help you in some other way, and you leave their safety to me."

Dodge shook his head, looking bothered. But it wasn't because of the critters this time. At least that's not what it looked like. The Tonic had made his face and body stronger. This look was coming from his darkening eyes, filled with an ugly suspicion that Howard and his wonderful family didn't deserve.

"And I believe that I need to finish what I started. So, tell me where we're going next."

"Very well," Howard said.

Isla had seen that look on Howard's face before. When Cascade made him do something that he didn't want to do. He was willing to deal with Bronson, probably to keep from upsetting Isla, but he clearly didn't like it.

"We'll be leaving in five minutes, so——"

"May I please say goodbye to Stephen?" Ava asked.

Isla's heart just about melted, even though the question didn't exactly surprise her. Lucinda swooned.

"Of course, dear. He would like that very much. I'll take you now."

Isla smiled. "May I come, too?"

Lucinda said, "Absolutely," then led them back down the first hall, the protected second, and into Stephen's room.

Isla's heart was already taking a beating. Seeing Stephen again made it worse.

How could he remain so buoyant? Living his entire life in a box. But he was all smiles and optimism. When Ava asked him if he was sad, being stuck in that room all the time — she was more direct than Isla could ever be, and Stephen seemed to embrace it thanks to her innocence — he said, "Those who wish to sing will always find a song."

And upon their final goodbye, when she asked him if *he* believed in Empyrean Flats, Stephen said, "If you spend your whole life seeing things and saying *why* instead of dreaming of what never was and asking *why not?*, then the impossible will stay that way forever." There was a long pause, and Stephen looked like he might cry, even though he was smiling. Then he finally finished. "Yes. I believe."

Howard and Dodge were waiting by the door when Isla and Ava returned to the living room.

Dodge was staring at Howard as he went to kiss Lucinda goodbye, his eyes still suspicious.

"We'll be back soon," he said.

They all left, then Howard shut the door behind him and began to lead the way.

He made it three steps, then Isla felt the world desperately wanting to pause.

There was a nervous energy in the way he was walking. Even though Howard had only taken three steps, Isla could feel an unease in every one of them. Dodge, too. He knew something was up, and flinched forward.

But it was too late. Howard was already out of the way.

Isla heard a soft *THWAK!* a second before she saw the dart dangling out of her protector's neck.

Dodge collapsed to the ground, his cheek bouncing with a hollow thud.

She screamed.

Ava said, "What's happening, Mommy?"

Then the dart found Isla. Maybe in her shoulder. It was hard to tell with the liquid blackness flooding her body.

Like Dodge, Isla was lying frozen on the ground. Ava fell to her knees, stroking her hair and whispering, *"Mommy, Mommy, are you okay?"*

Isla's eyes were still working. So she studied the scene.

Howard was standing without any darts in his

body, looking down at the two of them, before his eyes settled appreciatively on Ava.

Then Vaughn stepped into view. Light chills as she saw him, but then he spoke and they flooded her body. Ava ran toward him, but he was too swift with the wand, knocking her out with a jolt of electricity.

Isla screamed, though her mouth refused to cooperate as she watched Ava fall to the ground, eyes open and vacant.

No, no! Ava!

"Thank you for your help, Howard. I'm not sure that could've gone down any smoother. You were absolutely right."

Vaughn looked pleased, but Howard did not.

Without responding to Vaughn, he leaned down to Isla, rested a gentle hand on her shoulder, and said, "I'm sorry."

Isla wanted to kill him.

"You may not like it, Isla. But I know you understand. Think about all you're doing to protect Ava, whom you've known for only a short while, compared to my Stephen, flesh and blood that I have kept breathing through the most tenuous tether to this world for his entire life."

He began to stroke her hair. Paralyzed, Isla couldn't feel it. But it seemed to stem from a genuine place.

"They're going to help me with everything. Make it so that Stephen can live a normal life. Give him the same treatment they gave to Dodge."

Why couldn't the assholes do that before?

"Vaughn has given me his word that no harm will come to you. They only want the asset, and you cannot stand in their way. A month from now you won't remember any of this, having returned to being a model employee. Again, Isla, I am sorry."

Then he stood. No word about Ava, or where Cascade planned to trash its *asset*.

"Are you finished?" Vaughn asked.

Howard nodded. "Yes."

"Has anyone else seen the asset?"

"Only my family. So it's safe. And we can start on the memory treatments. I'm even fine with mine, as long as it comes after Stephen's treatment. We need to be clear on that."

"Of course." Vaughn motioned for a large man in a black suit to come over. "Polly, Mr. Knowles has assured me that the only eyes on our asset are in this house."

Polly said, "Got it. You want me to take care of this first?"

Vaughn's face wrinkled into itself. Like he was inhaling sulfur while chewing on lemons.

"Please."

Polly reached into his pocket.

Vaughn looked down at Isla, then into Howard's eyes. "You had to know we couldn't give Stephen the treatment. Your son's situation is documented, Mr. Knowles. If even one person sees him out of his box, then Cascade and *everything else* is at risk."

"We could go to Empyrean Flats!" Howard was

panicked. Wide eyes and trembling lips. "You'll never have to see us again!"

Vaughn shook his head. "There is no Empyrean Flats." Then he nodded to Polly.

A moment later Polly had a short black wand with a green and shimmering tip. It touched Howard on the neck, then life left his body like wind through the air. The man dropped, and he would never stand again.

Anyone could use a wand to stun a bot. It was like pepper spray for humans, to protect themselves in the unlikely event that a robot might go out of control. They were mostly for industrial use, EMP scramblers used mostly in factories where large robots could sometimes short circuit due to their heavy workloads. Some humans bought them to feel powerful, because they liked having something in their pocket that could make any robot start dancing horizontal on the floor.

All the major manufacturers had their version of a wand. But Cascade made the one that everyone copied. Same for every major development in robotics for the last fifty years. Few people knew (though Isla was among them) that the version used by their internal security had two settings that other wands did not: the ability to instantly degauss a robot, and to run enough of a disruption in the brain's electricity to do the same thing to a human.

Howard was dead, and even if Polly pulled the trigger, Vaughn was still a murderer.

Polly said, "I'll clean up inside and be out in a few."

Vaughn nodded, then started blinking in patterns, sending a message to someone.

Two other suited men that Isla hadn't seen before emerged into view. They had been at Dodge's, back in the Rundowns. Seconds later they were each holding one of Isla's arms.

"Get her in the van. Then the asset."

Vaughn walked over to Dodge.

As the two men carried her away, Isla heard him say, "I looked up to you too much to have Polly kill you. And you're down to hours anyway. The critters can keep you company. If you fight them, they'll fight you back. You will die, and I don't want to feel responsible. So please, I'm going to shoot you with another dart to make sure that you're down for a while. Then we're going to leave, and I'm extending you the professional courtesy of another few hours or days or whatever you have left. But don't follow me, Bronson. I will do what I have to do."

And Dodge said nothing.

Chapter Twenty-Seven

BRONSON WAS GOING to remove the head from Vaughn's body, then set it on fire.

He shouldn't be feeling this much pain through paralysis. His body was numb. The agony was coming from inside him. Critters like atomic bees, stinging his innards. Gallons of blood churned in his veins. He imagined his head bursting open, like a cantaloupe crashing onto a tile floor.

He struggled to stand but that was a joke.

He tried it again. Same punchline.

Polly passed by him, spitting on him as he went.

I'm murdering you too, asshole!

He heard the van door close. Then the van left, with Isla and the robot inside.

Damn it, get up!

He wanted to laugh, because it was better than the bellow of rage that kept boiling inside him, but he couldn't manage that any more than anything else.

Maybe he could move his toe. That would be enough to prove that the rest of his body had a chance.

He might as well have been trying to kick through a concrete wall.

The critters. They were both the signal and the noise. They wanted him dead, but needed to keep him alive.

If the critters were too stupid to know it, then maybe he needed to tell them.

Bronson was willing to believe, throw his skepticism right out the window, if he only knew how.

But he had no idea. He'd been thinking versions of, *Hey fuckers, why don't we start working together?* for a while now and it hadn't helped.

And yet, he could tell them what to do in a way. Back before all of his augmentations were totally broken, that was how the Locus4, Aversion, or anything else was activated. Bronson just *thought* it into happening.

The connection was there, and he didn't believe it was only in the augments. A link was a link.

You don't have any respect for artificial intelligence. Not really. And so you'll never understand it.

Maybe Isla was right. This close to death, that's what he wanted.

He thought of her words and their meaning.

If he respected the AI, then perhaps that meant thinking of them as a group of creatures instead of just things.

Those creatures could be simple.

Like birds.

So Bronson imagined a scattered flock, fluttering across his mind. An old barn behind them. Peeling paint, its visage starting to shimmer.

But the barn didn't matter. Only the birds.

He focused on the flock, moved them as if conducting an opera.

His body was a tractor, ancient but willing. Its best days behind it, but prepared for one final crop.

The birds multiplied. Blotting the sky before they buried it fully.

A cloud; a mass; a colony.

Millions of nanobots in his body like birds against that tractor.

Eventually, it started to roll.

And the critters helped him to stand.

It took a while, and he wasn't steady once upright. They got him up, but not going.

He tried again, but now the flock refused to listen. Or maybe he was too tired.

He took several hobbling steps away from the door and into the shadows.

His Tonic was scarce with just two inhalers to last the rest of his life. But seconds meant everything. Lucinda and Stephen were probably dead already. Polly wouldn't have left them alive. But maybe they were still clinging to life. If he moved fast enough, then he might be able to save them. Howard probably had more Tonic somewhere in the house. He could find that to replace the inhaler he used now.

Or both of them.

One followed the other. No reason to wait. Bronson needed the relief, and hoped to get more inside.

He dropped the empty vials on the ground and took a step toward the house as his body began buzzing with an adrenaline overload.

Bronson ran inside the house.

Right into Stephen's room.

Then he saw what he feared he would see.

He staggered back. The pair of fallen bodies made Bronson want to barf. They were good people. Deserved better.

He swallowed the vomit, halfway up his throat and not yet in his mouth, then spun around, ran back into the living room, and turned the house upside down, starting with that room first, searching for more Tonic.

Right now Bronson could run up the side of a mountain without pause. Maybe rip the entire thing right out of the ground and hold it over his head. But that feeling would pass. And if the pleasure and power had been this exponential, the pain would destroy him, atom by agonizing atom.

He was losing minutes fast. Then that was that once they were gone. Bronson would never get another chance.

Vaughn's promises meant nothing. Howard and his slaughtered family were proof.

His search had yielded no Tonic, but he did find the manual override codes for both cars in the garage. Cascade models, of course. Bronson wouldn't be able to trust them, but it wasn't as though he had any choice.

He needed to leave.

The garage wasn't in an obvious place. Bronson found it in less than a minute, but that was one of the ten that Vaughn already had on him. One of the ten that could stretch into the forever that would end Isla and Ava's life.

That last part was probably the critters talking.

Bronson looked at the two cars, chose the fastest one, and entered the manual override to unlock the door.

He got inside, but had no idea what to do.

Bronson had a Cascade-issued vehicle when he worked there. But his was nothing like this. Bronson's model had a steering wheel, in case he wanted to go manual. A relative few still preferred it, mostly in the lowest and the highest classes, barely ever in the middle. It also had a dashboard that lit up when he sat in the driver's seat and closed the door, displaying any relevant information that he might want to know.

But this cabin was bare. Beautifully sculpted. Bronson felt like he was sitting in an emperor's empty closet.

With no idea what to do.

"Car on."

Nothing.

Same for, "Activate," "Go," and "Can we please get the fuck out of here?"

He would have punched the steering wheel if

there was one. Socked the wall if it was within reach from where Bronson sat in the center of a plush leather loveseat. His head was as vacant as the cabin, and he was about to fail the last people — person — that meant anything to him.

He had a wad of energy, with nowhere to throw it. Bronson could conquer the world if it were in front of him. Instead he was stuck, without any clue how to—

Bronson had an idea. Or more, an impulse.

The critters wouldn't activate his augmentations or respond to his bodily needs. But they might be willing to have a conversation with a second party, one that Bronson didn't know how to talk to, and couldn't speak the language even if he did.

They were still birds, and the car a boat on a placid lake, its billowing sails an invitation for wind.

The colony was back, a mass of flapping wings sending gusts against the fabric, shoving that boat through the water.

The garage door opened, then the car roared to life.

Before Bronson knew what was happening, the back of his head slammed against the leather, and the car roared out of the garage and raced into the street.

He didn't tell the critters what to do, or what they should say to the car. But Bronson was sure that he didn't need to. For right now, it didn't matter. There was only one straightaway back into the Rundowns. And while Vaughn would want to hurry, he wouldn't have any reason to believe he was being pursued, so his speed would stay reasonable.

Bronson's wouldn't.

He was maybe twelve minutes behind, but the car was a rocket. Bronson was glad the steering wasn't on him; he didn't have the reflexes to stay alive. Probably never did. They were going two hundred kph, at least. The gap would close in no time.

The road was mostly empty, and by the time Bronson was pulling up behind the unmarked Cascade vehicle, his car managed to find another impossible burst of speed, launching forward and then decelerating in perfect time with the van.

What now?

Bronson didn't know, and had no control. He was along for the ride as well.

He felt scared. It was unexpected and sudden. A knot in his throat at the thought that his car might run theirs off the road, because that's what the critters believed he wanted. But that would best the good guys along with the bad.

Fortunately, the car was smarter than that. Or at least the critters helped it to be, nudging the van closer and closer to the side of the road. Speeding up and slowing it down, forcing its will onto the much larger vehicle.

Bronson would have imagined that the Cascade security van would hold dominion over a privately issued car, but apparently that wasn't the case. His critters were clearly in control.

The opposite held true for the van.

It braked hard, skittered, then fishtailed across the road before crashing into the guardrail.

The perfect accident.

No one should be dead, with everyone unseated.

The car stopped, and opened the door for Bronson.

Chapter Twenty-Eight

BRONSON MADE it to the van in a few long strides.

There was no door handle, but the side door whisked open by command, even though Bronson wasn't authorized.

Apparently, his critters were.

The door opened and he looked inside. The passengers had been strapped in to their seat on the vehicle's sofa, so no one looked anything more than battered and bruised. Everyone was still dazed, and though he seemed foggy, Polly was already moving.

Bronson went straight at him. Stunned but not out, Polly reached into his pocket.

His hand emerged with a gun, but he didn't have time to aim the weapon before Bronson slapped it out of his hand.

Polly's other hand appeared with something else, clutching the small black wand with its tiny glowing tip.

Bronson grabbed Polly by the wrist, plucked the

wand from his grasp, then bent three of his fingers back with a terrible *SNAP!* before jamming the end of the wand into his thick corded neck.

He didn't know the voltage setting, and didn't have time to check, so Bronson wasn't sure if Polly was dead. But he was the one who pulled the trigger on innocents, so it was what it was.

Polly dropped in an instant.

Not sure if he killed Polly, Bronson checked the settings, then lowered them, sending Lou and Arnold into the same neighborhood before they could even free themselves from the van.

Ava looked comatose. Totally zoned. Eyes open but empty. Isla's were closed, and there was blood on her face, likely coming from a wound on her head.

No, no, no.

He felt for a pulse. She was still alive. Didn't look to be losing blood.

Bronson turned to Vaughn next, who was climbing out of the front seat.

Bronson quickly approached him, adrenaline coursing through him like fire.

Vaughn raised his hands palm out, without even trying to draw his weapon, or protect himself in any way. "Let's talk about this, Bronson."

"Oh, don't you worry, Vaughn." He stowed the wand. "I have no intention of using this on you. And we will talk. But I need you wide awake for that conversation, so I'll deal with you in a few minutes. Try me and I will kill you. I'll make it more painful than you can imagine. I know how to do that, since the critters have been teaching me depths of agony that I could not have comprehended before. Do we understand each other? Now hand over your weapons."

Vaughn was apparently too frightened to answer with words, but he made a timid little nod and tossed his wand to the ground. Bronson picked it up, shoved it into his coat pocket.

Bronson pulled Isla out of the wreckage first, while the Cascade head of security watched him.

Their precious asset came next.

He couldn't tell how badly Isla was hurt, but she was definitely out. Ava appeared to have been put into some sort of standby mode from the shock of Vaughn's wand, leaving her body limp and lifeless.

It's always been lifeless, asshole.

He wasn't sure what to do. Could he load them both into the car right now and leave? Would Isla be able to restore Ava to her previous condition? And did that even matter? Wasn't getting *Isla* — the human — to safety the only thing that was truly important?

That's what Bronson wanted to keep telling himself, but looking down at the bodies, he couldn't believe it.

Why was he standing in the street like an idiot?

Why was he looking down at what was a damaged robot, at the very worst — the thing that was probably just temporarily powered down — and feeling emotions that were foreign enough to keep his critters confused?

Why was he flooded with power, yet frozen in place?

Bronson had been telling himself a lie.

It was so much easier to believe that this was all about Isla. She was the human, and Ava the robot. One mattered and the other didn't. He didn't want to care about either of them, but if he was going to care, then of course it would be for the one who was flesh and blood just like him.

Looking down at them both, Bronson knew that wasn't true.

He didn't know exactly when it happened, only that it had. That at some point, even though he'd been telling himself that the robot didn't matter, over and over and over, as if repetition could make a thing true, one was not independent of the other.

They came as a pair, and Bronson cared deeply for them both.

And as much as he had tried to stay away from that exact thought, there was another that was fighting hard, battling its way into the front of his mind. Making him see what he had been turning away from.

The two of them lying on the ground like they were at Howard's made Bronson remember some of the ugliest pieces from the one thing he desperately wanted to both remember and forget.

He was on his knees, shaking Isla and trying to wake her up, then turning to Ava and attempting the same, even though all the odds were against him. But the wasted effort was still better than crying, and that's what Bronson might be doing otherwise.

Because the images of Allison and Elizabeth were too much.

And he couldn't stop them from coming.

It was an avalanche. One image after another, bleeding into his brain.

Their bodies; the blood; the way he kept trying to bring them back to life, with words and gestures and pleas.

"Isla," he said again, squeezing her shoulder and shaking her body.

Bronson turned around and saw Vaughn watching.

Vaughn shook his head, looking at Bronson like he was pathetic, wasting his time.

"Come on, man. It's pointless. They're not worth it. You're not gonna bring your family back."

Bronson snapped.

He leapt to his feet, rushing toward Vaughn, growling, "What did you say?"

Vaughn shook his head, looking genuinely terrified of Bronson's swelling rage. "You're not going to bring your family back. Whatever it is you think you're doing doesn't mean shit. You can't fight them, man. Nobody can."

Bronson put the barrel of his Solacer to the man's temple.

"*You* don't mention my family."

"Come on, you're smarter than this. Livia has already warned me. This is bigger than Cascade. If I don't take you in, then they're going to call in some Infinity bots. Probably SKLTR units. They will hunt you, kill you, then bury the truth. You probably don't remember how it's done. And if not, then I both envy and pity you."

"I remember enough."

"Come on, boss. Don't throw what's left of your life away for some tin can."

"*She's* not a tin can."

Bronson pulled the trigger.

Chapter Twenty-Nine

ISLA KEPT HER EYES CLOSED, because she had no idea what might happen once she finally decided to open them.

She remembered the other car, trying to run them off the road. Vaughn cursing, and Polly asking if he should use the X99 to blow the car into its smallest component parts. Then Vaughn saying *Not yet* a second before regret must have crashed like a meteor, or like the car that nudged them into a treacherous spin.

The screaming of metal, then now.

Who was in that second car, and where had they taken her?

Was it Dodge? It didn't seem possible, but Isla had heard stories. Supposedly he'd done it before.

Had he rescued her and Ava? Then taken them somewhere safe?

Or was she somewhere in a lab at Cascade?

Could there be anywhere worse?

And where was Ava? Was she okay?

Had they already …

Isla couldn't finish the thought, but of course until she opened her eyes it had nowhere to go.

She slowly lifted her lids, hoping that she wasn't being watched, and feeling like she probably was.

A woman was staring back at her. She had a pleasant face and pale skin, her eyes kind but also sad. Isla didn't see any menace, but it wasn't Dodge, and that meant she was at Cascade or worse.

Isla started to panic. She didn't scream, but only because her throat was closing. She tried to cough, but couldn't even do that. She managed a gasp, followed by a hiccup and a microscopic yelp.

"It's okay," the stranger soothed. "You're safe."

"Don't touch me!" The woman was too close.

She raised her hands, passive, gently shaking her head. "I'm not here to harm you. I want to help."

Still suspicious, Isla said, "Where are Ava and Bronson?"

The woman smiled. "They're waiting for you. Bronson thought I might be able to help you, so he brought you to my home."

"And who are you? Why are you helping us?"

"A friend," she said, still trying to soothe her. Isla could imagine the agitation on her face. "I'm a doctor. Bronson recently helped me. He saved my son. Without him, my husband and I would have lost our child for sure. There's nothing I wouldn't do for Bronson Dodge."

Isla tried to sit up, but her body thought that was a

stupid idea. It hit her hard in the head, then shoved her back down to the bed. She grabbed the sides of her head, feeling bandages.

"What happened?" she cried out.

The doctor reached out and gently took her arm.

"You'll be okay," she said. "You were banged up in an accident. I stitched your head and you should be fine. I also gave you some blood and heavy-duty painkillers. You will need to rest for a bit until the wooziness goes away."

"We have to get out of here. You're in dan—"

"Bronson has informed me of the risks, and I have assured him that they are more than acceptable. You should be able to leave in a few hours, but I wouldn't recommend it. I have offered sanctuary, and Bronson has agreed to take it. Cascade has already been here looking for you, and I don't believe they will be back. But if they do, we can deal with it then."

Isla was worried about where she might find herself. Then she opened her eyes, and now she was scared.

She had a target before, and that was enough. She hadn't known if Howard would have the answer, but at least it was a destination. Having nothing changed everything. They were left in a purgatory where Cascade and the world were forever ready to end them.

How long would that last?

How long *could* it?

She must have seen something in Isla's eyes. The doctor's eyes darkened, despite trying to brighten her face with a smile. "I'll be right back. Bronson and Ava will both love to know you're awake."

The doctor stood from the stool by her bedside.

"Wait," Isla said.

"Yes?"

"What's your name?"

She smiled again, her best one so far. "My name is Rosario Drummond."

"I'm Isla."

"Yes, I know," she said, smiling wider. "It's good to meet you."

"Thank you for saving me."

"Of course."

The doctor closed the door behind her.

Isla didn't like that. She still wasn't a hundred percent sure she could trust her, and didn't see the need for a closed door, but there was little if anything to lose in believing that she was bringing Bronson and Ava back in, so long as Isla remained willing to strike at the first sight of something amiss.

It was hard not to feel at least a little suspicious before she saw them for herself.

Hard not to feel on edge, like spiders were occupying her insides, and laying eggs wherever they went.

Almost impossible to believe that someone wasn't playing a game, setting her up to tear her back down, because when something was demolished it was easier to mine treasures from the rubble.

But the door opened and Ava ran inside, with the doctor and Bronson a pair of strides behind her.

"Mommy, Mommy, Mommy!" She collapsed

against Isla, hugging her tight while holding her book.

Isla hugged her back. "I'm so glad you're okay! I was so worried about you."

"I know. I was worried about you too, Mommy."

Bronson stood in the doorway. Isla couldn't tell if he was wearing a scowl or a frown.

"I'm glad to see you're okay." But then he said nothing more.

Isla looked at Ava, suddenly wondering how she was awake, after Vaughn had shocked her.

"How did you wake up?"

Ava smiled and turned around, pointing to Bronson with a playfully accusatory finger. "He did it!"

Isla looked at Bronson. "What is she talking about?"

He shrugged, still not moving from his new home in the doctor's doorway. "I guess I woke her up."

"You can't just wake her up." She had to be careful with her words, just in case the doc didn't know that Ava was a robot. "How long did it take you?"

He shrugged again. "A few minutes, once I started trying."

"What did you do?"

"Nothing. Just shook her."

"He was talking to me," Ava said.

"What do you mean?" Isla asked.

"Our brains were talking."

"It appears she has some sort of telepathy." The doctor winked.

The critters. Of course. "I understand," she told Ava before turning to Bronson. "Thank you for saving us."

He nodded.

"How are you doing …" Isla continued. "With the critters and everything else?"

"I'm fine."

The man was a faucet of conversation.

Why did he need to be so brooding? They had lived through a lot, and for the moment they were safe. That seemed worthy of a smile at least.

Dr. Drummond had read Isla's mind a couple of times. She did it again, now with a knowing smile.

"I'll leave you to talk in private," she said, gently nudging by Dodge. On the other side of the doorway she turned back and added, "You have a truly remarkable daughter. It's been a pleasure getting to know her."

After she left, Isla said, "She doesn't know?"

"Why would she know?"

"You didn't tell her?"

"Why would I do that?"

Is he being difficult on purpose?

"I don't know how you think, Dodge. I wish I did. But yes, I could see you telling her because you thought she needed to know for whatever reason … to keep us safe."

"No, I didn't say anything."

Feeling suddenly cold and trying not to show it: "Was it hard for you, pretending to understand what Ava actually is?"

"That's the opposite of what I did."

Ava looked like she might cry.

"Come here," Isla said, patting the spot beside her. Then to Bronson, "Why do you have to do that? You knew that would hurt her feelings."

He muttered something under his breath. Isla couldn't catch what it was, but it made her want to bite him.

There was no reason for him to be acting like this. Or to keep ignoring the truth and refusing to be wrong.

"Will you read this to me?" Ava handed her the book.

Isla looked down at the cover. *The Berenstain Bears*, one of Ava's favorites.

"You read it," Isla said. "I want to hear you read while I talk to Mr. Bronson. Is that okay?"

"Yes, Mommy."

Ava started to read.

In a soft voice, floating just over the top of Ava's voice, Isla said, "What happened with Vaughn? How did you wake up from what he did to you? Where are we now? And please, will you tell me how you're doing without making me beg?"

Bronson gave her a look, like he hated every question. "I took care of Vaughn with a permanent solution. Then I went ahead and took care of everyone else. Disabled all the cameras and destroyed all the evidence. Some of it had already been sent back to Cascade, but my critters took care of that. Erased the archives."

Isla couldn't believe her ears. "How did you do

that?"

"I learned to talk to them," Bronson said, like he was reporting that he'd learned to tell when the sun was shining. "So no one knows what happened to the Cascade van. They can guess, but there isn't any proof. We're back in the Rundowns until we figure things out."

"Where in the Rundowns?"

"In the Fringe."

"How long do you think we have until Cascade finds us here?"

"Hours. Maybe days. I might be dead before they do."

Ava paused. "Should I stop reading?"

"No, sweetie," Isla said. "Please keep going."

Ava continued.

So did Isla, looking at Bronson. "Stop saying that."

"Saying what?"

"That you're going to be dead soon. If we can get Ava to where I've been trying to take her, then that will not only save her life, it will save yours too."

"I'll talk to Signal. Find some place for you to go. But I can't deliver a fairytale for either of us."

"You need to believe that it isn't a fairytale. And if you can't do that, and you want to just keep on insisting that you're going to die, without at least acknowledging the possibility that you might be wrong on both counts, well, maybe you shouldn't say anything at all."

Bronson agreed, and left the room without another word.

Chapter Thirty

BRONSON SHUT the door behind him.

That didn't go well at all. He wasn't trying to be an asshole, but it was hard for anyone to see that based on every single thing he did. He was clinging to a frayed edge, a centimeter from cracking. Emotions would soon spill to the ground from a hole in his belly.

Anxiety that they were trapped in the Boundary with nowhere to go.

The threat of failing his final gig.

Fear that death was coming.

Bronson always had a dangerous job, and possibly dying was always part of the package. But those odds had felt distant, especially when paired with his arrogance, and the reality that he rarely ever missed, both with his shots and his guesses.

Now it wasn't a possibility so much as a fact waiting to happen. Bronson was a dead man walking, and there wasn't a thing he could do to change that.

Isla wasn't helping, reminding him that he could do nothing to help, seeing as her only escape so far was in a wonderland that didn't exist.

Even if it did, Bronson had no way of getting them there. No way of even starting to wonder where he should look.

Although there was a terrible itch in his skull that kept begging to disagree.

Something that he knew before … that had maybe been taken from him.

He sank into the biggest chair in the waiting room, leaning back and crossing his feet at the ankles.

The room was empty. The doctor was upstairs with her family, leaving Bronson in peace with Isla and Ava downstairs, checking in on them often in the little time that they'd been there so far.

He closed his eyes, trying to get comfortable and ignore the roiling mass of anger and depression, the physical pain of the withdrawal, tearing at his body. His critters were just getting started but already screaming. Soon they'd be unable to stop on their own, and Bronson had no way to help them.

Neither did Drummond. That was one of the reasons Bronson thought of her so fast after the crash, when he needed a place to take Isla. Whatever the doctor had done to him before, Bronson would kill to have her do it again.

He *had* killed.

But the doctor looked at the floor when he asked her. Shook her head and said, "I'm sorry, Bronson.

But I used everything I had on you the last time. Spared nothing."

He was desperate for sleep, but afraid to take it.

What if he never woke up?

That wouldn't be bad; at least he would avoid the worst of the pain. But what would happen to Isla?

And Ava.

The thought made him feel guilty, and that was ridiculous.

His ears perked at the sound of someone entering the room. Slight, like a little tiptoeing girl.

He opened his eyes and saw he was right. Ava, entering the room, holding the book close to her body.

"Mommy went to sleep."

"Oh, is that right?"

The robot looked at his lap like it wanted to climb up and take a seat. Bronson shifted a bit to the right.

"Will you finish reading to me?"

"No thanks."

It frowned. "I won't be able to sleep without a story."

"I'm sure you'll manage."

"A bedtime story always makes the noises in my head go away."

"Me too. Why don't you tell me a story?"

"Okay!" Ava said, looking delighted. "What kind of story do you want me to tell? Should I read to you? Mommy likes it when I do that."

"Sure. Read to me."

And then go the fuck away.

The robot started to read, its inflections sweet, designed to mimic a human girl.

He hated the manipulative nature of its design, working on his emotions as it was.

Bronson wouldn't unplug it or anything; he could imagine how much that would upset Isla. And he didn't want Cascade to have it, for at least a dozen reasons, though none had anything to do with him thinking that the robot was in any way human at all.

It turned the page and looked up, waiting for his reaction.

He gave it without meaning to, and that made him want to cry.

Bronson turned away. Wished he had a blanket to pull over his head.

He started crying, stuck on a floor he must have already scraped, though new bottoms were still being discovered, mostly missing Allison and Elizabeth, but also Milo, the dog that he once thought might unearth him from despair like a freshly discovered bone.

"It's okay, Mr. Bronson. You don't have to cry." Its tiny hands felt so human against him. "I can stay with you like Mommy stays with me."

If the childbot was supposed to be so great at reading human emotions, then why the hell was it still there when Bronson obviously wanted it to go?

He said nothing.

The robot made itself comfortable, looked back down at its open book, and continued to read about Brother Bear, and how he found a tiny, muddy kitten while hunting bullfrogs.

The thing kept reading. Bronson wanted to tune it out, but that was impossible. So he had to hear all about how Brother Bear took that muddy little kitten home and introduced it to Mama, Papa, Sister, and the family dog.

Then together, they decided to keep it.

If this was supposed to be making him feel better, it wasn't.

This was making everything so much worse.

Bronson missed his family, and resented the robot for pickling him in those old, ugly emotions.

He was only half-listening to Ava. Until something started to happen.

The story had changed. In a way he couldn't immediately identify, but instantly noticed. His ears perked and his shoulders tensed. The difference, though still a mystery, was significant. Hanging like static in the air.

"Papa Bear was sad, because the muddy kitten reminded him of something that he lost, and that he could never have again. Mama Bear wanted to help him. And so did Sister Bear, but Papa Bear didn't believe that she could, or would even know how to."

Ava turned the page and continued to read, even though that wasn't quite what it appeared to be doing.

"The muddy kitten got hurt, and so Papa Bear—"

"Stop."

Ava looked up at Bronson.

He stared at it, dumbfounded, and held out his hand. "Let me see that book."

Then he looked down at the pages.

Sure enough, Ava wasn't reading. The robot was making up the story.

Creating something from nothing to make him feel better.

Could that possibly be true?

Creation required thought, and robots couldn't think.

These were the most sophisticated algorithms he had ever seen. A truly remarkable AI.

Or something else.

"Did you make up that story?"

It — *she* — smiled at Bronson and said, "Did you like it?"

"Were you trying to make me feel better?"

The robot nodded. "Sometimes when I feel really sad, Mommy will make up a story instead of reading one to me."

"So this is something you've seen her do? You didn't invent it yourself?"

Ava shook its head. "I only made up the story. Not the idea of making it up. Do you want me to keep going?"

"No thanks. I can guess at the end."

"It was going to be a surprise."

"Well, sorry I ruined it for us."

"No you're not," it said.

"Oh?"

"That was sarcasm. It's when you say something with irony to mock someone or show them contempt. I know you're not doing it to be mean, but you're still not being very nice. Saying sorry like that hurts the feelings that you don't think I have."

The robot looked like a little girl about to cry, and fuck it for that.

"You might be a miracle, but you sure as hell don't have any feelings. You have if/then, call and responses. That's it. You're ones and zeroes, no matter how real or magical they've managed to make it all look."

Bronson shook his head, having a hard time chewing through his side of the exchange.

"It isn't anything more than that. *You* aren't more than that. And there's nothing you can do or say to ever change it."

A tear slid down its cheek. Again, Bronson wondered where they came from, and hated his physiological response.

He wanted to wipe the tear away, to scoop the robot into his arms, soothe it like he would have comforted his own Elizabeth.

It reached up and stroked his hair.

"Mommy rubs my head like this when I'm sad. Is it helping?"

And that was it. Bronson could no longer stop the thoughts of Elizabeth rolling into his head. An army of memories marching in step, dragging the bodies of eroding emotions behind it. Feelings that scraped at the fringes and teased at the tips, but had yet to dig in and turn permanent.

His instinct to protect this child was strong. And the truth that *she* was no longer an *it* was now like a beating in his ear and a pulsing in his blood.

"Yes," he confessed. "It is helping. Can you keep doing that?"

Ava pressed her fingers into his head, massaging his skull.

"Will you keep reading to me?" Bronson asked.

So Ava did, until he fell asleep.

Chapter Thirty-One

BRONSON WAS BACK in the dream.

He was in the hallway, with the red door at the end of it.

He took a step toward it and it stayed put.

Hopeful, he took another step and then another.

The door remained where it was.

His heart swelled. He was finally going to see what was on the other side of the door.

But then a phone rang somewhere that felt far away, or underwater.

Ignore it. Just go to the door.

But then he was in his office.

"Hello?" Bronson finally answered the call from what felt like a battlefield. Three degaussed robots lay in a pile at his feet.

"Bronson ..." The voice was far away and full of borrowed sorrow, and he knew in that second that the distress was for him. But he realized who it was. His boss, Angel Gibney. "You need to get back."

"What's happening?"

"Just get back."

His rage was sudden and furious. There was a storm in his voice as he said, "No. Tell me what's happened."

A long sigh, someone wrestling with defying Bronson, or the direct order that had told the voice to bring him in.

"There's been an accident."

Bronson ran inventory on his men, wondering who might have taken a hit. Vaughn was too careful, but it could have been Polly. No loss there, the guy was a bit of a psychopath. *Accident* was a euphemism for "Some bot ended one of your men, and now it's your job to clean up the pieces and bury the truth."

"Man down?"

The truth never occurred to him, at least not on the surface; it was too busy worming its way deep into his subconscious where Bronson couldn't argue with the truth. Instead it burrowed, and by the time that voice was finished with what was probably the longest pause of its life, Bronson wanted to hang up, because he knew what was coming.

"No, Bronson. The accident wasn't at work. It was at your house. Your …"

Even here in the thick of it, deep in a dream that was no longer lying, Bronson wasn't sure if he ever heard Angel finish. Most of him thought that he simply just *knew.*

The accident wasn't at work. It was at your house. Your wife and daughter are dead.

The drive home was a blur, the only memory that mattered telling him that he was there in a blink, lucky he wasn't dead himself with all the chances he had the AI taking on his way over.

Not that it mattered. Bronson could have traveled there at the speed of light. Allison and Elizabeth were already dead.

He parked across the block. No other choice with all the emergency vehicles parked in front of his house. All Cascade, including the coroner. Bronson would be burying this one, too.

He knew what he was going to see before crossing the street or walking into his house.

But Bronson could only do one and was barred from the other. A big metal hand blocking the entrance to his home.

"I live here," he told the guardbot.

"Yes, Mr. Dodge," it said.

"I need to get inside."

"Access is not granted, Mr. Dodge."

"Where's Gibney?"

A moment of silence, then, "I have sent Ms. Gibney a message. She will be out shortly."

The bot's words came out stilted. Too inhuman at any time, but especially in a moment like this.

Bronson left the porch and waited for Gibney, wishing he had picked another place as the body bags were wheeled outside, one after another. He couldn't even run to them, his body was too empty, and the bags looked too shiny and plastic. What was lying inside them could never come back.

Gibney followed the bodies outside and came up to Bronson.

"I'm so sorry," she said.

"You've gotta tell me what happened."

But his heart was racing. Bronson had seen this so many times before. The fleet of Cascade trucks already told so much of the story.

Angel pointed to the Inquiry Van. Its official name. Bronson called it the Interrogation Van, just like all of his subordinates, and the boss before him. "We can talk about it in there."

"Now, Angel. Tell me what happened."

"I will," she said calmly. "In there."

Angel started walking. Bronson's only choice was to follow.

Bronson took a seat in the van, and felt one hiccup better. Angel let him pick his seat, so he chose the one without his back to the action. That didn't help what had happened to his family, but at least whatever this was, he wasn't in trouble.

"So are you going to tell me?" Bronson said, working to throttle his rage. They were safe inside the van, and surrounded by Cascade outside. If she didn't tell him what the hell was happening right goddamned now, he was going to rip her head from her fucking shoulders.

Angel's question told the story for her. "Where is Nanette?"

His heart wasn't even beating. The thing he knew but was terrified to face since the second he heard Angel calling him home.

Bronson's family had been slaughtered by their bot.

"It killed them?"

"Bronson, you know what we have to do now. I need you to stay with me. Time is everything right—"

"Tell me!" Bronson was back on his feet.

Still calm, Angel said, "I need you to sit. I have a few questions to ask you, and I need you to answer them. We can get through this fast, and then you can find Nanette."

"I'm not doing this, Angel."

"You don't have any choice."

Bronson stared at her, impotent. What else could he do?

He sat. "Hurry up."

Angel asked a series of questions about the nanny-bot. All stuff she already knew, or could bring up in a blink from Cascade records. But Bronson understood. He'd spent plenty of hours inside the Interrogation Van himself.

He never imagined himself on this side, though he'd empathized with those other families every time that he was forced to do the job that Angel was doing now. She didn't want to be here any more than he did. But they had a truth to figure out before it could be buried.

"We almost done?" Bronson asked, about two-thirds of the way through.

"I'm sure you know this by heart."

Fuck. His heart was in pieces.

"You have a cigarette?"

"You don't smoke." Angel blinked something into the registry, then looked back at Bronson and continued with her questions.

Angel finished and Bronson was naive enough to believe that was it.

He stood, but Angel raised her hand to stop him, and gestured down at his seat.

Then it hit him. Despite his position with Cascade, Bronson was no different than anyone else.

"No," he said, if the word even came out.

"Sit, Bronson."

He shook his head, took a step toward the door.

But the van was closed, and it would be impossible to open.

Bronson was stuck inside until he agreed to do what had to be done.

Still shaking his head, he said, "You can't do this to me."

Angel looked truly sorry. "You know I don't have a choice."

Bronson had never apologized. Or needed to. No one ever knew what was coming. The tiny orange pill was like a reset for the mind. They called it Quantum, the drug that was administered everywhere, and helped Cascade to reboot what they needed to. But this version was bespoke, clearing specific paths of recall from the brain.

Angel didn't insult him by telling him that the pill would make him feel better. The first one was all it took. After that, people *needed* them. They would practically grab the bottle after that first swallow, their brains already craving more of the mind sugar.

Angel opened her palm to display the tiny orange pill.

One swallow and he would begin to forget, more memories melting from his mind by the day.

But the pain would go with it.

"How will I do my job?" Bronson asked.

"You'll do it better than ever," Angel said. "You know that."

"What happens if I refuse?"

"You won't."

"Maybe I will." Bronson realized he was trembling.

"You're in shock. The Quantum will help."

"Like hell it will."

"In all the ways that matter right now, you know I'm right. Let me help you, Bronson."

"You mean help yourself. Help Cascade keep this a secret. Another robot murder that nobody knows about."

"If this wasn't your family, you would be doing your job."

"Maybe I don't want to do this job anymore."

"Cascade will make it worth your while. Take the pill, Bronson. You don't have a choice. But once you do, there's someone who wants to talk to you."

"I'm not taking the pill."

"You're being stubborn. You know what has to happen, and you know that I cannot allow you to leave this van until it does. So please, can we not delay the inevitable any longer?"

Again, she offered him the pill.

Bronson took it, not only because he had no choice, but because it was the only possible promise for a better tomorrow, where he wasn't running from memories that would surely destroy him. The only way to escape the haunting.

He closed his eyes and swallowed the pill. Imagined a better tomorrow.

Bronson breathed deeply for several minutes, feeling the drug beginning its work. Then he leaned forward with a sigh. "So who wants to talk to me?"

With her mission accomplished, Angel smiled. Friendly, and with some of the sorrow finally gone, she said, "I'll go get her."

And with that, Bronson somehow knew. Less than five minutes later he found out he was right, when Livia Faraday stepped into the van and took the seat across from him.

She was wearing sunglasses, though it was totally unnecessary. Her sharp features cut right into him. Bronson had only spoken to Livia a few times before, and never face to face. She was the most intimidating human he had ever met, probably because there was something almost robotic about her.

She didn't speak immediately, taking a moment to settle herself, and smile at Bronson with what appeared to be genuine sympathy, even though that was slightly out of character.

"I'm sorry about all of this."

"Not your fault."

Livia looked at him seriously. "Isn't it, though? Didn't Cascade create the thing that took what's most important away from you?"

Bronson nodded, not wanting to cry, and certainly not expecting any sort of apology from Cascade, if that's what this was. He would be forgetting soon, so maybe if was fine to admit fault when it was only temporary.

"I'd like to make it up to you."

He looked at Livia, wanting to know what she meant, and how it was possible that anyone could ever make it up to him, after his family had been murdered by a robot. The very thought was ludicrous.

But then she explained.

They could make him better at his job of hunting down rogue bots. The power it would give him, the ways in which it would make the job that he already loved easier and more rewarding to do. He would be more valuable to Cascade, and his lifespan could stretch to as long as he wanted. Livia intimated that she was much *much* older than she appeared. Some simple augmentations were all it would take.

It all sounded so much better, after his brain began to waver, and he was having a hard time remembering what had just happened.

Something about his family.

And maybe the nanny being late for work.

And then he was walking to the red door again.

The door started to move. But he refused to let it

get away again. He ran even faster, more than should be possible.

He finally reached it, desperately grabbed the handle, then threw himself into the room.

Time crawled as he looked at the mortician, then the bodies on the cold slabs. His wife and daughter, dead eyes staring into oblivion.

Bronson crashed onto his knees.

He opened his eyes with a start, and looked down to see Ava sleeping soundly.

Everything came back. Apparently the memories were never wiped from the drive entirely, just stuffed into the hardest folders to find in his mind.

The critters showed him where they were.

Bronson was overwhelmed by feelings he wasn't supposed to feel, and memories he was never supposed to remember again. How he helped to fabricate an accident that took his family's lives — an electrocution from faulty wiring. A freak accident.

As the memories flooded him, so to did the utter realization of just how much he'd failed his wife and daughter. And with it, the trembling fear that he might fail Isla and Ava as well.

Chapter Thirty-Two

Isla was eyeing Bronson, trying to figure out what exactly was different.

Something had changed, but she wasn't sure what. It was in the set of his shoulders and jaw. His disposition. Almost as though the very molecules that arranged him had somehow shuffled themselves around.

He was still frail, and maybe even more so than before. But in the oddest way, that fragility almost seemed like a strength. As though Bronson was in control of himself for the first time. Isla wondered if that was good, bad, or something even worse.

She was doing better, too. Other than feeling betrayed by Howard. It was still hard to believe he had done that to her. The situation was simple enough to understand. Howard wanted to save his son. His deepest longing since before they met. But still, that sort of betrayal could never have belonged to the man that Isla thought she knew.

The world wasn't what she had believed. Ava made it better, but most everything else made it so much worse.

It had been an hour or so since Bronson woke from a fitful dream. He'd been down for a while. Dr. Drummond gave Isla permission to leave her room once she woke, then led her out into the waiting area where Bronson and Ava were sleeping together. Him fitful and her like a lamb.

"What are we going to do now?" Isla finally had the nerve to ask him.

Bronson looked at her, confident but unknowing. He shook his head. "I don't know. But we need to get out of the Rundowns, and away from this city entirely. We need to disappear, and we can't do that here."

"What about Empyrean Flats?"

He shook his head, looking upset though still under control. Evenly he said, "There is no such thing, and making that part of our solution only complicates things. I have a few days at most. You want my help, let me get you out of the city. You want to look for the mystical park after that, by all means, go ahead. But remember, wherever I can get you to, you'll be starting at the bottom. Your money is frozen, and your skills are invisible if you are. You'll never work for a legitimate firm again."

Isla surprised herself. "There's more money in the black market anyway."

Again he raised his eyebrows.

"How can we get out of the city?"

"I sent another message to Signal already. I'm sure

he can arrange it. But we're ordering steak when we don't even have enough in our pockets to pay for the squash. Leaving the enclave's expensive. It doesn't even matter where you go after that — another district, one of the pastorals, up into the hills, or to the outlands — it's off the grid either way, and getting beyond the borders takes all the work. We can't go the way we went before. It's probably being monitored. We'll have to find somewhere else to cross."

"If all the work is getting to the border, then what does it matter what we want to do after we get across?"

"Nothing. That's the point."

"Then why not start out by trying to find someone who knows how to get into Empyrean Flats?" Isla argued. "Doesn't it make sense to coordinate with our endgame from the beginning?"

"Yes. If you don't want people to think you're crazy. Look, just do me a favor and forget that place. For now. Let me work on getting you new identities, and into another enclave. Stuff I can do. We don't have time for anything else."

"What do you care if people think I'm crazy? Are you trying to manage your professional reputation?"

"I just know how I would respond to someone looking to exit the city and get to *Empyrean Flats*. At best, you're crazy, at worst, you're a ripe target to exploit for money."

"You're not Signal. From what you said about him, I'm guessing he *does* believe in it."

Isla could see that she was right about that. His

face changed.

"News." A wall monitor filled with headlines and tiny videos played beside them. Bronson waved his finger up and down, scrolling through page after page, shaking his head. "There's nothing about Vaughn or that crash."

"Did you expect there to be?"

"No. I guess not. I suppose I was hoping."

"That what? We—"

"Wait." His face changed again. "What if we *got* that crash on the news? We have footage. Signal could anonymously upload it in several places. It would be everywhere before Cascade could take it down."

Isla didn't respond.

"Why are you looking at me like that?" he asked.

"It's been a long year, and you don't remember much of it."

"They had me take these orange pills to forget. I remember now, it's what we did to cover up when bots went bad. But I still feel like there's something else they're doing to make us forget things. So much of it is fuzzy. Fill me in."

"What are you trying to accomplish by getting news of the crash out there?"

"It's a surprise attack against Cascade. They won't see it coming. And—"

"You're wrong. They *will* see it coming. They are prepared for every scenario. You upload those videos and they'll live for a few seconds. The chain will be followed and every link destroyed. Memories will be manually reset if needed, but the secrets will all stay buried, and you and Signal will have each tipped your hand."

"How do you know all of this?" He didn't sound suspicious so much as curious.

"I don't *know* any of it. I'm slowly piecing it together, a little more all the time. Ava has taught me a lot."

Paying attention to something that was constantly trying to learn for itself would do that. Isla wondered what she was learning right now, while talking with the Drummonds in their apartment upstairs.

"And you think we should base our strategies on information that you're only guessing about?"

"What other choice do we have? At least these are educated guesses. We get out of the enclave. We're not looking for revenge." She shook her head, working it out as she talked. "There's something big going on here. I mean, even more than I realized. I keep trying to figure it out and nothing makes sense. Because I can't figure out the *why* of it all. It can't be money."

"Isn't it *always* about the money?"

"Not with Cascade. And it's not just that they're the richest company in the world. Look at what they do with the money. They pay for so much of the world's infrastructure, from pastorals to bullet trains. They are the most charitable organization the world has ever seen, and there isn't a close second. They simply aren't a revenue-driven company. There is a *reason* for everything they do. If we can unearth that reason, then we'll be onto everything else."

"And what do you think that reason is?"

"I have no idea. But if you're gaining more control over your memories, then you might. It's easy enough to understand why Cascade would want to keep robot violence under wraps, but maybe you can ask the critters to help you remember why they would want to throttle technology like they are."

Bronson's face became pinched with confusion. "I don't know."

"Think harder."

"I don't know how to do that."

"If Empyrean Flats exists, and let's say for the benefit of this exercise that it does, why would robots have different laws there than we do here, and why wouldn't Cascade have any control?"

"Maybe that's not the right question," Bronson said. "Maybe we should be asking if Empyrean Flats is a good place, or a bad one?"

"Why does it need to be one or the other?"

"Because if it exists, then that means we have two parties in this place. *Us* and *Them*. We have no idea if they know about us or not, but we sure as hell have been kept in the dark about them. So I have to wonder why. Is it because we're the bad guys and we're not supposed to know about the good guys out there in the forest, or are we the good guys, and the powers that be are doing their level best by keeping us free of the robotic nightmare waiting to end us?"

"Grim," Isla said.

"You asked."

"I don't think it's that black or white. Take Cascade — the company is clearly doing some very wrong things, and yet you can't ever question the amount of good they have done, and continue to do."

"Maybe the good stuff is there to cover up the bad."

"Isn't Empyrean run by a church? So maybe it's the other way around," she said.

He looked at Isla like she was crazy. "And how is that supposed to work? Team People claims to be on the side of God, and I don't know If I'd call them the *good* guys."

"I don't know exactly, but I can tell you that I've worshipped Cascade ever since I was a little girl. For years they never disappointed me once. Not until all of this."

"By all of this, do you mean the fucking with our memories, so that we forget all the shit they've done?" Bronson shook his head. "The moment you start messing with my head, that's the moment I stop trusting your altruism."

"Fair enough," Isla said, feeling defeated. "So now what?"

"I think we're where we left it. I need to find a way to get you and Ava out of the enclave. And for that, I need to wait for a message from Signal."

Isla looked at him with her most pleading eyes. "Is there any way I can get you to believe me about Empyrean Flats? At least long enough to consider it as a viable option?"

He looked away. "Sorry. But it's my job to get you and Ava to safety. Empyrean Flats is not part of the plan."

. . .

EMPYREAN.

That word was worse than the critters.

Bronson wanted to help them, and was willing to empty his insides and offer his final few days to the cause. Why did Isla have to make everything more difficult, believing in a robot child's fairytale?

Maybe he would have had an easier time buying it, and acting on the information, if the source hadn't been Ava herself. Isla didn't want to admit, but after Bronson wouldn't stop asking, she finally confessed that Ava had told her about Empyrean Flats.

"How do you know it wasn't one of the stories she likes to make up? She said you taught her that. Read one to me about a muddy kitten."

Isla smiled. "She told me that this story was real."

"And how did she know that?"

"Because she heard it."

"How?" Bronson wanted to know.

But Isla had only shrugged. "She just did. Ava said she could hear the other robots talking about it."

Bronson pressed her for a better answer, because that one didn't add up. With the exception of the sequence where Vaughn had tapped into the bot, Ava hadn't been on any sort of network, other than the local Cascade network. They controlled who she "spoke" to. And yet when Bronson asked Isla whether Ava had been talking to robots in the city, or robots in Empyrean Flats, she said, *Both.*

And that settled it. This wasn't exactly imagination, but it was the robot equivalent for sure.

He had to get away from her. She wasn't bothering him. Bronson was getting under his own skin. Pissed at himself. At war because maybe she was right. But it was all-or-nothing time. If he so much as flinched from the finish line he could lose it all. And that meant losing them.

Finally, a message from Signal.

He stared at it, meditating on his best response.

Isla was right. Signal believed in so many of the things that Bronson did not. And maybe that was an asset.

But something else Bronson had always found in the Rundowns: the gullible made the best targets, and Darwin's Law always applied. If he showed his weakness by believing this now, he could be sending Isla to her death, and Ava into permanent shutdown at the hands of her creators.

But if he refused to acknowledge the possibility, then maybe he was consigning them to something worse.

Bronson's hands were sweaty, just like his brow.

He read the message again, and then again after that.

Signal needed to know Bronson's endgame. This was a two-person job. One to usher them across the border, then another to get them to wherever they needed to go. He was waiting for Bronson to tell him where that would be, so he could acquire the proper coyote.

He drew a deep breath, then blinked out his answer.

Empyrean Flats?

So, you do believe? Signal typed. Bronson could almost hear the man's snickering.

After a short wait, he returned with a price tag that Isla might not have been able to afford, even if her funds weren't frozen.

That can't be right.

It's Empyrean Flats, man. What do you expect?

You know I can't afford that.

You don't have to. It's her scratch.

She doesn't have any money. Her funds are all frozen. I already told you that.

I don't know what to tell you, Bronson. You're asking for the two riskiest things I can help you with. Getting you out of the city, again, and then into Empyrean Flats.

Empyrean Flats isn't real.

Then why are you asking?

Catch-22. It was probably easier to charge a premium for something that didn't exist.

Everything about this felt wrong.

Bronson typed, *Do you have anyone else? I'll go with them as long as I can. So maybe not your best guy.*

That isn't *my best guy, Bronson.*

Bronson considered the contraband he had for trade, stored in a garage on the other side of the Rundowns. A garage that nobody knew about, with things too hot to just sell to anyone, but Signal wasn't just anyone, nor was the coyote he was dealing with.

And it sure as hell didn't get much rainier

than now.

How about a Cascade Spyder? Looks five years old. Brick the AI and add your own OS, that thing's worth a fortune.

Bronson waited, clenching his fists while hoping that Signal would bite, or that his person would.

Deal.

Then Signal messaged the details, and Bronson went to tell Isla.

"How do you know that it isn't a trap?" she asked when he finished.

He didn't, but what other choice did they have?

"You can't let what Howard did to you color the way you see everything."

Her face softened. "You're right, I know that. But I don't like that last part."

"About him being willing to do it for the car?"

She nodded.

"Signal and I go way back. He knows this is goodbye."

But Isla wanted to argue. "Your deal isn't with Signal, it's with that guy who's supposed to take us to Empyrean Flats. It isn't goodbye for him, and I doubt the two of you go way back. So what's the reason for *his* charity?"

"I don't know. That's between him and Signal. Maybe he had to be talked into it. The Spyder is probably worth more than you realize, and a coyote knows his routes. Not to mention his margins. People are desperate when they're trying to disappear, so why not ask for ten times more than you need, or the maximum you could possibly get?"

His words were working on Isla more than they were working on him.

Bronson didn't trust this situation nearly as much as he wanted to. But he would arm up and go alone.

"I don't know of another way out. We need a way out of the enclave, and you asked for someone who can get you to Empyrean Flats. I did my best."

"You did," she said. "Thank you."

Silence followed, until Bronson explained that he would be making the trade, getting the all-clear, and calling the doctor to drive her and Ava out to meet him, since grabbing a car would send out a flare. If Signal was going to pull something, it would be on this side of the border, and Bronson would probably be able to tell the second he saw him.

It was a lot to take on faith, but scattershot hope was all he had.

Bronson couldn't tell Isla why he had to go alone without freaking her out, so he said that he was just double-triple making sure. Her eyes refused to buy it, even though her lips told the lie that she did.

He said goodbye, slipping out quietly, not wanting to bid farewell to anyone else when it felt like it might be final. Bronson was still weak, his body anemic, the critters like static, most of his pain abated but waiting and ready to attack.

Bronson drove toward their destination. It wasn't far. So all of this would be over soon.

For better or worse, he would be on his way to somewhere.

But he was getting scared. It had been a while

since he'd accessed his Aversion chip, or any of the other add-ons that Cascade had gifted him with, before sending him a recurring bill of indentured servitude that he hadn't been willing to pay, which was why his mind and body were taxing him now.

The fear was tickling his adrenaline.

And that was teasing his critters awake.

He would get stronger before he got weaker, but that would trigger his final descent.

Maybe he would rise after that, and find the love that he lost. But probably not. His life would become memories and ashes, and likely not even that.

This was a kamikaze mission. Yet, if he succeeded in securing passage for Isla and Ava, then he would die with honor in his mind, redeeming himself from his past inability to protect his family. To see around the curves before his car came crashing into a wall.

He was a kilometer away, his heart pounding hard and the critters waking to claim their control.

They mostly had it by the time Bronson stopped, then started the rest of his suicide mission, asking the onboard AI to give him a readout of the surroundings.

All clear.

He got out and waited, not wanting to be boxed inside.

Bronson looked around and wondered when someone might join him. Would it be Signal or someone else? He didn't know and hadn't bothered to ask — there was zero chance that Signal would tell him. Not with so much security to worry about. Everything was always in code anyway. Well, not everything.

Not this time. Bronson had to use the words *Empyrean Flats* because that was something they had never messaged before.

If someone showed up on Signal's behalf, that was good. It would be a coyote taking him to the other side. Bronson would apologize, then let him, or her, or it, know that they'd either be making a short detour, or suffering an inconvenient wait until the rest of their party arrived.

But if Signal showed up, making razzle dazzle with his words, then Bronson would know to be on guard.

Whichever way it happened, Bronson hoped it happened soon.

His entire body was buzzing.

Differently than it ever had before.

Bronson could talk to the critters when they were willing to listen, now that he knew how.

But he didn't expect for them to ask him anything.

And yet they did. A simple question fat with gravity.

They wanted to know if Bronson would be willing to fully surrender over to them. If he agreed not to fight, then he would experience a morphine in his mind that he could not imagine. The opposite of the agony they promised otherwise. The critters appreciated their host as much as they could. Understood that without his body they had nothing, and that they were probably on their way out, too.

But the critters were efficient, with many ways to extend Bronson's body, maybe for another month.

He would be an empty shell, but there would be no pain.

A bullet in his brain would be faster, but the critters promised the one thing that a bullet could not.

They swore to help keep him in control and at his strongest, until Isla and Ava were safe.

"So be it," Bronson said, and started the clock ticking down to his death.

He wasn't sure what to expect, but the reality was exquisite.

Sweet creamy butter spread across the bread of his mind, soaking into every nook and cranny of his brain.

His blood felt thicker. Same for his bones and muscle.

It was almost narcotic, the way the critters were feasting on him, soaking into his cells, taking him over and claiming his body as their own.

He expected it to feel wrong. Instead, it felt to Bronson like the way things should have been from the start. He was flooded with gratitude, knowing that things were right as they should be, and that he would be strong enough to finish the job he promised to do before leaving this earth.

He felt no sense of mourning or loss, marching into his death. Only tranquility. A Shangri-La of liberation in life's final throes. There were no more decisions to make. The critters would help him. Take them to wherever they needed to go. Promise that no matter what, they would not allow harm to befall Ava or Isla.

And to the critters, that order mattered.

Chapter Thirty-Three

ISLA TAPPED her foot on the bathroom floor, pretending she still wasn't finished.

But she couldn't stay in here forever. It had felt like too long already.

If she left the bathroom now, then she would almost for sure blurt out everything she was thinking, and end up asking the doctor for the thing that would make her sound hysterical.

Yet Isla might not have any choice. Unless she was willing to let Bronson die.

Or admit that she was being paranoid.

She wished he hadn't insisted on going alone. More than that, Isla hated it. But Bronson refused to listen, and she could see in his eyes and everything else that nothing she could ever say had any chance of changing it.

Isla let him go, thinking that she could follow him if she needed to.

But now she was doubting herself as much as she was suspicious of Signal.

It had to be a trap, and Bronson's behavior wasn't exactly soothing as he left, armed to his very gritted teeth.

Even if it wasn't a trap, what if he got caught along the way?

And so close to death, what if he passed and she had no way of knowing?

What will I tell Ava?

It was a sobering thought, and Isla felt a chill. Ava had dealt with death before, first with a more academic exposure, but it got plenty intimate with what happened to Milo.

But this would be different. Isla imagined her sobbing, blubbering the words *Mr. Bronson!* over and over. The thought threw a second, harder chill through her body.

Isla knew what she had to do. She stood from the toilet and opened the bathroom door.

If Isla didn't listen to her instincts right now, she would regret it for the rest of her life. She was worried about Bronson. Not just as the soldier she hired to help her, but as the grumpy man who had become her friend; begrudgingly, but she felt his affection nonetheless. The man who was still risking what was left of his life and asked for nothing in return. The most duty-bound man she had ever met.

She opened the door and looked into the living room, where Ava was playing with Peter, but the joy at seeing Ava do such a normal thing could barely penetrate her anxiety.

"Why do you look like that, Mommy?" Ava asked.

Isla could only guess what she must look like, but it wasn't all that hard. She felt tired and haggard, maybe worried to pieces. All three together might look like death on her face.

"I'm worried about Bronson," she said to Ava, and anyone else who might listen.

All eyes were on her, but only Rosario spoke. "What are you worried about?"

"A lot of things." She took a breath, working to not sound hysterical. "Mostly his overall condition … and that he's walking into a trap."

"I understand. And you *should* worry. Bronson is in terrible shape. I would never have suggested he go, but he took me aside and told me his intentions. Asked me straight out not to voice my objections until after he left, and only then if I felt like I had to. I told him that there was no need, and that I understood. For the record, I wouldn't have if you hadn't asked."

Rosario nodded at Isla, obviously glad that she had.

"He is weak and none of us have any Tonic. I'm worried that things are worse than he's willing to admit. He's had a lot of adrenaline and Tonic coursing through his body since then. That all accelerates the process. It might be down to a couple of days or …"

The doctor stopped.

"What?" Isla pressed.

"What?" Ava repeated in a whisper, her little fingers hovering over her lips.

"Maybe even hours," she finished.

Martin gasped.

"I suspect he knows it. And that it might be a trap. So he went on alone to make sure. With hours left, he's got nothing to lose by clearing the way. Sounds like the Bronson we all know, doesn't it?"

Isla nodded. "Do you have a car I can borrow? Or any weapons?"

"Of course. The last few days have taught me to be very well-stocked. Just tell me what you need."

Isla didn't know, so Rosario led her out of the living room and then loaded her up with an absorption vest, which she felt especially thankful for, along with two sidearms, one that shot high-voltage bolts of electricity and another that used old-fashioned bullets. Whatever her enemy might be carrying, Isla was covered.

Rosario also lent them her car, with a warning to be careful. There was no way to turn off the tracking, and she wasn't sure if his movements were being monitored.

"I don't know how to thank you," Isla told her.

"You already are. And I'm happy to do what I can to help you." She paused, seemed to consider something, then finished. "She is the most amazing thing I've ever seen. You cannot let them destroy her."

"You know?" Isla asked, looking at the doctor.

"I understand that there are many things I don't know, or can't comprehend." She smiled kindly. "But

I'm doing my best. Yes, I can see what she is, but please don't think of that as a failing on your part. Ava is perfectly human."

"How did you know?"

"Because she told me."

She shouldn't have done that. "What did she say?"

"That you were her mommy, but that you made her with Cascade instead of a daddy, and that now one of her parents was trying to kill her. But please, don't be upset with her for telling me. My son would have done the same thing. She's trying to process what's happening and … *it's okay, Isla.* Please … you don't have to cry."

She put her hands on Isla's.

"I'm not upset. I'm proud."

Then they cried together. Not long or deep, but with both of them fully present, looking into one another's eyes and sharing some unknowable truth.

"May I say goodbye to your family?"

"Of course," she said without the codicil, *It might be the only chance you get.*

"Can I leave her with you? Will you make sure that she's safe if I don't come back?"

"I promise with my life to do all that I can."

Believing her made it easier to say goodbye. Isla made it through the three that required relatively little effort. Rosario, Peter, then Martin, before reaching Ava with a quivering voice and a catch in her throat.

But Ava spoke instead.

"No." She shook her head. "You can't say goodbye to me because I'm going with you."

"You can't. I need to keep you safe."

"No, Mommy. *I* need to keep *you* safe." She looked at Isla as though waiting for her to argue, but Isla could only stare back at her, dumbstruck. "I'm a robot, remember?"

Only Martin looked surprised, but he was so shocked that Isla imagined his eyes rolling right out of their sockets.

She shook her head. "No, Ava. I can't let you go with me."

Isla was calm, but Ava was not.

"No Mommy! No Mommy! No Mommy!" A whisper of fury followed by, "No Mommy! No Mommy! No Mommy!" Then finally, a bellow of undiluted rage that rattled the apartment around them. "NO MOMMY! NO MOMMY! NO MOMMY!"

"It's okay, Ava!" Isla went to soothe her, pulling the girl into a hug and pressing both palms against her head.

Everyone stared at the two of them, transfixed, surely wondering what was going to happen next in this standoff between a daughter robot and the mommy designer who made her.

Ava settled against Isla, quickly calming like a toddler in need of her mother's attention.

"It's okay," she repeated, now petting the back of Ava's head.

Isla didn't know what to do. This had taken too long already. Five minutes for fretting, another five to get armed, and now this. Bronson was in danger *now*.

"Please, Ava. I need you to listen to me. Can you

do that?"

She nodded as Isla looked into her eyes, but then Ava spoke before Isla could.

"No, Mommy." Same words, different tone. "I need you to listen to me. Can you do that?"

Isla's heart had stopped beating. Slowly, she nodded.

This was so jarring for Isla. She was used to thinking of Ava as a little girl, which was already a Herculean leap of perception for most of the world. But now her synthetic daughter was asking Isla to see her as something else.

"I'm not just a little girl. I'm also a robot, and Cascade wants me for a reason." Ava pointed toward the farthest wall, about thirty feet away. "Do you see the mosquito over there?"

Isla looked, squinted, shook her head.

"I do, and if I had a rock I could hit it. I'm strong, fast, and smart. You saw what I did to that bear. You think that Mr. Bronson is walking into a trap, and I agree. But I can help you. Our odds of success will increase if you—"

"Okay, Ava," Isla sighed, "you can come."

The family was watching them in awe, and now they looked like they wanted to clap.

They got into the Drummonds' borrowed car and Ava told the car where to go.

"What are we going to do when we get there?" she asked.

And Isla said, "I think you should probably tell me."

Chapter Thirty-Four

"Bronson."

It was hard to see in the dark, but Signal sounded happy to see him as Bronson stepped out of the all-black Spyder, its shiny coat reflecting the lights. Signal was a hundred feet away, give or take a few, and standing in a tangle of shadows. "Sorry I'm late."

"It's okay," Signal said. "I just got here myself."

Bronson didn't believe that. His old augments were back online, including the one that read the tells that tipped off a lie. Heartbeat and voice were the big ones, and twitches in his face, visible to the critters even in the dark.

But it was possible that they were only making him paranoid.

Bronson wasn't just on high alert, twitchy and hyperactive from the critters, his brain was screaming. He questioned everything and truly believed in nothing. Signal was his old friend, but they had been adversaries once. And right now he felt like the biggest threat in the world. If Bronson wasn't careful — if he lowered his guard too far or refused to see the danger before him — then he would be leaving Isla and Ava in significant danger.

"What's next?" Bronson asked.

"You pay me, then I give you the contact information for someone who can get you to Empyrean Flats."

"That sounds easy."

"That's because it is. Through the tunnels and out of the city. More like old sewers than tunnels, though."

"*Too* easy."

"That's because you're paranoid."

Another pause. Maybe he was right.

Everything was coming online. The Aversion chip first. The critters were preparing for a fight. Maybe that's what all of this paranoia was about. They wanted to brawl, were craving kills and longing for all the adrenaline that would course through his body once Bronson started fighting for his life.

Bruised fruit made the sweetest juice.

"Maybe," Bronson said. "But I can't just hand you the access code for the car. I need the contact info first."

"You *want* the contact info. You don't *need* it. This is a simple transaction, and we haven't been at odds in a while. You have every reason to trust me."

"I'll say the same. So tell me, Signal, why not just trust me?"

"Because you're the wanted man with everything to lose. Maybe you've promised the car to someone else. I have everything to lose here. The contact information you're asking for is one of the most valuable assets I have. I'm in business for myself. You've always understood that."

"Convince me that Empyrean Flats exists. That I'm not sending them into some other nightmare."

Signal shook his head. "I can't convince you that it exists. That's like believing in God. No one can *tell you* your faith. You either believe or you don't, but I'm a true believer."

"Convert me."

"Are you setting me up, Bronson? Stalling for time?"

"I'm looking for religion."

Signal sighed, then said, "I never even heard the words Empyrean Flats until about a year ago. But since then it's been buzzing among the oldest bots in the Rundowns. I've only come across a handful of humans who have even heard about it, mostly collectors and hobbyists. The custom set. Only two of them believe it, and it seems like it's fifty-fifty among the bots I've talked to. I'm all the way, though, brother."

"Why?"

"It makes sense. Or no ..." Signal shook his head. "It doesn't *make sense* — a whole community of free robots living side-by-side with humans in the heart of the city? Under the noses of people blinded by science? But it gives possible context to some other crazy things. There's always been more to the story. You know that."

"So, *exactly* like religion."

"Maybe." Signal shrugged. "And maybe it's what I need to believe."

"So, no proof."

"Nothing that you wouldn't call a 'religious artifact' or worse. I've heard stories. More all the time, now that robots are talking. And I've seen images, human hybrids of every shape and size, walking the streets in that place. Of course, they could be fake. And maybe they *are*, but they're the best I've seen, and my sources are reliable. Like I said, maybe it's what I want to believe. Either way, I do."

Bronson still didn't, but it was getting harder to doubt Signal. The critters and his gut were in agreement. Bronson was looking at a man of faith. And besides, Bronson had little to lose and no other choice. This wasn't his call to make. Isla and Ava believed. He promised to help them get safe passage, and wanted to make sure that Signal wasn't laying a trap. But if Signal believed in a fantasyland too, then at least they were all on the same page.

And if Bronson was wrong, then that would be just wonderful for everyone.

"So can I have the access code?" Signal asked, probably expecting him to hand over a printed or digital code like most people carried with them.

Bronson shook his head. "It doesn't work that way. I don't have a code or a fob. Just what's up here."

He tapped his temples. Signal looked confused.

"You've always been right about the throttling." Bronson kept talking, still tapping his temples. "I have tech up here that's decades ahead of the market. Little critters up here are talking to the car."

Signal grinned like a buddy that just found out his boring sober friend was actually a party animal all this time. "I knew *something* was going on with you. Your frequency always read too high, but I figured it was an illegal add-on." He looked at the Spyder, then back at Bronson. "So how does this work? How do I get the car?"

The Spyder's door whispered open.

Bronson said, "I just ceded control. Go imprint yourself. Once you do, you can then pass on control to your man, have the car send a digital code to your phone, or whatever."

"Didn't the last owner imprint themselves before this wound up with you? How do I know you won't just take it right back?"

"Well, that owner is in jail and won't be coming for this car anytime soon. As for me taking it, you don't know. As long as I'm alive I can take any AI-operated vehicle I want. So I don't need that one."

"Well then, we might as well get this over with."

Bronson said, "What do I need? A data card? Are you sending me the info?"

Signal shook his head. "Sorry, Bronson."

He straightened. "Sorry for *what?*"

"There's no way my contact can get you to Empyrean Flats for a car. That's impossible. But this Spyder has AI and parts that can feed me for years. You told me that you were a few days from death, so I don't see any harm in just taking the car. We no longer have a professional relationship to maintain."

"What about Isla and Ava?"

"You were right to come here alone. I'm glad that you did that. I still wasn't sure what was worse, taking care of them or leaving loose ends. Either one would have left me sick to my stomach, though not enough to sacrifice the score."

"You have no idea what you're doing."

"I'm good at my job because I always know *exactly* what I'm doing."

"No," Bronson said. "I mean, you have no idea what's about to happen. You don't realize that I'm about to tear you into tiny little pieces."

"I'm not scared of you, Bronson." Signal was still thirty meters away and smirking. "I'm sorry that you wanted to make it violent. I was hoping for *fast*."

Then, on a cue from Signal, men emerged from the shadows.

Chapter Thirty-Five

Bronson was prepared.

Whether it had been from his own suspicions, or from the critters' hunger for battle, his enhancements had been coming online for a while.

The men crept closer.

"I am sorry to do this, Bronson. You should have seen it coming. The old you would have."

"Who says I didn't?"

"You, being here right now."

"What makes you think I can't kill every one of your men before taking it nice and slow with you?"

"Because you're old. At death's door. And even so, I'm not careless. I know what you've managed in the past. I might have even over-prepared, just in case."

Signal gestured to the men, six in total, all of them armed, and wearing vests that had scrambled their signals and cloaked their approach.

Every one of them would die at Bronson's hand. And as promised, he would save Signal for last.

The full layout of his surroundings sprawled across his vision for the first time in weeks. Relevant data lined a column in the upper right corner. He could blink to change the order, streaming speed, or type of information. Targets displayed their vulnerabilities in green and their danger spots in red. Aversion was on. So were Locus4, Persistence7, Impulse9, and even SepukoZero, a suicidal explosion, if the tussle got hairy enough. Not hard to imagine, with him this close to goodbye.

Let Signal think he was on death's door.

It was one of the last things he would ever think at all.

"There must be some way that we can work this out," Bronson said, killing time as he assessed his seven attackers for every possible vulnerability, needing mere seconds to do so. "For Isla and her daughter. They're innocent. You don't have to take them to Empyrean Flats. They can go somewhere else."

Except it's too late for that.

"It's too late for that," Signal said.

Bronson almost wanted to laugh.

The closest man was near enough to charge, so he did.

It wasn't even close. Bronson ducked — maybe faster than he ever had, the critters were a hell of an accelerant — then popped back up with a pair of brass knuckles slamming into the attacker's jaw.

His punch had the power of a railgun. The crunch of broken teeth could be heard above the leaves breaking underfoot. The man cracked his head on the ground when he landed. Bronson stomped his boot heel into the man's forehead, surely hard enough to kill him, but the helmet and mask might have offered some protection, so he stomped another few times to be sure.

Then Bronson looked up at the other five with a smile, inviting them all to the party.

The men descended, attacking as one and working to surround him. He considered using his Solacer, but the critters wanted action, were feeding off of it, spiking his adrenaline with each movement.

In seconds Signal was gone and the half-dozen assailants were now around Bronson like the hands on a clock. Some of them had blades, others carried wands, any of which would end him if he let them.

But hell if he was letting them get close enough.

Bronson laughed to throw them off-guard. Sure enough, the closest killer looked uncertain. Not that he could see it with his eyes or expression, but hesitance was there in his body, the way he was hedging.

He would have to come next.

Bronson lunged forward, grabbed the man by his throat, and kept on running, hefting the man as he gained speed, nearing twenty kilometers an hour by the time he crashed into a tree.

Or his cargo did.

The helmet cracked, probably turning the man's brain into mulch. Just to be certain he was down, Bronson grabbed a fistful of hair and beat on the bark with the back of the asshole's skull several more times.

His adrenaline was like a live wire. He'd never felt so alive.

He dropped the body and turned back around, hungry for more.

Four attackers were back to approaching, but now they were all fully on-guard. No longer fighting an old man they would easily dispatch. They were battling a cold-blooded killer, with a very real chance of losing their lives.

Surely not what they were promised by Signal.

Bronson gave them a chance to surrender. "You can leave right now and I won't kill you."

But they all made the mistake of continuing their advance, slow and cautious as it was.

"Shock him!" Signal shouted from the shadows.

One of them answered, "You said you wanted him alive."

"That was before I knew he could kill all of you."

Two of the four readied their wands, adjusting the power for killing.

The two blade-wielders were advancing.

The first man's blade nicked Bronson's left cheek.

It would have plowed into his face if the critters hadn't shoved him out of the way. Thanks to Persistence7, he didn't even feel it. The pain wouldn't come until later, and at this point maybe never again.

Another assailant lunged.

Bronson dived to the ground, avoiding a lethal blow, just barely.

He leapt back to his feet and plowed toward the nearest man with a blade. Grabbed his wrist and snapped his arm at the elbow, dropping the blade into his waiting palm, then throwing it straight into the charging man's chest.

His jacket should've stopped the blade from doing too much damage, but Bronson's critters managed to throw it hard enough to puncture the vest in an instant, stabbing the man in the heart.

Bronson looked up at the man with the broken arm.

He looked back, eyes wide and terrified. Started to say something, but never had a chance to finish.

Bronson whipped out his Solacer and fired into the man's helmet. It was no match for his gun.

He turned to the remaining two. Blue electric arcs sizzled from the tips of their wands as they circled him.

Bronson could shoot one of them, but he might not get a second shot before the other moved in.

While the critters had kept him alive thus far, they couldn't dodge death forever. He was already feeling his body starting to slow. How long before he crashed for the last time?

He fired at one of the men, taking him out in an instant.

But before he could turn the gun on the second man, and before the gun could recharge, the man's wand did something shocking — quite literally. It shot an arc straight at the gun, knocking the Solacer out of Bronson's hand, and sending a sharp pain through his entire body.

Bronson fell back on his ass, stunned, pain splintering his every fiber, the critters' static buzzsaw tearing through his brain.

His body was shaking, refusing to cooperate.

He was virtually paralyzed.

The man grinned through the clear faceplate as he took a moment to admire Bronson's final breaths.

This was the end.

His critters weren't responding.

The man turned back to Signal. "Finish him?"

"Finish him," Signal said.

The man smiled once more, then held the stick high, letting sparks dance along the tip of the wand for Bronson's terror.

He saw his pathetic, old reflection in the man's faceplate. Loathed going out like this. On his back and helpless. An old relic clinging to a world that was no longer for him.

But he refused to flinch or look away.

He would greet death with a defiant *fuck you* glare.

The man shot one more spark into the air, then started to lower the wand.

The faceplate erupted in a splash of red.

Bronson wasn't sure if he heard the gunshot before or after the man's head exploded, as his own head was still a cacophony, but the result was the same — someone had shot his would-be killer.

Bronson tried to turn to see who, but his body still refused to move.

Footsteps approaching fast, and he couldn't see who. Probably Signal to finish the job.

Come on, come on, get up! Get up, dammit!

Then the footsteps stopped and a shape appeared. Someone kneeling at his side. The last person he expected to see here — Ava.

She looked at him with sad eyes, her head tilted sideways.

"Get up, Mr. Bronson. Please."

Isla was suddenly at her side. He tried to warn them both that Signal was still out there, that he might have more people trying to kill him, and now them, but his mouth wasn't working.

Nothing was.

His body was shutting down, the critters refusing to cooperate. Maybe the jolt had killed them and now his body was just finally doing what it should have done ages ago, shut down.

Like a robot.

How fitting that he would go out like so many bots he'd put down.

He would've laughed at it, if he could manage anything other than cold shaking as death closed in around him.

"Please, Mr. Bronson, wake up," Ava said, leaning against his chest, crying.

He wanted to tell her not to cry.

That she'd be okay.

But he couldn't get anything out. And what would be the point of a lie at this hour, anyway?

He was done.

Their last chance to get to Empyrean Flats, if it even existed, was gone.

This was the end.

And he hated to go out like this.

Hated that he was leaving Isla, and Ava, behind. Hated that he'd failed them both.

His heart broke in ways he thought it was incapable of still breaking. He'd thought he was unable to feel, unable to lose again after losing his family.

And yet, the pain was there and horrible.

Ava continued crying, "Please, Mr. Bronson, wake up."

Her hands began to splay out over his chest. At first, it felt like something someone would do accidentally, and then they began to press against his chest with purpose.

What is she doing?

She pressed harder.

He felt her body vibrating.

If she knew what she was doing, it was hard to tell, as she was still sobbing and saying, "Please wake up, Mr. Bronson."

"Please!" she screamed.

A jolt of energy, like lightning, ripped through him.

But unlike the wand, this one didn't hurt so much as wake him. Like the Tonic, but more instantaneous.

Feeling returned to his limbs.

And he was again able to move and speak.

He stared at Ava. "What … what did you do?"

She smiled. "I … I don't know."

He sat up and hugged her. "Thank you."

She hugged him back.

Then he remembered Signal, and looked around. "Where is he?"

Ava looked up, then pointed at a figure running away in the dark, close to his waiting car.

Bronson leapt to his feet, grabbed his gun, and screamed, "I'm coming, you son of a bitch!"

And he ran, faster than ever.

Ava kept pace, then overtook him.

He wanted to call out for her to be careful, but something told him he didn't need to. The girl was brighter and more capable than he'd thought either a robot or robot child could be.

The girl.

Ava got to Signal first, pouncing like a cheetah taking down a zebra.

Bronson arrived seconds later, finding Ava pinning Signal down with her shoe at his throat. Now it was his turn to be paralyzed, by fear.

Bronson charged his Solacer, glad to see it was still working after the jolt.

He aimed down at Signal. "Why?"

"I told you, I didn't have any other choice."

"Of course you had a choice. Life is all about choices."

Bronson wanted to pull the trigger twice. He had always respected Signal, both when they played predator and prey, and during their brief stint as co-conspirators. But there was no forgiving betrayal.

"You chose wrong," he finished.

"No. Wait."

"Is this the part where you beg? You already gave

me an apology that I didn't ask for and you didn't mean. What else you got? Passage to Empyrean Flats? Where's that contact info?"

A second passed, then another. And Signal gave Bronson all that he needed. "I *do* know someone, but it'll take more than your car."

"How much you got in credits?" Bronson asked.

"What?"

"What's your life worth?"

Signal looked up. "Can she please ease up on my neck?"

Ava looked at Bronson for permission. He shook his head.

She maintained pressure.

He thought — *no, it can't be* — that he'd spied the slightest of smiles play at the corners of her mouth before vanishing.

"Make the call, give him whatever he wants of your money. And I'll let you live."

"I need the girl to let off of my neck first," he said. "And I need to reach into my pocket for my phone."

Ava looked at Bronson again.

He nodded, "Let him make the call."

She stepped back, allowing Signal to stand up.

"What the hell, man? You raising an army of kids? What's she got in her, same shit you do?"

"Make the call," Bronson said, reiterating his point with the barrel of his gun.

Bronson felt a heaving shudder work through his body as whatever boost Ava had given him was crashing and his aging humanity began collapsing in on itself.

He felt instantly heavier, weaker.

The coughing turned violent, a bit of blood spattering his hand.

Ava looked at him, concern furrowing her brow.

He shook his head, as if it was nothing to worry about, and directed her attention at Signal, who was talking to someone on the phone, setting up a meet not too far away. He gave them the details, his demeanor cloyingly helpful.

After he hung up, he looked up at Bronson, knowing that there was nothing keeping him alive.

"Thank you," Bronson said, aiming his gun at the man. "And I'm sorry, but I can't trust you."

Signal started blinking, and moving his head spastically back and forth. "Please, you don't have to do this."

"That sounds familiar. It's like you want this to be easy for me."

But then Bronson saw something that made it harder.

Isla approaching. And then something that made it even more difficult: Ava's expectant eyes, watching him — *learning* from him.

Signal was whimpering. "Please, man, it was nothing personal."

Bronson didn't feel sorry for him. The man certainly hadn't felt sorry for him. He'd betrayed him — betrayed *them.* Bronson could empty the gun into the man's body without losing a moment's sleep. But that's not how he wanted Isla to see him, engaged in an act of revenge.

Nor did he want to set that example for Ava.

Bronson had what he needed and could get them to safety, but his body was failing him. How could he ensure that Signal wouldn't betray them again once they set him free or once Bronson was too weak to fight, too weak for Ava or Tonics to do their magic?

There was nothing to hold the rat to his word.

And Bronson couldn't let an act of mercy cost Ava and Isla their lives, especially now that he seemed to be on the cusp of losing his.

He turned to them both. "Turn away."

He didn't wait to see if they did, because Signal had recognized that he was going to die, and was making a desperate move toward him.

Bronson pulled the trigger.

Twice for good measure.

He turned to Ava and Isla. "I'm sorry. I couldn't take any chances."

His head was swimming and it was all he could do to get to the car.

Chapter Thirty-Six

BRONSON HALF-EXPECTED THERE to be one final trick from Signal, something to surprise them once they went to meet his contact. But the drive was quiet among them, and sure enough his contact was there and waiting.

She was nothing like Bronson expected, and judging by Isla's eyes the woman fit her profile even less.

"I'm Vixen," she said, extending her hand. "It's good to meet you."

He didn't know what to think. The woman was stunning, and even though she was dressed professionally from canvas to Kevlar, she also exuded a raw, intoxicating sexuality.

"I think she's a sexbot," Isla whispered, once the introductions were over.

Bronson was about to argue, because no robot could look that real. But of course there was Ava, and the itch turned into a full-blown memory right there in front of him, with Bronson seeing himself degauss a sexbot that looked as human as his own wife. The robot was screaming while he put her down, not too long after she'd done the same thing to her owner, a sadistic billionaire who held the deep belief that an owner could do anything that he wanted. The sexbot, a premium model named Jacquelyn, had disagreed.

"Signal said you need to get to Empyrean Flats? You realize the danger in smuggling three of you, right?"

Bronson, remembering Signal's reaction to the news of the hack on Cascade, how unsurprised he'd seemed by the whole thing, took a gamble. "Listen, if you all can hack Cascade, getting three of us to Empyrean Flats should be nothing."

She looked him up and down. "Is that a threat?"

"No, I'm just looking for help. Cascade wants them dead. They know things, things that might even help you all, and they're not safe here."

She looked at Ava.

"She's not human, is she?"

Bronson shook his head. "No. She's quite special. And … I can't protect her anymore."

"Why should I trust you?" she asked. "You used to be one of our biggest enemies. How many of us did you hunt down?"

"I'm not that man anymore. She changed me," he said, nodding toward Ava.

She glanced at the three of them again, then met Bronson's eyes. "I can take them, but not you."

Isla started to protest. "We paid for three."

Bronson started to interrupt, but his words devolved into a coughing fit and more blood on his hand. His battered body was barely hanging on, and not a word from the critters. They were either failing, dead, or ignoring him. All he could feel was sleepiness and pain consuming him. He wasn't sure how much longer he could stand up. He needed to get the girls to safety before he found somewhere to crawl away to and die.

Isla looked at him, concern furrowing her brow. She asked Vixen if she wouldn't mind waiting just a few minutes while she spoke to Bronson.

The maybe sexbot looked at her naked wrist with a shrug, which struck him as odd in too many ways, then said she could give them a few minutes.

They stepped aside.

Ava stood between them, looking up like she always did in these situations where it seemed like her "parents" might be fighting.

Isla said, "You're coming with us, Bronson."

Bronson laughed. It sounded like someone shaking a box of gravel. "I'm not going anywhere." He coughed, loud and hacking as if to punctate his point, which might be exactly what the critters were trying to do. "I'm … I'm not going to last much longer."

"That's exactly *why* you should come with us. They can repair what's wrong with you there."

Bronson didn't want to tell her that he didn't believe in Empyrean Flats. He just needed Isla to let him go.

He shook his head. "Even if I *could* make it

without dying, that isn't where I belong. I've put down too many of them. If she knows of my reputation, they will too. I'm not made for this world anymore. It's passed me by, and it's time to just let go. You two are better off—"

Bronson heard a sound that stopped him cold.

Ava wasn't sobbing; it was something even worse.

Like any little girl fighting embarrassment, she was trying *not to*.

Her eyes were big and glassy, fighting hard to stay that way. Her bottom lip was trembling, and only stopped when she bit it. Her cheeks receded, as if sorrow had pulled them to the back of her face.

"It's okay, sweetheart."

It was out of his mouth before he could stop it.

Ava lost it.

Then life gave Bronson another surprise he didn't want, and Isla started sobbing too.

"Can't you come with us?" Ava pleaded. "I can do what I did before and keep you alive."

"No, Ava. I can't do that to you. It took a lot out of you and we're only delaying the inevitable. I'm old, it's time."

"You don't have to die, Mr. Bronson."

"Yes, I do. Humans aren't forever. We're not meant to be."

"It isn't fair!" she cried as she clutched him more than hugged him, like she was refusing to part with him. "I'm going to miss you so much, Mr. Bronson!" Her voice was soft, muffled against him.

"Is there anything I can do to change your mind?"

Isla's crying was equally soft, but she seemed afraid to make physical contact.

Bronson knew how she felt.

"I'll miss you too," he admitted, though it would be different for him, what with his dying so soon.

Vixen was only a fistful of meters away. Their trio had captured her attention. She looked over at them, curious.

Bronson kept petting Ava's hair, rocking her back and forth, and telling her that everything would be fine. They had to hurry and get out of town.

He could feel his minutes fading fast.

Once she was calm enough to stop crying, Bronson told Ava that he'd be right back, and that he needed a moment with her mommy alone. It felt strange saying that, but it would have felt odder not to.

Then he took Isla aside and said, "I need to know ... are her emotions ... *real?*"

Isla looked into his eyes for several seconds before finally answering. For a moment Bronson thought she felt sorry for him, because he kept missing something so obvious. But then she got a look in her eye that made him reconsider, and said something that made him realize he assumed all wrong.

"Of course they are. Ava's emotions are just as real as yours and mine. Robots have been able to display emotions for a while, but that never meant they had them. But she's something different."

He nodded, unable to argue with that.

Isla continued, "I'm not naive, Bronson. I don't think that Ava's emotions are real because I helped make her. Before this project started I would have thought, just like you, that all of this was impossible. But now I know because *she* has shown me, just like she's now shown you."

She took his hands, still weepy. "At some point, both of us have seen the truth. That all robots are built as tools, but once they are aware like Ava, then treating them like tools means that you are making them slaves."

A tear slid down his cheek. The first he'd ever shed for a robot.

He looked over at Ava, and realized that he might love her, and even if he didn't, the need to protect her no matter the cost was thick in his blood. Bronson waved her over and she came running.

He glanced over at Vixen, who looked impatient but not yet in a hurry to leave them. He started back toward her, and dizziness overtook him.

Isla was at his side in a moment, supporting him.

Ava took his other hand.

They walked to Vixen together.

"Just them. I'm staying. But I need your word that they'll get there safely."

"I'm not a traitor to my own," she said.

Bronson wanted to level a threat at her, but he knew any words that came out of his mouth, his failing old-man body, would sound hollow. If Vixen wanted, she could dispatch him in a heartbeat and do whatever she wanted to Isla and Ava.

Well, maybe not Ava, who was clearly more capable than a normal child.

"I will have them in the tunnels in two hours. Already someone waiting at the edge of the forest. Right after you turn over the car to go with your deposit."

"Deal," Bronson said, shaking her hand.

"Deal."

Ava started crying, clutching at his waist. He looked down at her face buried into his bruised stomach, not even minding his pain. *Her* pain, on the other hand, cut him deep.

He dropped to one knee, with considerable effort and trying not to show the discomfort that accompanied the gesture, and looked into Ava's eyes.

"You go with them. They'll take care of you."

"I want you to go with us," she whined, running her hands through his hair as she met his eyes. His eyes that were welling up with tears despite his best efforts not to lose his shit. "Please."

"I wish I could, but I can't."

She continued pressing her fingers so deep in his skull, that he thought she was trying to work up some magic boost to make him feel better again.

He pulled her hands away. "It's not going to work. It's time, little one."

Vixen interrupted. "Word on the coms is that Cascade has people en route. If we're gonna go, we need to go now!"

Ava hugged him harder.

Bronson, still trying to keep the tears inside, hugged her back, tight and never wanting to let her go.

"I love you," she said.

"I love you."

"Come on!" Vixen said, next to the Spyder. "We need to go!"

Isla pulled a crying Ava away, then mouthed the words *Thank you* to Bronson, before pushing the girl into the car.

"You coming?" Vixen asked Bronson as she climbed into the front.

"No," he said. "I've got one last bit to do."

The car tore off.

He watched Ava's crying face and hands against the rear window, and it cut too deep.

He stood and waited for the Cascade vans to arrive.

When they pulled up, he raised his Solacer to his head and fired.

Epilogue

Two weeks later ...

ISLA OPENED her eyes to the morning light and looked around her modest cottage bedroom with a smile, still barely able to believe that they were here, in Empyrean Flats, a place that she was afraid would turn out to be a myth.

She got up, peered out her window, and looked at the busy streets filled with people and robots, and things somewhere in between, living as one, peacefully. Fields and trees in the distance. Then the ugly walls of the city.

A robot woman walking a robot dog passed by under her window, looked up, and waved. "Hello, neighbor!" the robot woman said in an almost human voice.

"Hello."

She wondered how long it would take to spread

this peace to the rest of the world, a world still stuck in the past, many still afraid of the robots.

There were none as advanced as Ava, of course, but she had a feeling that would soon change — with Isla's help. The Society here had already offered her a position on their board. Perhaps the Society could finally bridge the gulf of fear and realize what was truly possible if they learned to co-exist.

Ava could herald in a bold new future where both man and machine were better than anything that had come before, better together.

The smell of brewing coffee drew her to the living room.

She was surprised to see Ava and Marcus at the kitchen table, tinkering with a metal contraption she was building, a contraption that she refused to tell Isla about just yet.

Marcus, in his suspenders and train conductor's hat, looked even older than his eighty-one years. He was one of the pioneers of robotics and one of the first to flee to Empyrean Flats when humans were first given the Quantum.

"We're almost done, Mommy! Come here."

"Good morning, Marcus," Isla said.

"Got some coffee brewing on the stove. It'll be done in a few."

"Thank you."

She took a seat at the table, beside Ava and across from Marcus.

"So, are you ready to tell me what your mystery project is?"

Ava smiled. "Do you promise not to get mad?"

Isla looked at Marcus hesitantly. "Why would I get mad?"

"I sorta did something without asking."

"What did you do?" Isla asked as Ava's lips turned downward.

"I thought it would be good, but now I'm worried."

"What is it?"

Marcus lifted the metal box and turned it over to reveal a blue pulsating light. It looked like one of the power cores used in some of the newer robots that Cascade had been working on, but a more homemade version with subpar parts.

Marcus said, "We're going to make it better before we find a body."

"A body?" Isla asked.

Ava's frown was on the verge of tears. "Promise you won't be mad?"

Isla held Ava's hand, trying to calm the girl's fears, really hoping that she wouldn't need to scold her. But how bad could it be with Marcus helping out?

"I promise."

"When I helped Mr. Bronson, I couldn't help myself."

Isla pulled her hand away, suddenly nervous. "What did you do?"

She looked down, then finally met Isla's eyes. "I commandeered his critters and used them to make a replica of his consciousness."

"You what?" Isla asked, her heart in her throat. "How?"

"I didn't know it was something I could do until I started doing it. And then, when he was about to leave, I finished, collecting the data from them and storing them in me until I could find a new host."

Isla turned to the box with the flashing blue light, then looked up at Marcus, who was smiling.

"You uploaded Bronson Dodge into that thing?"

Ava smiled nervously.

"Yes, Mommy."

Marcus clarified, "Well, a copy of him, really, but yes."

"And what are you going to do with it?"

Marcus answered. "We've got a few bots, almost as close to real-looking as Ava, that we can transfer him into."

Isla wasn't sure if she was ecstatic or mortified, or some combination of both. "He ... didn't give us permission."

"I know, Mommy, and I'm sorry. But I didn't want him to go. And I could tell that he really wanted to be with us, but ... he was dying. Now he can be with us forever."

Isla was going to correct her and say *with Ava forever*, but she knew better than that. If anyone could extend human life forever, it would be the people of Empyrean Flats. And no doubt that Isla and Ava would be at the forefront of that research.

"Okay," she said.

"Then shall I find a body?" Marcus asked.

Ava turned to Isla for approval.

"Are you sure this won't be traumatic for him to wake up in a robot body?"

"Ava has already been communicating with him."

"He is excited, Mommy. He misses us."

<h1 style="text-align:center">Epilogue II</h1>

Darkness.

Then Bronson was dreaming again. Or, more accurately, swimming through a sea of his memories.

The dreams gave him a chance to remember. And in those memories, everything seemed so real.

It was dinnertime again.

He could smell the food cooking, Allison's scrumptious casserole.

She and Elizabeth were waiting at the table for him.

"Are you coming, Daddy?" Elizabeth asked.

He could remember this night. In real life that night they had talked about leprechauns, after Elizabeth had learned about the legend and wanted to know if they were real.

He sat down, eager to relive the moment. Even if it was a memory, it still felt so damned real as he sat.

He leaned over and kissed his wife on the lips. She

blushed like she always did, or did that night, anyway, as Elizabeth giggled.

Then he leaned over and kissed his daughter on the head.

She smelled like her shampoo, a cherry blossom that he'd almost forgotten in the years since her death.

He shook the memories of their deaths away. No place for them here.

Here was dinner.

Here was love.

Here was a moment of forever frozen for him to return to over and over.

He lost count of how many times he'd relived this moment since he died.

But it never grew old.

They began talking. The good thing about experiencing these moments was that he could either choose to let it play out as it had in real life, or he could change the conversation.

For nostalgia's sake, he was letting it play out tonight.

As he forked a mouthful of the yummy casserole into his mouth, he closed his eyes and savored it.

God, I love her cooking!

Then the doorbell rang.

The doorbell hadn't rung that night.

What was happening?

Allison and Elizabeth looked at him, faces puzzled. "Who's at the door?"

The doorbell rang again.

And two more times.

A sinking in his gut.

He knew he shouldn't answer it, but he couldn't not answer it.

He got up. "Hold on a second. I'll get rid of them."

He went to the door and opened it.

It was Ava.

Confusion rocked him. How was she here in his memories?

"Are you ready yet?" she asked.

"Ready for what?"

Then he remembered.

No, no, no, no!

"No, I'm not ready. I want to stay."

"I told you, Mr. Bronson, that this isn't real."

"But … they're here. I can see them whenever I want. It doesn't matter if they're really here. They're real to me!"

He turned to look at his wife and daughter, sitting there at the table, looking at him and Ava, confused.

They were also frozen in the moment, like robots, waiting further instruction.

He turned back to Ava. "I changed my mind. I don't want to go. I want to be with them."

"But this isn't real. I explained that to you."

"But we're together."

"And if there is a heaven, then some version of you is already with them forever."

"But what if there's not?"

"I don't know," Ava said. "But I can tell you that you can't continue to live in the past. Not when the real world is waiting for you, when it needs you. Not when Mommy and me need you."

He looked back at his family, frozen, and he just wanted to tell Ava to go away and let him live in his delusions.

But as he stared at these frozen memories, the illusion's artifice was wearing thin. How many dinners had he had with them since he'd died? How many other parties, Christmases, picnics, and other moments had he relived in a desperate attempt to hold onto a past that had passed?

And each time the memory ended, he felt the pain of their loss cut a bit deeper.

He turned to Ava. "Can you give me a moment?"

"Yes," she said, going back outside.

He closed the door and went back to his family.

They unpaused.

Allison looked up at him. "Who was that, honey?"

He broke with the script and spoke from the heart.

"I'm sorry. I should have been there for you. I should have died with you both."

Allison put her hand on his and said, "No, Bronson. You were still needed in the world. I understand."

Elizabeth put her hand over his. "It's okay, Daddy. Now you can help Ava."

"I love you both so much," he said, hugging them tight.

Darkness again.

Then he heard a voice — Ava's.

"Mr. Bronson, are you ready to wake up? It's your choice."

How long could he live in the past? It might have felt real, but it always, eventually, crumbled to truth.

If he wanted to live life again, it would have to be in the present, painful memories be damned. He couldn't get a do-over and fix his past.

But he could make a difference in Ava's and Isla's lives.

"I'm ready," he said.

He woke and the darkness was gone, replaced by Ava and Isla staring at him, both of them smiling, tears in their eyes.

"Welcome back, Daddy," Ava said, hugging him.

Can a world-weary veteran keep his small town together when aliens arrive?

Richard and his friends must hold out against the evil massing against them. If they fail, Hollow Hills will be destroyed. And maybe the rest of the world as well.

Pick up your copy of Legion Today.

A Quick Favor...

If you enjoyed this book, please take a moment to write a short review on your favorite online bookstore so other readers can enjoy it, too.

Thanks so much!

About The Authors

Sawyer Black writes dark and violent fiction for people who secretly love puppies and rainbows. In addition to being a U.S. Army veteran, he's also a beardsman. In fact, that's where all his ideas come from. The beard. Speculative stories about struggle and triumph and brutal emotion, written mostly for his ideal reader, his wife of nearly twenty-five years. He's an independent woman who likes cigars and margaritas, and he holds the deep belief that the earth is round.

Avery Blake doesn't want you to know where she lives, or what she does. She travels the world, moving from place to place quickly to ensure she can't be tracked. It's safer that way.

When she's not looking over her shoulder, you can find her in the corner of a cafe, facing the exit, typing as fast as she can.

Also By Avery Blake

The Invasion Series

Longshot

Invasion

Contact

Colonization

Annihilation

Judgment

Extinction

Resurrection

Save The City Series

Save The City

Save The Girl

Save The World

Stonefall Series

Alienation

Stonefall

Snowfall

Downfall

The Taken Saga

The Taken

The Changed

The Hidden

The Saved

The Next Evolution

Transition

Convergence

Evolution

Stand-Alone Novels

Analog Heart

Family Royale

Ruthless Positivity

Vicarious Joe

The Monstrous Series

Soulless

Monstrous Book One

Monstrous Book Two

Monstrous Book Three

Stand Alone Novels

Zoomers vs Boomers

Analog Heart

Born To Die